Cold Case

A Florida Keys Mystery

Book Four

Carl & Jane Bock

Habent Sua Fata Libelli

ABSOLUTELY AMAZING eBOOKS

Manhanset House
Shelter Island Hts., New York 11965-0342

bricktower@aol.com • tech@absolutelyamazingebooks.com
• absolutelyamazingebooks.com

Library of Congress Cataloging-in-Publication Data
Bock, Carl & Jane.
Cold Case
p. cm.

1. FICTION / Thrillers / Suspense. 2. FICTION / Mystery & Detective /
Hard-Boiled. 3. FICTION / Thrillers / Crime. Fiction, I. Title.
ISBN: 978-1-1955036-74-0, Trade Paper

Author photo: Katie Ramirez

July 2024

Cold Case

A Florida Keys Mystery

Book Four

Carl & Jane Bock

Other books by Carl & Jane Bock

Coronado's Trail
An Arizona Borderlands Mystery, Book One

Death Rattle
An Arizona Borderlands Mystery, Book Two

Grace Fully
An Arizona Borderlands Mystery, Book Three

Day of the Jaguar
An Arizona Borderlands Mystery, Book Four

The Swamp Guide
A Florida Keys Mystery, Book One

The White Heron
A Florida Keys Mystery, Book Two

Death of a Glades Man
A Florida Keys Mystery, Book Three

Dedication

To all those individuals working to restore
and save the Everglades and Florida Bay.

Prologue

The man had been looking forward to this particular day for better than a week. A chance to get out on the water alone was a reward in itself. But to make things even better, a fisherman friend had told him about a creek that had just opened up in the backcountry of Everglades National Park. A strong tidal surge—they called it a king tide—had washed out some dead mangroves left over from the last hurricane. This made it possible to get back into a part of the glades where few fishermen had been before, including him.

He knew the waters of the Park better than most people. Among the myriad creeks and back bays and open waters, there were particular spots where fish would hold: places with bottom structure or trenches or the right tidal currents, or—better yet—all three. Such knowledge was essential, especially in times of declining fish populations. He was familiar with a trove of such places. But the chance to fish somewhere new? Well, that was special.

The trick was finding it. His friend had given him only a general description of the point where the new creek emptied into the lake. Had that been deliberate? Probably. Fishermen were known to keep their secrets.

He made an early start, leaving the dock before the sun had cleared a bank of clouds touching the eastern horizon. He had two reasons. First, he hoped to be the first fisherman out there, and to get up into the creek before anybody saw him. But equally important were the tides. He'd checked the charts the night before. If he timed it right, the waters of a rising tide would push him back into the glades without having to paddle his canoe very hard. Then, if it went according to plan, by the time he was ready to head for home the tide would have turned so it would help push him back out.

The trip would be complicated by two factors, but he was used to both of them. First, he understood that the creek was too narrow for his boat. Therefore, he would need to tie a canoe on the gunwale and move over to it when he reached the creek mouth. Second, he had a dog with him. It belonged to a neighbor who made frequent business trips and asked him to look after it when he was gone. The man didn't mind. The dog seemed to love being out on the water almost as much as he did, or maybe even more. He just sat there, presumably enjoying the fish and the birds.

The day's route took him west along the southern coast of the Florida mainland. Then it turned north into the East Cape Canal, leading up into Lake Ingraham. The lake had always been there. The canal was a human construction, but much widened since it had been dredged out more than a century ago. The creek mouth was supposed to be somewhere along the north shore of the lake, but his friend had said it was a tight fit and nearly hidden by a canopy of mangroves that had survived the tide. He wasn't worried about getting in once he found it because his canoe was narrow, with a shallow draft.

He hugged the shoreline, moving west, looking for any sort of opening. A flock of roseate spoonbills suddenly lifted up above the wall of mangroves, their pink plumage bright against the azure sky. He gave them only the briefest glance, even though he liked watching birds and other wildlife almost as much as fishing. Keeping an eye out for the entrance to the little creek took his full attention.

The search was so intense that he failed to notice the other boat. When it first came out onto the lake it was about three hundred yards behind him. It sped up and started to close just as he discovered the creek mouth, but still he didn't see it. He ducked down under the overhanging branches and tied his boat to a thick mangrove trunk. Then he off-loaded the canoe and the dog, and began paddling back into a part of the glades he'd never seen before. He looked forward to the day's fishing adventure, believing he was alone.

Chapter 1

Twenty-five Years Later

Robert Portman gaveled the meeting to order with more enthusiasm than necessary to get the attention of his fellow board members. I happened to be there with other residents attending the quarterly meeting of the Gulf Shores Homeowners' Association, of which Robert—"don't call me Bob"—happened to be president. We'd gathered in his living room because our development had no community center. Mrs. Evelyn Portman had provided refreshments consisting of ice water and cookies. Robert, who had a pair of bulging eyes and a pointy nose that in combination made him look like a giant mouse, was sitting behind a desk with his back to a picture window that looked out on the darkening waters of the Gulf of Mexico. The rest of us—perhaps thirty people in all—sat facing him in a variety of mismatched chairs apparently collected from different parts of the house. The sun had nearly set, and I had a hard time paying attention to Portman. Instead I watched as the fiery orange globe neared the horizon, hoping to see the fabled and illusive green flash.

We'd all been handed copies of the night's agenda, and I couldn't help but notice that my reason for being there didn't come until the very end. This seemed to preclude the possibility of an early departure that I found disappointing. Before our president started to speak I raised a hand to get his attention. "It's Sam Sawyer, Mr. Portman, and I have a favor to ask."

"Yes, Sam?"

"My main purpose here tonight is to introduce a new neighbor, as the agenda notes. But I was wondering if we might move it up a bit? As a favor to him, that is."

Portman frowned and shook his head. "No. I'm sorry. Parliamentary procedure requires that we begin by reading the minutes of the last meeting, and then move on to the budget. I'm sure we're all anxious to meet your friend, but these things must happen in the proper order."

With that he turned to Gladys Townsend, who was both secretary and treasurer of the HOA, and had been for many years. "Gladys, will you proceed please?"

My wife Katie once pointed out that it was women who usually did the actual work on things like committees and boards, while men were the self-appointed "huffers and puffers," as she had put it. I expect she was talking mostly about academic settings that were the bulk of her life's experience. We'd both been professors at one time, at a university up in Fort Lauderdale, where she was a forensic botanist. That's the use of plant materials in solving crimes. I'd been an ornithologist and conservation biologist, until I had a mid-life crisis and moved down to Islamorada in the Florida Keys and became a fishing guide. Katie commented that, at age thirty-five, I must have had the earliest mid-life crisis on record. We could joke about it now, five years later, but it hadn't been funny at the time because it had nearly broken up our marriage.

Fortunately for us, Katie had found a way to join me in Islamorada when a position in forensics opened up at The College of the Florida Keys. It was a step down the academic ladder for her, but at least we were back together and we no longer had issues such as who got to keep Prince, our Pembroke Welsh Corgi.

In addition to fishing, I'd also found myself involved in criminal investigations since coming to the Keys. I sometimes help Katie in her forensic studies, or work on my own in cases involving poaching or the sale of contraband wildlife products.

We live in a little wooden house up on stilts that my uncle had built back in the 70's. I'd inherited it after he died. Our place stood in contrast to the concrete and glass mansions that increasingly lined the canals of the Gulf Shores Development, including the one presently occupied by our board president. Robert Portman had moved here five years ago, after retiring from a career selling stocks and bonds someplace in Ohio. Stock brokering must have been pretty lucrative, given the current price of real estate in Islamorada, and considering both the size and quality of their new home. I'd taken him fishing a couple of times, but he hadn't seemed all that interested.

Anyway, back to the meeting. Once Gladys Townsend finished reading the minutes and all five board members had voted "aye" to approve them, she then went on to review—in painstaking detail—the state of the current budget, consulting a personal computer sitting on her lap. "So, as you can see, we are well within our planned expenditures. *However*, we have two members seriously in arrears in paying their monthly dues. We've sent them three reminding letters, to which they have not yet responded. Therefore, with President Portman's approval and over his signature, we have notified the law office we have under contract, and they are to initiate legal proceedings."

"Who are these homeowners?" somebody asked.

Ms. Townsend glanced at Portman, who appeared to be cringing. "We would prefer not to say at this point," he replied. "But rest assured we will pursue this matter to a successful conclusion. And thank you Gladys for that excellent report."

Katie rarely attended Homeowners Association (HOA for short) meetings, and I didn't come all that often, except for the annual event where we voted on the budget and elected new board members. My reason for being here on this particular evening was to introduce a friend and client, Rashaan Liptan. He was a celebrated Miami *Heat* basketball player who'd recently retired, and had moved into the neighborhood along with his wife and twin daughters. But, as President Portman had pointed out, introductions of new residents belonged in the "new business" category, which was last on the agenda. Therefore, we had to sit through the entire proceedings, including all the requisite huffing and puffing. I felt sorry for Rashaan.

The Gulf Shores HOA actually didn't have all that much to do. Individuals owned and maintained their own lots and improvements, albeit under constraint of codes and requirements enforced by a design review committee, of which Portman was the self-appointed chair.

"The next item on our agenda for this evening is a report from the design review committee," Portman announced. He then described a handful of matters the committee had dealt with since the last board meeting, mostly involving who would be permitted to repaint their homes in one or more of several board-approved colors.

The Gulf Shores community did have responsibility for two properties: a stretch of beach along the gulf, and a boat ramp with an adjacent picnic area beside one of the canals that wound through the development. In my limited experience while attending board meetings, these were two perennially hot-button items. I noticed that Rashaan had begun fidgeting in his chair, and I hoped that he wouldn't lose patience and bolt from the room before I had a chance to introduce him to everybody.

"The next item on our agenda is a report from the Beach and Ramp Committee," Portman went on, as he turned to another board member, a man named Allen Grimsby.

Allen stood up and cleared his throat. Then he let out a conspicuous sigh, which I took as a bad sign. "The sand itself is in good shape, and the maintenance people have done a good job raking away the dead seagrass. However, we have three problems."

I nudged Rashaan. "Here comes the part about dog poop."

Grimsby shot me a look. "First, on several occasions I have found dog feces on the beach, even though—as you know—we have signs at the gate stating in no uncertain terms that dogs are not allowed." He stopped talking to let that sink in, but started up again before anybody had a chance to comment. "And second, people keep dragging our wooden Adirondack chairs out into the water, even though they are *clearly* marked that it's not to be done because it causes them to rot. I may have to ask the budget committee to appropriate funds for new chairs if this keeps up."

"What about getting plastic ones?" somebody asked.

Allen nodded knowingly. "That could work, but some members of the committee, including me, think they look kind of tacky."

I got the clear sense that tackiness—however he imagined it—was high on Allen's list of homeowner transgressions. "But let's move on to an additional problem, which I really feel is at the heart of all the others. And that is the matter of the beach and ramp keys." He paused for effect. "You people just aren't keeping track of them like you're supposed to. Just this month we've had four reports of supposedly lost keys, and I myself have accosted several parties using the beach or launching their boats, who had no business doing either. They all claimed to be somebody's guest, but when I pushed the matter they weren't able to come up with any names." Allen pivoted in the direction of Robert Portman. "And so, Mr. President,

I move that we raise the fee for getting a new key from its present one hundred dollars to five hundred."

Rashaan's fidgeting ramped up. "Is this for real?" he said under his breath.

"Yeah, sorry."

At President Portman's suggestion, the board voted to increase the key replacement fee to three hundred dollars.

Finally, we had come to the "new business" part of the agenda. I started getting out of my chair to introduce Rashaan, when another man beat me to it. A wizened old guy with a handlebar mustache rose in the back of the room. "I'd like now to make my patrol report," he said.

Robert Portman rolled his bug eyes and sighed. "Yes, Nate?"

I knew this guy. Nathaniel Sturm was a long-time resident of the community who made it a point to cruise the neighborhood on his vintage Indian motorcycle, often with a miniature white poodle on his lap, looking for what he called "transgressions and suspicious behaviors." I'd chatted with him on several occasions as he motored past my house. I learned that he'd lived in Gulf Shores almost since its inception, more than forty years ago. In spite of his eccentricity, or perhaps because of it, I liked him a great deal. What I didn't know yet was how useful he would turn out to be.

"Since our last meeting, I have seen no sign of criminal activity," Nathaniel began. "However, I must once again point out several flagrant violations of our covenant about not displaying offensive signs at any time, or political ones except during the month prior to an election. I'm not aware of any scheduled elections."

I hoped that would be the end of it, but then somebody asked "What sort of signs?" and Nate took that as an invitation.

"Okay, then," he said. "First, over on Palm Avenue there's a notice on a gate that says 'Trespassers will be shot. Trespassers who survive will be shot again.' Then, down on Poinsettia Court there's a bumper sticker on a pickup that says 'Dump Trump.' And on the next street over—I forget its name—there's another bumper sticker that shows a little boy peeing on the word 'Obama.' I don't know about you, but that seems both offensive and political at the same time."

Rashaan leaned over and whispered in my ear. "At least the guy's being fair and balanced, to borrow a phrase."

Suddenly there was a scraping sound coming from the back of the room, and we both turned to watch a fat man called Will Stebbins lift up out of his chair. "Now just a goddam minute!" he said. "I think that's *my* pickup you're talking about, and I'll put any sort of bumper sticker on it I have a mind to. Who does this Nate person think he is, anyway?"

Nate Sturm whirled and started to say something, but Portman put his hand up. "Now let's all calm down, everybody. Thanks for your report, Nate. We'll have to check the covenants to determine if there's anything in them about bumper stickers. The board will get back to you on that, okay Will? Meanwhile, *please* sit down and let us get on with the rest of the meeting."

Stebbins muttered something about "the next time I see that motorcycle," but he did sit back down.

Portman went on: "And, now, last on our agenda, I believe Sam Sawyer has somebody he wants to introduce. Sam?"

Finally.

I rose from my chair and nudged Rashaan to stand up beside me. "Yes, thank you Robert. I would like you all to meet Rashaan Liptan, who has just moved into our development along with his wife Julie and their twin daughters Serena and Candace. They bought the house at 150 Bayshore Drive. As I'm sure most of you know, Rashaan is recently retired from a long and storied career with the NBA's Miami *Heat*. I also can vouch for his skills as a fisherman."

As a way to toss the ball into his court, so to speak, I next asked Rashaan if he could tell us a little more about his daughters, "in case some of you here tonight might have kids or grandkids with similar ages and interests."

"They just turned sixteen," Rashaan replied. "Serena is into sports, especially tennis and track, while Candace likes to draw and paint. Best I can tell they're more interested in their phones and boys than they are in either basketball or fishing." That got a few chuckles from around the room. "And thank you, Sam, for this opportunity. Let me say that it's a great pleasure being here. Julie and I and our girls look forward to enjoying our new home and meeting you all individually."

"Welcome to our neighborhood," Robert Portman said to Rashaan, after which he initiated a brief but polite round of applause. I may have been listening too hard for it, but had there been just a hint of restraint on the part of some people in the room?

Portman next asked for a motion to adjourn, got one, and gaveled things to a close. Rashaan and I stayed around to mingle with those members who didn't leave immediately. He answered some obvious questions, like:

"Do you miss basketball?"

"Yes, but it was time to leave."

"Why did you choose our neighborhood?"

"Julie and I got tired of the rat race up around Miami. We thought this would be a better place to raise our daughters. The twins had a great time last year when we spent two months at a local resort. And, as Sam mentioned, I really like to fish."

At this point a man came forward, clearly prepared to introduce himself to Rashaan. It was Patrick Henry Simpson, a fishing client of mine who lived just down the street. He almost matched Rashaan's six foot six, but he was heavier, with a full shock of gray hair and a deep tan. Simpson wasn't my favorite client. He lacked the inherent patience I usually found in the very best fishermen. But he was a generous tipper, he knew how to handle both spinning and fly gear, and he paid double whenever we had one of our backcountry canoe trips.

"Rashaan, this is Patrick Simpson, a neighbor of ours."

The two shook hands. "Pleased to meet you, Mr. Simpson."

"Please call me Hank."

"Then please call me Rashaan."

"Of course," Simpson replied.

Simpson was a developer who had been responsible for much housing construction in the Florida Keys including many of the homes in the Gulf Shores Development. But I didn't know all the details, some of which he proceeded to provide.

"I'm a *Heat* fan, so I know a lot about you, Rashaan. But it probably isn't reciprocal. I build houses. Sometimes whole developments. As it happens, the very first one I built is the one you just bought. That was back in 1997, and I built that one for myself. I was just a start-up architect back then. Came up through the school of hard knocks in Miami. Of course your place has been sold a few times since then, and I expect there've been lots of upgrades."

"We love the house," Rashaan said. "The classic Spanish-style architecture, the red tile roof, the courtyards. It's just perfect. And Julie says a woman must have designed the kitchen and cupboards. All the right heights and arrangements."

"That would have been my ex-wife. I'm glad you like the house, and welcome to the neighborhood. Are you a fisherman?"

"Just getting started on that."

"Well you couldn't do better than to go out with Sam, here. He's the best. And if you like shallow water angling like I do, I highly recommend one of Sam's canoe trips into the backcountry."

~ ~ ~

It was dark by the time the meeting ended. Rashaan and I found ourselves walking part way home together because we lived in the same direction from the Portman's house.

"Thanks for coming to the meeting," I said. "Sorry it went on so long. They always do."

"No problem. The world is run by committees. The NBA is full of them. But what can you tell me about that guy Nate? Is he some sort of rent-a-cop for the development?"

I knew what he was asking. We all remembered a case up on the mainland where a self-appointed vigilante gunned down an innocent black kid walking home from an ice cream store.

"No, Nate's not like that. I think he's harmless. Probably just bored and a little bit nosy. He's lived here a long time, and he was friends with my uncle."

"Good to hear. Actually, he looks familiar, like I've seen him someplace before. I just can't remember when or where."

"You'll likely find out because he'll probably stop by your house one of these days. He loves to meet new people."

"And what about that Stebbins fellow?" Rashaan said. "The one with the special bumper sticker?"

"That may be another matter. He's a charter fisherman, specializing in offshore trips for sailfish and the like. I've heard rumors he may not always pay attention to things like size and catch limits."

"Which doesn't necessarily translate to his being a racist redneck, does it?"

"No, I suppose not. But I'm pretty sure his bumper sticker is the one with the little boy peeing on Obama."

"Oh."

We continued walking together, our feet crunching on the gravel beside the road. There was no wind, and no other sound except the harsh call of a bird someplace off in the mangroves.

"Suppose that was a yellow-crowned night heron?" Rashaan asked.

This was something new. Before I quit the university, I'd taught and studied ornithology. He must have known that. Likely it had come up during our fishing trips together.

"Could be. Didn't know you were interested in birds."

"It's recent. Both Julie and I have taken up bird watching."

"What about Serena and Candace?"

Rashaan laughed. "So far the girls haven't gotten past rolling their eyes about it. Maybe if they found some boys who liked it, we'd have a chance. But next time you and I go out on the water, could it be for birds? Or maybe fishing *and* birds?"

"Sure, and I may know just the place. The Park Service just opened up an area back in the glades that's been closed for years. We'd have to take my canoe because they don't allow motors. You up for it?"

"You think I'd fit in?" he asked.

I hesitated. Why would a black man actually wonder if it was okay for him to go birdwatching in Everglades National Park?

Rashaan must have picked up on it. "What I mean is, would somebody my size fit in your canoe?"

"Oh. Yeah, I think so. Hank Simpson's been out in it, and he's about your size."

I'm an idiot, I thought to myself.

"Any chance we might spot a flamingo?" he asked. "I think you told me you found some not long ago."

"Maybe. There've been a few sightings lately."

"How soon could you fit this into your schedule?" he asked.

"What about tomorrow?"

"You're on."

Chapter 2

We didn't find any flamingos on that trip. But even if we had, we might not have remembered it, given what else happened that day.

Florida Bay is a roughly triangular corner of the Gulf of Mexico, wedged in between the south Florida mainland and the Keys archipelago. Much of the bay is inside Everglades National Park, including nearly all the water we crossed that day. Our final destination was a small nameless creek flowing south out of the everglades into Ingraham Lake at Cape Sable. The cape forms the far western corner of mainland Florida before the coast bends north toward Everglades City and on up to Naples and Fort Myers.

Straight-line from my home in Islamorada to Cape Sable is about 45 miles, approximately an hours' boat ride. But it took us longer than that for more than one reason. First, you can't do it by a straight line even if you wanted to, because of numerous small keys and shallows that get in the way. Second, my Maverick skiff couldn't make top speed with a canoe strapped to its port side gunwale. But even if there were a straight-line route, and even if we hadn't had a canoe, it still would have taken most of the morning because Rashaan kept asking me to stop so he could look at birds.

First, he wanted to glass a small key not far from my house where a colony of frigatebirds regularly roosted. As we approached, a bunch of them lifted up off the mangroves and began circling the island.

Rashaan pointed up. "Those white-headed ones are the juveniles, right?"

"Right."

Then we came to a key where hundreds of white pelicans had gathered on a beach. I pulled in closer so Rashaan could take pictures with his phone. "The kids are gonna love seeing this," he said. "These birds aren't here in summer, so they must have just gotten here, right?"

"Right."

Next we passed an area where white herons and great blue herons were hunting the shallows together. "Aren't those herons actually the same species?" he asked. "Just different color forms?"

"Right again."

Rashaan clearly had gone full in when he'd taken up birdwatching.

Once in sight of the mainland, we turned west, following the coast toward Ingraham Lake. We didn't see any unusual birds on this stretch, which gave us time to chat about other things.

"I understand you sometimes help Katie on criminal matters," Rashaan said. "How do you find time to balance that with guiding?"

"I'm still working on that. Part of it is seasonal, or at least it will be. In the fall—like now—the fishing business is pretty slow. That gives me more time to pursue other things. Actually, Katie and I just formed our own LLC. We call it 'Upper Keys Investigations.' We've also taken and passed the examination to become licensed private investigators in the State of Florida. Katie's the mainstay of the operation, given her credentials as a forensic scientist. But we're planning to expand our services to include such things as tracking down missing persons. And I've had some luck with that, if you can call finding dead people lucky."

Rashaan laughed. "Speaking of luck, I guess this trip counts as lucky for me, given your new career."

"That all depends."

"On what?"

"On whether we find any fish to go along with all those birds you've gotten so interested in."

Rashaan laughed again. "No worries. Whatever else happens today, it's still a solid ten."

Even though we'd left my dock in the half-light of dawn, by the time we reached the mouth of the creek the sun already was high overhead. We tied the flats boat to a mangrove and off-loaded ourselves and our gear into the canoe. Next came a critical first step before we started fishing or birdwatching. The mosquitoes and the noseeums had already found us, and I knew it would only get worse the farther we moved back into the glades.

I handed Rashaan a clear glass bottle that I always kept in the center console of my boat. "That's industrial strength DEET. Lather up good because it's gonna be wicked in there. But don't touch anything such as your glasses frame. This stuff melts plastic."

Once we'd doused in repellant, we ducked under the overhanging mangroves and paddled inland.

Rashaan and I fished hard for the next three hours. Or I should say Rashaan fished hard while I handled the canoe. We worked our way through a variety of narrow creeks and open lakes, all of which were loaded with fish. He caught and released a half-dozen each of snook and redfish, along with a couple small tarpon, using both fly and spinning gear. It could scarcely have been any better. Even the bugs were tolerable as long as we were out from under the mangroves.

There also were plenty of crocodiles. Some were in the water, showing only snouts and tails. Others were sunning on shore, their mud-brown eyes open but seemingly staring at nothing. "Are they taking naps?" Rashaan asked.

"If they're moving then they're not napping. Otherwise it's hard to tell."

"Speaking of telling, I've always wondered: how do you tell a crocodile from an alligator?"

"In Florida, alligators are mostly in fresh water, while crocodiles prefer salt water. What we've got here are crocodiles. But if you happen to see a pair together in the same pond, it's easy. The alligator is the one next to the crocodile."

"Hah hah. But seriously, are crocodiles dangerous?"

"Not in my experience, but I wouldn't go sticking my hand in the water."

Rashaan was about to cast toward a tailing redfish, when we both heard a low guttural "*gaw, gaw, gaw*" coming from somewhere back in the trees.

He stopped in mid-cast. "What was that?"

"Not sure," I said. "Obviously some sort of bird."

"Let me try something," Rashaan volunteered, as he pulled out his cell phone and tapped on it.

The bird kept calling.

"Huh," Rashaan said.

"Huh what?"

"My phone says it's a mangrove cuckoo? Could that be correct?"

"That's possible. We're definitely in the right habitat. Southern Florida is the only place it occurs in the U. S. I've seen a couple before in Everglades National Park."

14

I knew about an app you could get from the Cornell Laboratory of Ornithology that would identify birds by their calls, but I'd never seen it work. Rashaan obviously had loaded it into his phone.

"Can we go check it out?" he asked. "Mangrove cuckoo would be a new species for me. But I'm reluctant to go strictly on what the app says because sometimes the thing gets it wrong." Rashaan chuckled. "Like one time I used it in my back yard up in Miami, and it told me I'd just heard an African hornbill. Which seemed pretty damned unlikely. Turned out it was a neighbor's dog."

The bird kept calling from somewhere behind a wall of mangroves. I paddled along, looking for an opening where we might be able to squeeze the canoe in under the canopy. I found one, but it was going to be a tight fit. "You sure you want to do this?"

"I'm sure."

I started paddling slowly back into a narrow channel. "Be ready to hunker down. And watch out for spider webs."

"Spiders?" Rashaan asked.

"Yeah, they'll be thick in here. That's one of the reasons you're in front."

"And all along I thought it was because that way I'd get first crack at the fish."

We were about ten yards into the trees, pushing overhanging branches out of the way, when suddenly there was a loud *thunk* that I felt as much as heard. The canoe lifted up, teetered precariously from side to side, and then settled back into the water.

"What the hell was that?" Rashaan asked.

I looked back over my shoulder in time to see a big tail sculling back and forth in the dark water. "That was a croc. Guess we interrupted its nap."

We could still hear the bird.

"Want to keep going?" I asked.

"Uh, sure, we've come this far."

In another twenty yards the creek widened out into a small lake. Rashaan lifted his binoculars and scanned the bank of mangroves lining the right-hand shore of the lake. "Good grief," he said. "Looks like we're not the first people to get in here."

"What do you mean?"

"There's a boat over there, back in the trees. At least I think it's a boat."

15

"Guess we'd better go take a look," I said, starting to paddle.

"And forget about the cuckoo, right?" Rashaan asked.

"Afraid so, at least for now. Maybe another time we can come back and look for one."

The boat Rashaan had spotted turned out to be a canoe, jammed up into the mangroves and tilted hard to starboard. Plant debris, mostly dead leaves and twigs, nearly filled the hull, suggesting it had been there for a very long time.

I handed the paddle to Rashaan, along with my wallet and phone. "I think we need to check this out. Hold the canoe here, and let me know if you see any sharks or crocodiles."

I eased out of the canoe, set my feet on the bottom and gently stood up, ready to hop back in if the bottom proved too soft to support my weight. But it held reasonably firm, so I waded into the mangroves and got up next to the canoe.

It took a while to clear away enough debris to be able to check things out. To my relief, there was no sign of a body. But neither was there much of anything else, not even a paddle let alone any fishing gear. Based on the remnants of a decal still visible on the hull, the canoe was an "Old Town" model, ten or twelve feet long, and colored red. There were no registration numbers on the hull, but that wasn't surprising. I knew registration wasn't required for vessels without motors that were less than sixteen feet long, at least not in Florida. What was required was a Hull Identification Number (HIN), the boating equivalent of a car's VIN. It would have been stamped into the hull at the time of manufacture. In a regular sort of fishing boat the HIN would be on the transom next to the outboard motor. But since this canoe was pointed at both ends, I knew the HIN would have to be someplace else.

I found it on the hull, just below the starboard side gunwale.

"You got a way to write something down?" I asked Rashaan.

"Yeah, a pen and a little notebook. You know, for my bird notes."

"Okay then, take this down. It's a combination of letters and numbers."

"Ready when you are."

"XTC62508D292. Now read it back to me, so we're sure we got it right."

Rashaan did that. Then he asked the obvious question. "What's that gonna tell us?"

"I had to learn this stuff as part of the exam to get a captain's license. The first three letters are a code for the manufacturer. The next five numbers are like a serial number unique to that particular canoe. The last part tells us the date it was built. I'm not sure about all of it, but the '92' stands for 1992. So we know this canoe is better than thirty years old."

"That's great," Rashaan said. "But now I think you'd better get back in *our* canoe. There's a big croc coming our way, and he's looking kinda pissed. Like maybe he wants us out of here."

"How can you tell it's a 'he' and how do you know it's pissed?"

"I guess I can't. But it's definitely *not* taking a nap. So hurry up, okay?"

"Yeah, I just want to take another look around. See if there's anything else that might give us a clue who might have left this thing here."

Rashaan muttered something I couldn't make out, but I could tell he wasn't happy.

"I'll only be a couple of minutes, Rashaan. This could be important."

"So is my ass. What should I do if that croc comes for us?"

"Don't make a noise like crocodile food."

"You're just a bucket of laughs today, Sam."

"Only when it comes to crocodiles."

The area back beyond the canoe was higher and dryer and opened up into a sort of grassy meadow. I walked out into it, making a big circle, scanning for anything unusual. It wasn't a very thorough search because I didn't want to leave Rashaan alone much longer.

After about ten minutes I gave up, waved to Rashaan that it was time for him to come and get me, and wadded back out into the water. There was no sign of the crocodile.

"Did you find anything?" he asked as soon as I was safely on board.

"Nope. Just the canoe itself."

"What happens next?"

"First, I'm gonna get the coordinates of this location using the GPS on my phone. Next we call Mike Nunez. He's head ranger for Everglades National Park and a friend of mine. He needs to know about this."

Was the Park Service already familiar with this canoe? It didn't seem likely. In my experience, they were pretty good about removing derelict vessels and other debris.

Chapter 3

Cell service can be tricky in remote parts of south Florida, and we definitely were in one. But this time I got lucky. There were two bars on my phone when I turned it on. I punched in Mike's number and got lucky again. He answered on the second ring.

"Nunez here. Is that you Sam? How's fishing?"

"Not bad, but that's not why I'm calling. I'm out in your backcountry today with a client, and we've found an old canoe. From the looks of it, it's been here a long time."

"Where are you?"

"We're in that no-motor zone you just opened up north of Ingraham Lake. The boat's an Old Town canoe, red. Thought you should know about it, if you don't already."

"Doesn't sound familiar. You have any sort of ID?"

"There's no registration, but I've got the HIN. Says it was built in 1992."

"And there's nothing else? No personal items?"

"Not that I could find."

"Okay. Read me the HIN, and I'll run a check."

I gave him the letters and numbers. "I've got the coordinates too, but getting in here was complicated. We found the thing completely by accident."

"If you have time to wait, I'd like to come out and have you show me."

"Be happy to. We'll paddle back out to where I tied up my skiff and wait there. It's along the north shore of the lake."

"Who are you with?" Mike asked.

"Rashaan Liptan."

"No kidding? The basketball player?"

"The very same. He's also a fisherman and—more recently—a birdwatcher."

"It'll take me maybe a half hour, Sam. See you in a bit."

Rashaan spotted a green heron on the way back down the creek. We stopped to watch it dive on some glass minnows, but we still beat Mike Nunez to our tie-up on the lake shore. Rashaan did some more birdwatching and I fiddled with fishing gear while we waited.

"You known this ranger long?" Rashaan asked.

"Uh huh. For several years. We've worked a couple of cases together. He's a good guy, really dedicated to the glades, probably because of his Seminole heritage."

Rashaan nodded like he understood. "Guess this place was all theirs once." He looked skyward as a dozen roseate spoonbills flew overhead. "Beautiful birds. Do they nest around here?"

"They do, but not in their former numbers."

"Why is that?"

"Spoonbills were almost exterminated by plume hunters in the 18th and 19th centuries, but they have largely recovered from that. Threats today involve habitat loss and degradation of their crustacean foods, likely due to declining water quality."

He started to ask for more details, when we both heard the sound of an approaching vessel. Pretty soon Mike came around the corner, driving a Hell's Bay skiff painted light green with a Park Service logo on the side. We'd joked before about the logo: the silhouette of a bison in the foreground, with a snow-capped peak behind it. "I suppose Indians are supposed to know all about those buffalos," he'd said. "But in my experience they're scarce as hell in the everglades."

Mike waved as he pulled along side. He was a stocky middle-aged man, barrel-chested, about four inches short of my six feet. He wore a deep tan, and his short bristly hair had more gray in it than the last time I'd seen him. I introduced him to Rashaan.

"Honored to meet you," Mike said. "You might not guess from looking at me, but I played basketball in high school. Ever since I've been a big Miami *Heat* fan." Then he turned to me and pointed back into the mangroves. "So you found an old canoe back there? Guess we'd better go take a look."

"Sure. But we might want to go in my canoe," I replied. "The no-motor rule may not apply to you government people, but it's really tight back in there."

"That works for me, Sam. You got an extra paddle?"

"I do, but we won't, . . . oh I get it. You're thinking of bringing that old one back out?"

"Uh huh. We have a policy of confiscating abandoned vessels. I'll tow it back to Flamingo and try to get in touch with the owner. There'll be a fine involved."

Rashaan stayed with the boats while Mike and I paddled back into the mangroves, me in the lead to point the canoe in the right direction. There still were plenty of crocodiles around, but I no longer heard the mangrove cuckoo, assuming that's what it had been.

"Its great to see so many crocs back in here," I said.

"Uh huh. And spoonbills, both of which are in some trouble. With sea level rise, there's more salt water pushing back in here every year, which is good for the crocs because they pretty much avoid fresh water. And the spoonbills are nesting farther inland too. Apparently it's getting too deep near the lake for them to reach their prey."

We ducked under the mangroves at the mouth of the little creek, just like before, but this time we didn't bump into anything. Then I directed us to the spot with the old canoe.

"Boy, it looks like that thing has been here awhile," Mike said. "I'm actually surprised nobody's seen it before now."

"Maybe they did, and just didn't give a darn."

"Yeah, maybe. Let's get in close, then I'll jump out and tend to this thing."

"You want some help?" I asked.

"Probably not. Just stay here, ready to lead me back out to the lake."

Mike climbed out of my canoe with the spare paddle, and waded ashore. Then he tugged on the canoe and slid it out from under the mangroves. He started to pull himself up over the gunwale, but suddenly he stopped and began fumbling around inside the hull. After a while he straightened up and turned to look at me.

"Looks like we'll have to go with Plan B," he said.

"What's Plan B?"

"We're gonna leave it here."

"Uh, okay. But why?"

"There are holes in the hull, at least three of 'em. If I tried to paddle this thing back out, I'd turn into shark food. Or maybe lunch for a crocodile."

This was embarrassing. "How in hell did I miss those holes?"

"Probably because they were plugged with mud and debris. I didn't see 'em until the hull started to fill up with water and I rooted around looking for the leak. But there's another reason we're not moving this thing. Unless I'm way off, those holes were made by bullets."

"What do you want to do?"

Mike didn't say anything for a while. He slapped at a mosquito that had landed on the back of his neck. "Right now, nothing. If this is a crime scene, we'll need to get a forensics team in here, with metal detectors for sure, and maybe scuba gear. That will be up to Investigative Services, and I don't want to involve them, at least not yet."

I knew that the Investigative Services branch of the National Park Service handled major crimes in Federal parks. I also knew that Mike wasn't all that thrilled to call them in, probably because they tended to take charge and push regular Park staff aside. That's how they'd behaved another time when he and I had worked a case together.

"Before we do anything else, I'm gonna follow up on this canoe's hull identification number that you already gave me. I was going to do that back in the office before coming out here. But without an actual registration number, I knew it was going to be tricky, and I didn't want to leave you out here until it meant you'd be taking a trip home in the dark."

"I appreciate that, Mike."

He sighed and looked around. "You know, maybe we'll find out the canoe belongs to a guy still living in the area. Maybe he had some sort of an accident and just left it back here. Maybe those aren't bullet holes. Maybe we can get this whole thing solved without having to bring in anybody from the outside."

Maybe, I thought to myself.

Chapter 4

When Rashaan and I got back to my dock, he helped me clean out the boat and stow my canoe on sawhorses in the side yard. We agreed to go fishing and birdwatching again soon, but we didn't agree on the "arrangement" as Rashaan called it. What he meant was that he insisted on paying my guide fee, while I told him to forget about it. After a brief back-and-forth we left that part hanging, since it didn't seem worth risking our friendship.

Rashaan left to walk home, while I went up on the back deck with Prince the Corgi. Just then Katie pulled into the yard. Prince had learned to recognize the sound of her Prius (what little there was), and he dashed off around the house to greet her.

They came upstairs together and joined me on the deck. It was late afternoon but still sunny. Katie gave me a quick kiss, and asked how my day had gone. I told her about finding the old canoe back in the glades, and about Mike Nunez' discovery of possible bullet holes.

Being in the forensics business, this naturally got her full attention. "Sounds like a possible crime scene," she said. "Could Mike trace it to any particular missing persons case?"

"Not yet. He's looking into it."

Normally before dinner Katie and I shared snacks and drinks out on the deck, along with Prince. But tonight she had something else in mind. "I don't have anything prepared for dinner. And besides, it was going to be your night, remember?"

I wasn't completely sure about that, but it was a fact that we shared cooking duties. I was fully responsible on Tuesdays and Thursdays, when Katie had a seminar class than always ran late. She usually cooked when I had all-day fishing clients because I was pretty wiped out after eight or nine hours in the boat. The rest of the time we shared cooking. One of the reasons our arrangement worked was that we could eat out on days when we both were too tired to cook.

There were a handful of restaurants in Islamorada favored especially by locals. They had good food at reasonable prices, the latter being increasingly hard to find. One we particularly enjoyed was the Safari Lounge. The place included a unique (at least for the Keys) collection of stuffed African wildlife hanging on the walls and from the ceiling. Regulars called it the "Dead Animal Bar," where—as some wag once put it—"the extinct meet to drink."

We liked the Safari for a bunch of reasons. It was only five minutes from our house, it had good basic fare, and two of our friends owned and ran it. Flora Delaney, who went by Flo, had tended bar there for years, until an inheritance enabled her to buy it. She did the cooking, mostly sandwiches and salads, while her partner Snooks Lancaster tended bar and handled the snacks. I'd known Snooks since I first moved down to the Keys. He was a former fishing guide who taught me most of what I knew about the business. He was one of the best, but he didn't fish much anymore now that he was in charge of pouring drinks at the Safari.

And then there was Prince. Flo and Snooks had two cats called Mocha and Gringo. They didn't like leaving the pair at home while they were cooking and bar tending, but it obviously wasn't going to work having the cats running around loose in the restaurant. Instead Snooks built a room in the basement below the kitchen just for them. By a special arrangement, our Corgi Prince was allowed to visit the "cat house" (as Snooks called it) when we came for food and drinks. At first there had been the usual dog vs. cat issues, but by now they had it pretty much worked out.

Because Flo always threw a handful of dog treats down the stairs to lure Prince into joining the cats, he always was at a fever pitch to get out of the car when we went to the Safari. Tonight was no exception, and he'd already disappeared by the time we came in and took our usual seats at the bar, which was a large rectangular structure that filled the center of the room. We waved at Snooks, who was in the process of serving drinks to a couple seated at one of the tables next to a big window. Windows at the Safari looked out on a palm-lined beach and—beyond it—the Atlantic. During daylight the view from the Safari was spectacular, but by now it was completely dark outside except for a few lights coming from boats moored at a nearby marina.

Snooks waved back and signaled that he'd be right over. Just then Flo came out of the kitchen carrying a big platter of burgers and fries, headed for a family of four seated at another one of the tables.

Once they'd finished delivering the food and drinks, Flo and Snooks came over to join us. Katie and Flo exchanged big hugs, while Snooks and I made a sort of feint at it, neither of us having gotten used to the idea of men greeting each other with more than a handshake.

Whenever Flo and Katie got close to each other, I couldn't help comparing them. I wasn't proud of it, and didn't plan on it, but it just seemed to happen. One time a few years back, while Katie was still up in Fort Lauderdale, Flo and I had a one-night hook-up. Alcohol was a factor, neither of us was proud of it, and it never happened again. I never was sure whether Katie or Snooks knew. They certainly hadn't heard about it from me.

Flo was a couple of inches shorter that Katie's five-eight and maybe five years older. She was a bit curvier than Katie, though both were well-endowed in that department. Her hair was a rich chestnut brown while Katie's was jet black. Flo's most distinctive feature by far were her emerald green eyes, while Katie's were hazel.

"What's up?" Flo asked. "Haven't seen you two in a while."

"We're good," Katie replied. "Except neither of us had the energy to cook tonight. You have anything special?"

Flo quickly responded. "How about baby-backed ribs, coleslaw, and baked beans? Snooks likes my attempt at barbecue."

We nodded and Flo left for the kitchen.

"What are you guys drinking?" Snooks asked from behind the bar.

"Two of your house margaritas, rocks and salt," Katie replied, without giving me a chance to speak first. It was fine with me.

Snooks walked over to a newly equipped island in the center of the bar and set about mixing our drinks. He had thinning gray hair tied-up in a ponytail held in place by a red rubber band. Even though he now worked mostly indoors, he had a permanent leathery countenance: doubtless the result of too many years on the water with too little sun block.

We watched him work. "You gonna tell Snooks about what you found today?" Katie asked.

"Thought I would. He's been fishing around here for most of his life, including canoe trips into the backcountry. Maybe he'll remember something."

Snooks came back with our margaritas and set them on coasters in front of us. We both took a first delicious slurp. Then I put my glass back down and brought up today's event.

"Went out with Rashaan Liptan today. We took my canoe into an area the Park Service just opened up off Ingraham Lake."

"How was fishing?" he asked.

"Pretty good, but it got cut short when Rashaan spotted an old wrecked canoe way back in the mangroves."

"Huh."

"I got out and had a look. The thing was full of debris, as if it had been there for years. And it was one of those vintage Old Towns I've only seen pictures of."

Snooks began fiddling with the rubber band holding up his ponytail. It was a familiar gesture. He usually did it when he was thinking hard about something. What was different this time was the look on his face. It was as if he'd left the room, as if he'd gone someplace else mentally.

I went on with my story. "I called Mike Nunez, their head ranger, and he came out with the idea of towing the canoe back to headquarters. But that didn't work out because it turned out there were holes in the hull. Mike guessed they might be from bullets."

Snooks came back from wherever he'd been. "Did he get an ID?"

"It had never been registered, or at least there was no sign of it. But we got the hull identification number put on by the manufacturer. Mike's gonna try to track it down that way. He'll let me know what he finds out. But I was wondering. Do you remember any Old Towns around here going missing, probably way back?"

Snooks shook his head. "No, not really." He briefly glanced back at the kitchen, then excused himself and went off to tend to other customers.

"That was odd," Katie said, after Snooks had left.

"Yeah, it was. It was almost like he didn't want to talk about it."

Just then Flo came out of the kitchen carrying a big tray with our ribs and sides. She served our food and then took the bar stool next to Katie. "Rashaan Liptan was out here a few days ago with his whole family. He and Snooks had a long conversation about basketball numbers, which I ignored. Their two daughters were a lot more interesting than who got the most three-pointers in the 2019 playoffs, or whatever it was they were arguing about. Have you met Julie and the kids?"

I had but Katie hadn't.

"Serena and Candace are absolute delights," Flo went on. "They loved our cats, said they hoped to get some for themselves, and asked if they could bring them here for a visit. It must have embarrassed Julie because she started to say something. But I said that would be fine."

Snooks came back after he finished washing some glasses. "How's the guide business?" he asked.

"Busy. Whenever you're in the mood, I could send some clients your way. You're still the best, my friend. They wouldn't be disappointed."

It was true, but it also was an attempt to butter him up. The man had gone to some dark place when I mentioned the wrecked canoe, and I wanted to get him back.

"No, I don't think so," Snooks said. "Too much to do around here."

So much for my charm offensive.

We finished our dinners, paid the bill, and then went out into the kitchen to retrieve Prince for the ride home. Except for us, the Safari was empty. Snooks was busy washing glassware when we came out of the kitchen, but he stopped to say something as we approached the door.

"If I were you, Sam, I'd forget about that old red canoe. There probably are lots of them wrecked over the years, scattered back in the glades. It can be a dangerous place. Probably you should just leave it to the Park Service. It's their land, after all."

We were almost home when something occurred to me. "Did Snooks just say something about a red canoe?" I asked Katie.

"Uh huh. Why?"

"Because I don't recall mentioning the color, just that it was a vintage Old Town."

"Were all of them red?" she asked. "That could explain it."

"It could, but they weren't."

Chapter 5

I spent a good part of that night trying to figure out what was up with Snooks. We were long-time friends, and I'd never known him to be standoffish. Yet when I mentioned finding that old canoe he'd pretty much gone silent, other than spilling the fact that it was red when I was pretty sure I hadn't even mentioned that. Did he know or at least suspect who might have left a red canoe back in the glades? If so, why wasn't he willing to talk about it?

Katie must have wondered the same thing because she brought it up while we were enjoying coffee and donuts together the next morning. We were out on the deck, having given Prince the first of his twice-daily constitutionals, followed by his breakfast. The sky was clear blue, and the air had a crisp fall feel to it—or as close as we ever get to that down here in the Keys. I watched as a little blue heron worked along the edge of the mangroves lining the canal across from our house. It stopped, stabbed, and came up with a small crab in its beak.

"You think Snooks knows something about that canoe you found?" she asked.

"Good question. I've got half a mind to track him down today and push him about it." I took a swallow of coffee and ate a bite of glazed donut. Donuts were a secret indulgence. "What are your plans for the day?"

"I think I'll go up to the lab. Stella Reynard gave me the stomach contents of a homeless woman they found dead last week in the trees behind the Publix supermarket."

Stella was a detective with the Monroe County Sheriff's Department. We'd worked a number of cases together, and she knew Katie was an expert at identifying plant foods in the stomachs of dead people, based on the fact that each plant species has unique cell arrangements. Katie often could determine a victim's last meal based on the combination of cell types present.

"You think the woman ate something from that grocery store she shouldn't have?" I asked.

Katie laughed. "Of course not. But I suppose she could have been dumpster diving. And the point—as you well know mister smart guy—is not necessarily to determine what killed her, but to find out something about her last meal before she died." She drained the last of her coffee. "You fishing today?"

"Nope. I just need to give my canoe a better scrubbing than we had time for yesterday, and then straighten up some fishing gear. Also, I might get hold of Snooks and try to find out what was bugging him yesterday."

"Any chance you'd want to take a drive up to the mainland this afternoon?"

"I could do that. Why?"

"I've been meaning to pay a visit to 'Robert Is Here.' You know, the fruit stand up in Homestead? Wanna go along?"

"Sure. I could use one of his milkshakes. We haven't been there in over a year."

"That's because you never take me anywhere."

I decided to ignore the jab once I caught a twinkle in her eyes. "Is that why you want to go, Katie? To have a milkshake?"

She laughed. "Well, that could be one reason. But actually, I was hoping to get samples of some of the tropical food plants they have for sale, in order to get photos of their cell types for my reference collection. Tropical fruits and vegetables often are regular parts of peoples' diets in this part of the world. One of my students was up there recently and she said the place had some new stuff for sale."

"Okay, good. I'll be ready when you are."

Katie stood up, ready to leave. "See you in about three hours then?"

"I'll be here, and I'll have Prince emptied out in case we run late."

Sometime later I was hosing off the canoe when my phone chirped to life. It was Mike Nunez.

"Hey, Mike. What's up?"

"Had some luck tracking down the owner of that Old Town canoe. Thought you'd want to know."

"Damn right I do. What's the deal?"

"I ran that HIN and came up with a name." I heard the sound of paper rustling. "It was purchased by somebody named Rolando Cabrera, and his mailing address was a place about five miles west of Homestead. I checked the map and it looks like the address might be for one of those farms out there. Of course that isn't necessarily who owned it when it got left back in the glades. But he definitely was the man who bought it back in 1994."

"Sounds like you've really done your homework."

"Sort of. But here's the weird part. I ran a search for somebody with that name and came up with nothing current. No driver's license, no phone number, no address, no nothing. It's like the guy just vanished."

"What about the address linked to the HIN? Is anybody there now?"

"Yeah, actually there is." More paper rustled. "Somebody named Royce Holland. And there's a phone number."

"You gonna call him?"

"I tried that at least six times, but nobody answered. And the mailbox was full so I couldn't leave a message. I'm thinking of driving over there this afternoon. I'll let you know what I find out."

Being naturally nosy, and not inexperienced at crime fighting, this was too good an opportunity to pass up. "Any chance I could come along, Mike? It turns out Katie and I have planned a trip to Robert Is Here this very afternoon, so we'll be in the area."

"That sounds like a plan, Sam. I'm a sucker for their milkshakes. Give me your ETA when you know it, and we'll meet up and go from there."

~ ~ ~

Katie chose banana-mango-dragonfruit, Mike ordered guava-pineapple, and I had papaya, my regular favorite. The milkshake line stretched out into the parking lot, as it often does at Robert Is Here, but as usual it was worth the wait. We sat at a picnic table under a tiki top and watched the animals in a little zoo out back as we worked on our shakes. "This place is amazing," Katie said between slurps. "I can't wait to get a look at all the unusual fruits they have for sale here."

"This is about your forensic work, isn't it?" Mike asked.

I recalled that Katie had helped Mike solve the murder of one of his fellow Park Service employees three years ago, by identifying some unusual fruit cells in her stomach that suggested where she'd had her last meal.

"That's right," Katie said. "Each kind of plant cell has a unique wall pattern, and since those walls are made of cellulose, which humans can't digest, I can identify what was in a victim's stomach long after they've died But only if I can match those cells to ones in my photo collection."

Mike grinned and nodded. I was pretty sure he already knew all this.

"Uh, sorry for the lecture," Katie said. "You push the right button on a professor, and out it comes. Anyway, I've heard that Robert has some new fruits for sale that I might not have analyzed."

"You want to look around here while Sam and I go visit the guy we hope knows something about that red canoe?" Mike asked.

"Sounds good," she said.

Mike and I went back out through the fruit stand and got in his Chevy Blazer with a Park Service logo on the front door. We drove west on Palm Drive for about a mile, then headed north on a narrow paved road bordered on both sides by fields with tidy rows of tomatoes, onions, and some sort of green crop I didn't recognize. Mike slowed at one point, and turned down a gravel lane. At the end of the lane stood an unassuming wooden house, painted white with a shingle roof and a small covered porch. There also were two metal outbuildings, each of which was bigger than the house. A door at the end of one of the buildings was open, and I could see a large John Deere tractor inside. As soon as we pulled to a stop, two dogs came bounding down off the porch, barking like they meant trouble. We sat in the Blazer, waiting for the dogs to calm down by themselves or for somebody to come out of the house and make them do it.

After about two minutes, which seemed longer, a man appeared at the door, squinting against the sun. I guessed his age at somewhere between late sixties and early seventies. He had on bib overalls and a t-shirt that might once have been bright green, but the color had long since faded out. He had a farmer's tan: dark face and neck, but with a white stripe across his upper forehead where a cap normally sat.

"Can I help you?" he said.

Mike identified himself and asked if we might come over and ask a few questions. The man fidgeted and frowned and looked out across the fields that I assumed were his, almost as if he had been expecting somebody else. "Sure, I guess so," he replied without enthusiasm.

"Then would you mind calling off your dogs?" Mike said.

The man yelled a couple of names I couldn't make out, and then barked out "Shed!" The dogs immediately went off into one of the metal buildings.

"Are you Mr. Holland?" Mike asked as we walked up.

"That's right, Royce Holland. Is there some sort of a problem?"

"No problem. But we're looking for somebody who might once have lived here. Thought you might be able to help."

"And who would that be?"

"Rolando Cabrera," Mike said.

"Haven't heard that name in a lot of years. What's this about anyway?"

"Would it be alright if we came up on your porch?" Mike asked. "Then I'll explain."

"Sure, I guess so," Holland said. "But I don't know if I'm gonna be much help."

We sat on a couple of rickety old benches on the narrow porch. Mike introduced me and then explained the reason for our visit. "Yesterday Mr. Sawyer here found an old red canoe by itself back in the glades inside the Park. Based on the ID number, Mr. Cabrera is the one who purchased the canoe and then listed this place as his address. So we're wondering if he's still around, and if we could talk to him about why his canoe might have been left out there."

Royce Holland shook his head. "Rolando used to work for me. Worked here for a lot of years. But then he left."

"Where did he go?"

"We were never sure, but we always assumed he'd gone back to El Salvador where he came from. One day he just didn't show up for work."

"When was that?" I asked.

"Well now let's see," Holland said, scratching at the bristle on his chin. "More than twenty years ago. Must have been 2001 or thereabouts. I can't remember exactly."

"Did you ever try to find Mr. Cabrera, or maybe file a missing persons report?"

"Nope. Didn't do either."

"And you never heard from him again?"

"Nope."

"What about the canoe?"

"What about it?"

I could tell by his expression that Mike was getting tired of this. "What happened to his canoe? Did he ever sell it?"

"Couldn't tell you. I remember when he got it, but then he took it over to the marina at Flamingo and kept it there. For all I know it's still there, and frankly I couldn't care less. Never have liked the water. Don't even own a boat. All those gators and crocs scare the shit out of me."

That seems to be that, I thought to myself.

Mike must have agreed because at this point he got up, thanked Holland for his time, and said we might be back in touch if we had any more questions.

"I wonder why that man never reported Cabrera as missing?" I asked as soon as we were back in Mike's Blazer.

"My guess is Cabrera was an illegal farm worker, and Holland didn't want to get in trouble for hiring him."

"Yeah, that makes sense. And if he did go back to El Salvador, that would explain why you couldn't find anything recent about him."

"That's one possible explanation," Mike said. "But we both know there's another one."

"Yeah. Is there any way to search for the man in El Salvador?"

Mike sighed. "That's way above my pay grade, Sam. But either way it's time for me to get in touch with our Investigative Services division. We need a forensics expert or two to check out that area where you found the canoe."

We drove back to Robert Is Here. Katie was standing next to our Jeep. The hatch was up and I could see two big paper bags in the back. Based on their bulging shapes, she must have hit the fruit and vegetable jackpot. Mike rolled down his window. "How did it go?" he asked.

"Very well, as you can see," she replied. "How did it go with you two?"

Mike summarized what we'd found out, while I got out of his vehicle.

"Which means either the man went back home to El Salvador or maybe he's dead somewhere out in the glades," Katie said.

"Which means we're gonna do a forensics search in the area where Sam found that canoe," Mike said.

"I'd be glad to help," Katie said.

"Thanks. But I'm not sure a corpse that old—assuming there is one and we find it—would have a stomach, let along anything still inside it."

Cold Case

Katie shook her head. "No, that's not what I'm talking about. Another thing we forensic botanists do is search for clandestine graves. Of course maybe the Park Service already has somebody who knows how to do that. There must be lots of searches for missing persons in the National Parks."

"Tell me a little bit more about this," Mike said.

"If a body gets buried, but not in a coffin, it fertilizes the soil as it decomposes. That can change the above-ground vegetation. We look for those patterns. Of course it wouldn't work in areas with standing water, which includes a lot of the glades."

"But not all of it, so that could be useful," Mike said. "And thanks for the offer. Unfortunately it won't be my call. Once the Investigative Services team gets on board, which will be pretty soon, they'll be in charge of who does what. But I'll be sure to let them know about you."

Chapter 6

When Katie and I got back home there was a familiar old Toyota pickup in our yard. The door opened as we pulled in behind it. Snooks got out of his vehicle as we got out of my Jeep, and we exchanged hellos. It was close to dark, but even in the low light I could see that his face lacked its usual smile.

Snooks tugged at the rubber band holding up his ponytail. "Can we talk?" he said.

"Sure, come on up. You got time for a beer?"

"Uh, no thanks."

The three of us went up the stairs. Prince naturally went nuts as soon as I opened the front door, since he'd been cooped up for the better part of six hours.

"This little guy needs a walk," Katie said. "And he'll want dinner as soon as we get back. Let me handle that while you guys have your talk."

Katie took Prince's lead off the hook where we keep it next to the door, leashed him up, and the two of them went back downstairs. Normally it was my job to walk him in the evening. Katie must have guessed that it was me Snooks wanted to talk with more than her.

"I need to explain something about yesterday," Snooks said, before we even had a chance to sit down.

"Something about that canoe Rashaan and I found?"

"Uh huh. I know I acted kinda weird when you brought it up, and I owe you an explanation."

"You don't owe my anything, Snooks. But I must admit it made me curious." I pointed over to the living room. "Let's go sit. You sure I can't get you anything?"

"No, I'm fine, thanks." He tugged again at his ponytail. "See the reason I tried to shut you up was because I was afraid Flo would hear us even though she was out in the kitchen."

"Hear what?" I asked.

Snooks took in a breath and let it back out. "Years ago—way back before you came down here—a man named Sebastian Brophy made an unwanted move on my brother Andy."

I knew about Andy: that he'd worked for the Audubon Society investigating a ring of shark fin poachers, and it had gotten him killed.

"Did this have anything to do with the shark fin deal?" I asked.

"No, this was way before then. Anyway this guy Brophy used to hang out at a bar up in Largo, as a bunch of us did. I ran into him one night up there, just after I'd found out about the deal with Andy. We were both pretty drunk and we got into a tussle." Snooks stopped and shook his head. "Actually it was a lot more than a tussle. I pretty much beat the crap out of him, put him in the hospital. Then the cops got involved."

"How did that turn out?" I asked.

"Badly. I was convicted of assault, and they sentenced me to a year in the county jail."

"But you did your time, and that was that, right?"

"Not exactly. I got paroled after four months, and then while I was out Brophy disappeared along with his boat and his canoe. That was back in 1998."

It was all beginning to make sense. "And that canoe was a red Old Town, right? And the law suspected you of being involved in Brophy's disappearance?"

"Right on both counts. Nothing ever came of it because they never found him. And there was nothing to tie me to the case except a possible motive." Snooks paused and fiddled with the rubber band holding up his gray ponytail. "But if that canoe you found turns out to be Brophy's, the whole thing could open back up."

"But if you had nothing to do with it—and I'm sure you didn't—then why would that be a problem?"

"Because of Flo, Sam. She doesn't know anything about this, and I want it to stay that way. It could break her heart if she learned about my record."

I had a decision to make, but it wasn't all that hard. "There may be some good news here, Snooks."

"Oh yeah, what's that?"

I proceeded to fill him in on what Mike Nunez and I had learned today, that the canoe belonged to a farm worker in Homestead and not to Sebastian Brophy. The look of relief on Snook's face was palpable, but it didn't last all that long.

"Did that canoe have registration numbers?" he asked.

"No, all we have is the hull ID."

"Which means that guy from El Salvador could have sold it to Brophy before he went back home, and there wouldn't necessarily be any record."

"That's true. But let's not get ahead of ourselves here. The Park Service is gonna do a thorough search of the area where we found the canoe, and we may know more after that's done."

Just then the door opened and Katie walked in with Prince.

"Uh, sorry, I should have made his dinner, but I forgot," I said.

Katie must have caught something in the air because she smiled and said that was no problem. She picked up Prince's bowl and went off down the hall to the closet where we kept a bag of kibble. She came back in a little bit, laid the bowl on the floor in the kitchen, and sat down next to me.

We sat silent for a while. I wasn't about to bring Katie in on what was going on, at least not until Snooks had left. But he beat me to it, and repeated the whole story for her, right then and there. After he finished he looked at the two of us and asked: "In the meantime, what should I tell Flo?"

"That's your call," Katie chimed in before I had a chance to say anything. "But I know what I'd do."

"What's that?" he asked.

"I'd tell her exactly where things stand, and I'd do it for a couple of reasons. First, she deserves it. And second, I wouldn't want to be in your shoes if she finds out you've been holding out on her."

"Yeah, but . . ." He trailed off.

"Flo's a tough lady and she loves you, Snooks," Katie said. "Take my word for it."

Chapter 7

The next day I fished with a married couple from Cleveland. She was a medical doctor in a big hospital where he kept the books. They wanted to catch mackerel on a fly and then some other kind of fish to eat. We agreed that mackerel were okay if you smoked them, but otherwise they were a little dark and oily. Snappers and porgies were much better eating. I knew about a spot out in the bay where fish congregated around an old sunken boat. Both Spanish mackerel and mangrove snappers gathered there. My clients were experienced anglers who knew how to cast, so it was an easy and enjoyable day. They fought and released three mackerel apiece, and kept four good-sized snappers for their dinner.

I was back at the dock cleaning my skiff when I heard the sound of shoes crunching on gravel. I turned around and spotted Rashaan Liptan coming around the house. He was puffing and sweating heavily. At first I thought something might be wrong.

He must have caught the look on my face. "Just out for a run in the neighborhood. I like to keep in shape, but these old legs aren't what they used to be." He had a hand towel around his neck, which he used to wipe the perspiration off his face. "Thought I'd drop by and see if you had any news about that canoe we found."

"Mike Nunez and I had a talk yesterday with a farmer named Royce Holland up by Homestead. It turned out he used to employ a Salvadoran who bought that canoe back in the mid-1990s."

"You sure it was the same canoe?"

"Yup. Mike traced it back through the Hull Identification Number. The buyer lived at that same address, or at least that's what the Old Town records showed."

"And you're sure the buyer was the Salvadoran and not the farmer?"

"That's what the farmer said, and it's consistent with the record. But here's the frustrating part. The Salvadoran disappeared a few years later."

"Did the farmer file a report?"

"Apparently he didn't, probably because the guy was illegal."

"Still, it sounds like you might be getting somewhere."

"Maybe. We'll know more after the Park Service does a search of the area."

"You gonna be in on it?"

"Yeah, I think so. Me and Katie, but I don't think it'll happen for a couple of days."

I thought about telling Rashaan about Snooks and Sebastian Brophy but decided against it. No point in spreading a story that might be irrelevant to the case.

Rashaan took another swipe with his towel. "You know about the Islamorada Hump?" he asked.

Talk about a change of subject. "Yeah, and I've heard all the jokes."

Rashaan grinned. "Wanna go fishing out there?"

"Not in this little skiff of mine. The hump is an underwater mountain out beyond the continental shelf. The seas usually are way too rough. You'll need to find somebody else."

"I already have. My next-door neighbor, Rusty Montrose, has a big enough boat, or at least he says it is. I happened to mention that Julie is crazy about ahi tuna, and he said we could get some out there. Said he doesn't get to fish that often since his wife died, and he doesn't like to go out alone. Anyway, we're headed there tomorrow. Want to go along? Rusty says he's got all the right kind of gear, so you'd just need to bring yourself and maybe something to eat and drink."

"Actually, that sounds interesting."

"Good. Be at my house by 6:30."

~ ~ ~

Rusty Montrose turned out to be a seriously old codger, with a seriously old boat. It was a vintage Grady-White Sailfish model with twin two-stroke Yamaha outboards. Plenty big enough to take on the Atlantic, assuming everything still worked.

Rusty himself was thin and bent, with a shock of frizzy white hair tinged with a hint of red at the temples. Rashaan introduced us and we shook as he invited me aboard.

"Any relation to Fred Sawyer?" he asked.

"He was my uncle."

"Oh yeah? You live here now?"

"In his place, after he left it to me. Did you know him well?"

"Sure. Back in the 70s when this development was just getting started, we all pretty much knew each other." He turned his attention to the controls, and lowered the outboards into the water. "Let's just hope these old boys fire up. It's been a while."

One of the Yamahas started much quicker than the other, but they both eventually got going. I was glad he had two, just in case. It wouldn't have been good to get stuck out in the blue water without a way to get home. Rusty asked Rashaan and me to cast off the bow and stern lines, and we pulled away from the dock. Once out in the Gulf, he motored down to the Channel Two Bridge, then went under it and out into the Atlantic. The day was clear and calm, with only a moderate swell. The Grady-White made good time, so far without a hitch, and after about twenty-five minutes a cluster of boats came into view out toward the horizon.

"Are they on the hump?" I asked Rusty.

"Yep, and it looks like we'll be anything but alone."

In fact, the place was a damned zoo. There must have been at least a dozen boats moving around in an area not much bigger than two football fields.

"What's the plan and what are we likely to catch?" I asked Rusty.

"The fish will be feeding where the ocean current hits the slopes of the hump, moving food around and up into the water column. That's why everybody's in this one little area. Our best chance is for blackfin tuna."

"Are they good eating?" Rashaan asked. "My wife really loves ahi."

"Absolutely delicious," Rusty replied.

"What about methods?" I asked. "It looks like some boats are trolling while others are holding in place."

"We'll try both methods, but my favorite is to troll plastic worms of different colors, right up on the surface. It can be exciting as hell if one of those big fish streaks up and grabs the bait."

We let out two long lines, one with a black worm and one with a bright pink version, set the rods in holders built into the hull, and began working our way around the area. Given all the company, it was a little like fighting your way through rush-hour traffic. The good news was Rusty seemed to know what he was doing. The not-so-good news was that nothing was happening, to us or to anybody else from what I could see.

"Rashaan tells me you're a fishing guide," Rusty said, maybe just to pass the time waiting for a hit.

"Yeah, but I'm strictly a backcountry fisherman, or sometimes the Gulf. There's no way my little Maverick could handle the open ocean. And besides, I'm mostly interested in fly-fishing."

"Oh yeah? Sounds like a guy I used to know who lived in our neighborhood, Bash Brophy."

"Bash?"

"Yep. His actual name was Sebastian, but we called him Bash."

"Short for Sebastian?" Rashaan asked.

Rusty shook his head. "I suppose maybe, but the main reason was the way he played linebacker. Never saw anybody hit harder."

I sensed a gold mine that day on the Islamorada Hump, if not for tuna than at least for information. "You two knew each other for a long time?"

"We both went to Coral Shores High School in Tavernier, and then we ended up buying houses in Gulf Shores. So we definitely knew each other, but I wouldn't say we were all that close. Even back in school Bash was sort of a loner."

"Is he still around?" I asked, even though I was virtually certain I already knew the answer.

"No, he . . . say, why are you so interested in this guy?"

I knew it was time to fess up or shut up. "A fishing buddy of mine happened to mention him the other day, that something bad happened."

"Yeah, what happened is he disappeared. I'm thinking you already knew that."

If this case was about to get re-opened, whether or not it involved Sebastian Brophy, the last thing the sheriff's department would want was rumors getting started. And I may already have spilled too much. It went against the grain, but I decided a little white lie was necessary.

"I know he disappeared, but I don't know anything about the circumstances."

"Well, he didn't run off, if that helps. Or if he did go away on his own, it must have been in his boat. It was gone too, but his pickup was still at his house when the cops showed up."

"Was there a missing persons investigation?"

"Sure was. But nothing ever turned up."

"Did they suspect foul play?" I asked.

"I imagine they did. We all did. Bash didn't have a real good reputation around here."

"Why was that? Something to do with fishing?"

Rusty shrugged. "Maybe. He was way into conservation; always grumbling about somebody or other that wasn't following the rules. But Bash also worked for the Village of Islamorada as a building inspector. It was a pretty wild time back in the 1970s, with lots of shady developers. He was always getting in the way of some project or another."

"I can see why that might have been an issue. But as a motive for murder?"

"Who said anything about murder? And anyway, this all happened a long time ago. Why are you interested now?"

I shot Rashaan a look that I hoped said *Don't go there.* Rashaan evidently got it because he kept quiet.

"No reason in particular," I said to Rusty. "Except that my friend brought it up the other day and I—"

Suddenly Rashaan let out a yelp. "Look at that!" he shouted.

I spun around just in time to catch the end of a big swirl about a hundred yards off our stern, and then one of the rods bent nearly double. Rashaan and I looked at each other and hesitated.

"Hey, come on!" Rusty said. "One of you guys needs to get on it! That looks like a good blackfin!"

I pointed to Rashaan. "Your fish, man."

He grabbed the rod and played the fish masterfully through a series of deep and powerful runs. Fifteen minutes later we had a nice twenty-pound tuna on board. Rashaan looked down at the fish flopping around on the deck. "Looks like Julie's gonna get her ahi," he said. "She and I both thank you for that, Rusty."

We trolled for another hour without getting a hit, and then tried some deep water jigging, but that didn't work either. Nearly all the other boats had moved off by then as well, and Rusty announced that it was time to call it quits. I was grateful he didn't bring up Sebastian "Bash" Brophy on the boat ride back home.

41

Chapter 8

Two evenings later, Katie and I were out on the deck enjoying an after-dinner decaf, when my cell lit up. It was Mike Nunez. I put the phone on speaker and told him Katie was on the line. We exchanged hellos.

"You guys available for a backcountry trip tomorrow?" he asked. "The Investigative Services team wants to go take a look at that canoe wreck. I told them about Katie and clandestine graves, and they're up for you two coming along. But it's gotta be tomorrow."

I had a client booked for the morning. Bill Swanberg was a local who owned a True Value hardware store in Marathon. We'd fished a lot together and I didn't want to disappoint him. I thought of two possibilities: either he and I could go another day, or I could pass him off to Snooks. I really didn't want to miss out on the National Park deal.

Tomorrow was a Saturday, so I knew Katie had no classes. I looked at her. She nodded "yes."

"Let me get back to you, Mike. It should be okay, but I need to untangle myself from something."

"Good. I hope you can work things out. Sorry for the short notice, but when the Feds take charge of something—which they definitely have—it's their way or the highway." I could hear the edge in his voice. I also thought it was odd he referred to the Investigative Services people as "the Feds." Wasn't he a Fed?

I made two quick calls, got Snooks and Bill hooked up, and called Mike back in less than fifteen minutes. "Okay, we're set. What's the plan?"

"Two things for openers. First, we'll need your boat as well as mine, both outfitted with canoes, because there'll be five of us going out. And second, Rhonda Wilcox wants us all to meet at my office in Flamingo before we head over to the site. Can you be here by eight tomorrow morning?"

Katie frowned but shrugged.

"Yeah, we can do that," I said. "See you in the morning."

I remembered Rhonda Wilcox from a couple of years ago when the Investigative Services branch got involved in a case in Everglades National Park. She seemed competent and no-nonsense, but I also remembered she'd left no doubt about who was in charge.

"This could take most of the day," I said to Katie, after disconnecting from Mike. "We should try to find somebody to give Prince an outing. I'm thinking Rashaan's daughters might be available."

"Good idea. Why don't you handle that, while I take a quick run up to my lab. There's some equipment I'd like to bring along."

"Like a clandestine grave detecting device? Is there such a thing?"

Katie laughed. "I wish. No, just ordinary stuff like plant field guides, a notebook, and my fancy camera. Oh, and also a metal detector."

~ ~ ~

Setting out across Florida Bay in the pre-dawn light has always been a magical time for me: the sun just a faint glow to the east, the dark waters ahead full of promise. But that was the way it looked and felt through the eyes and mind of a fisherman. Today was going to be different. We were on a quest and full of hope, but for what exactly? Certainly not for a body. But if not that, then what might we find that could put Snooks' mind to rest? Ideally we would find something connected with that old canoe that ruled out Sebastian Brophy as ever having been there. Then we could forget about the whole thing and get back to our regular daily lives.

As we motored in toward the marina at Flamingo, we passed maybe a half-dozen fishing boats going out in the opposite direction. One was a skiff with a platform above the outboard, and a guide who probably would be poling his client across a no-motor flat in search of redfish or snook. At the other end of the vessel spectrum was an old-time Boston Whaler with a family of five crammed in under a blue canopy. Most likely they hoped to drift into a school of speckled trout and bring home dinner.

Mike met us at the dock and helped me tie up. He had on hip waders, just like the ones Katie and I were wearing. I wondered how Rhonda

Wilcox would be dressed. The last time I'd seen her she'd been wearing a white short-sleeved shirt, black slacks, and low heels. Definitely not dressed for the field.

"Morning Katie," Mike said. "Thanks for coming. And you too Sam."

We walked together across the parking lot to the low Park Service office building. Mike led us into a room that afforded a good view out on the bay. A long table with eight chairs dominated the center of the room. A high bench next to the wall held two Keurig coffee machines. Above it an array of cups hung from pegs on a rack. There also was a small refrigerator like the ones you find in motel rooms, and a bowl filled with coffee and tea containers ready to pop into one of the Keurigs.

Rhonda Wilcox was seated at the head of the table, with a younger man perhaps in his late thirties sitting to her left. She wore an olive tunic that said "Police; Federal Agent" across the back in big black letters. She had on blue jeans and white rubber boots that came up to her knees. The man with her was wearing ordinary tennis shoes. I wondered how he expected to stay dry in a swamp, assuming he was going with us.

Mike made introductions. We learned that the man with Rhonda was her assistant, Elon Tharpe, and that he was an expert at crime scene investigations and reconstruction. He had curly red hair, an easy open face, and a stubbly "I forgot to shave today" beard. He reminded me of Prince Harry. Rhonda was severe looking, which I remembered from the last time, her face seemingly in a perpetual frown. She seemed unable or unwilling to smile, even when she rose to shake our hands. Her dark hair was pulled back in a tight bun that only heightened her aura of humorless severity.

"Please be seated, everyone," Rhonda said. "Let me begin by thanking the Doctors Sawyer, both for contacting Ranger Nunez to report what you found, and for coming along today." Then, with a nod to Katie: "At Mike's suggestion, I researched a bit on the sorts of things you have contributed to criminal science, and I must say it is most impressive."

I sensed a "but" coming from Rhonda, and then it did.

"That having been said, I'm sure you will appreciate that this is a Park Service investigation, that any and all evidence we might collect today is our property until we determine otherwise."

Mike rolled his eyes, but Katie acted as if this were the normal state of things. "Of course," she said.

"Before we head out," Rhonda continued, "I want to describe what I think should be the key parts of today's investigation, including who does what. As I understand it, we have a canoe at the edge of some open water with a mangrove swamp behind. Is that right Mike?"

"It is."

"And you think there might be bullet holes in the hull of the canoe, correct?"

"That's right. Can't be sure, but it looks that way."

"Good. Elon should be able to determine that, but in any event he'll start by examining the canoe and its immediate vicinity. Once that is completed, we'll move on to the second two phases." She paused to look at Katie. "Dr. Sawyer—actually both Dr. Sawyers—you should inspect the land beyond the canoe for a clandestine grave, and any other objects of possible relevance."

"I have a metal detector," Katie volunteered.

"Good," Rhonda said. "And while you're doing the land search, Elon will look under the water. He brought along a wet suit, scuba gear, and a waterproof metal detector with an extra long handle."

I raised a hand. "The place is full of sharks and crocodiles, Mr. Tharpe. You sure you want to get in with 'em?"

Elon grinned. "I will if I have to. That's why I brought the wet suit. But if the water's less than five feet deep, I can reach the bottom with my metal detector without having to get out of the boat. And I have a fishing gaff with a hook on the end that we can use to lift things out of the water. Of course if we suspect something's down there that's not metal . . ." He trailed off.

Rhonda cleared her throat. "The last thing we'll do today, once we've completed our search, is to get that old canoe out of there. I know it's Park Service policy to remove abandoned watercraft when possible. Mike, are we prepared for that?"

"Yes we are. I have an extra paddle, and some duct tape."

"Duct tape?"

"For the bullet holes, or whatever they are. It wouldn't be a permanent fix, but the tape should hold back the water long enough for us to paddle the canoe back out to the lake shore, where we can pick it up later."

"Good," Rhonda said. "Then just one more thing before we head out. Should any of you happen on *anything* that might be related to this case, no matter how trivial you think it is, please do not touch or disturb it. Instead, immediately call it to my attention."

She didn't finish by saying "and then stay the hell out of the way," but she might as well have said so.

We walked back to the marina and out onto the pier where our boats were moored, each with a canoe strapped to a gunwale.

Rhonda Wilcox frowned. "What are those canoes for?"

Mike explained about the narrow creek. "Too tight for our boats."

We waited while Elon struggled into his wet suit. I wondered why he didn't wait until he needed it, but that was his business. Once Elon was ready, we loaded up and pushed off from the dock. Mike led and I followed, as we motored out into the bay and then turned west toward Cape Sable.

I knew Katie was a fan of Prince Harry. We had a copy of his autobiography on our coffee table. Once Mike had moved ahead of us, I asked her if she thought Elon looked like the prince. She laughed and said "Sort of."

"And what's your impression of Rhonda?"

"Something that would be politically incorrect for you to say, but okay for me."

"What's that?" I asked.

"Tight-ass."

I laughed and shook my head. "That seems about right."

It was a struggle offloading our gear into the two canoes for our paddle rides back into the glades. Not only did we have the two metal detectors, but Elon also had a pair of large metal toolboxes and the fishing gaff along with his scuba outfit. Plus Katie had a small backpack and everybody brought bottled water. We lathered up with DEET, got into our canoes, and started paddling back into the mangroves. Mike led again because he had marked the route on his GPS when we'd been there before, and I wasn't sure I remembered the series of creeks and lakes we needed to get through. But I recognized the narrow opening in the wall of mangroves when we got close to it.

"We're going in *there*?" Rhonda asked.

"If you want to see that old canoe," Mike replied. "Just duck down. The creek will get us through, or at least it did last time. Sam, you want to go ahead, maybe push some of those branches out of the way? Feel free to break some off if you have to."

I did as he asked, with Katie doing most of the branch breaking since she was sitting up in the bow. The bugs were nasty until we broke out into the little lake.

The Park Service people paddled up beside Katie and me, and I pointed out the red canoe.

"Good," Rhonda said. "Let's get on with it." She looked back over her shoulder at Elon, who was sitting behind her. "You go in first and do your thing with the canoe. We'll wait out here until that's done. Then, no matter what you find, the rest of us will spread out and work the area back in those trees, while you search in the water with your metal detector." She paused to look around at all of us. "Everybody got that?"

We all did. But I could tell Katie was getting fidgety. Why couldn't she and I go ashore and start looking for a clandestine grave right away? She was a pro. She knew how not to mess up a crime scene. But it was Rhonda's call.

We'd spotted the dorsal fins of a couple of sharks farther down the lake, and one good-sized crocodile was sunning itself on a sandy bank. Elon understandably wasn't all that anxious for a big wade. "Don't worry," Mike said. "We'll get you in close."

We paddled over next to the mangroves and watched as Elon sloshed ashore with his metal detector and his toolboxes. It took him two trips.

"See anything obvious?" Rhonda asked, even though Elon barely had time to get started.

"I see the holes in the hull, alright, along with a bunch of debris. I'm gonna poke around in there. Then I'll slide it off to one side. There's a chance we could find slugs in the ground under the canoe, assuming it hasn't been moved since the shots were fired."

"And assuming those holes were made by bullets," Mike said.

"Correct."

We watched and waited, while Elon fired up his metal detector and worked the business end back and forth over the area. It seemed longer, but it couldn't have been more than ten minutes before he stopped scanning and went down on his hands and knees. He took a probe or perhaps a pair of tweezers out of his shirt pocket—I couldn't tell which—

and began poking around with it. Time passed slowly. Finally he said "bingo" and held something up about three inches from his nose.

Evidently Rhonda's admonition about "if you find anything get out of my way" didn't apply to Elon. "What is it?" she asked.

"Definitely a bullet," Elon replied. "Can't be positive, but I'm guessing it's from a .38 caliber weapon." He went over to where one of his toolboxes lay open, picked out a small tan envelope, and dropped the slug into it.

I don't know about Mike, but I actually was relieved because this meant we hadn't dragged everybody back in here for no reason. On the other hand, it clearly was an ominous sign about the fate of the person who'd brought that canoe back in here however many years ago.

"Good work," Rhonda said. "Any more than just that one slug?"

Elon didn't answer, but instead he went back to work with his metal detector.

In the end he found three more slugs, but nothing else. Before he was done, he'd dug a hole about six inches deep and shaped like an Old Town canoe. It was an impressive job, tidy and thorough from what I could tell.

"You guys might as well come ashore," Elon finally said. "Looks like that's it for right here."

We paddled in, tied our canoes to mangrove trunks, and got out. The bugs found us as soon as we made our way up next to Elon. His face was flushed and beaded with sweat. It must have been hell for him dressed in that wet suit. It was bad enough even in the hip waders I was wearing.

Rhonda asked Elon for the envelope and got it. Then she took a look inside, and scratched her head. "You know, there's something odd about this."

"Yeah, I'd been thinking the same thing," Mike said. "There are holes in the canoe and slugs in the ground. If somebody was trying to kill somebody out here, then they must have been a lousy shot."

"Or they could have had some sort of rapid-fire weapon, and just sprayed things around," Elon replied.

"I guess there's no way of figuring that out," Katie said. "Unless we find a body."

Potentially, there was both good and bad news for the rest of the search. The good news was for Katie and me: the thick wall of mangroves at the edge of the lake quickly gave way to relatively open ground with grasses and scattered trees. Searching there for a clandestine grave or anything else would be relatively easy. The bad news was for Elon: the water was murky, with no more than two feet of visibility. If there was anything down there that wasn't metal, it was going to be next to impossible to find without getting in the water. It also would be hard to see a shark or a crocodile until it was too late to get out of the way.

Rhonda must have realized the risk. "Mike, I want you to go with Elon and paddle the canoe while he works his detector. But Elon, don't go in the water if you find something. Just mark the spot with your GPS. If it looks like something important, we'll figure out what to do later."

It wasn't at all clear to me what "figure out" would entail, but one thing did occur to me. If—somehow—a body had ended up in that lake a bunch of years ago, between the sharks and the crocs and the tide it would be long gone by now. Our only real hope was on land.

Rhonda slapped at a mosquito that had landed below her left ear, leaving a bloody smear on the side of her neck. "Okay, everybody, let's get to it."

For Rhonda herself, "getting to it" apparently meant waiting until somebody else found something. She sat herself down on a fallen mangrove trunk and pulled a pen and a small notebook out of her vest.

We left Rhonda where she was, as Katie and I moved inland while Mike and Elon went back out in the Park Service canoe. I had a general idea what we were searching for, but I asked Katie just to make sure. "Some sort of unusual clump of vegetation, right?"

"Yep. Out here in this prairie, it could be something as simple as extra tall grass, but more likely a cluster of trees or shrubs."

I scanned across the clearing ahead of us. There were numerous patches of woody vegetation sticking up out of the grasses. "I see a bunch of those clusters out there. How are we gonna tell which one might be a grave?"

"That'll be the tricky part, Sam. But because these coral-based soils are relatively infertile, a decomposing body should provide a major nutrient boost. So what we're looking for is a patch that is relatively lush and likely taller than the others, but also covering a smaller area."

"Something body-sized?"

"Exactly. If we find something like that, then I'll check it with the metal detector. If we get a hit, then I suppose we have to call in Rhonda."

"What if there is no metal, but your botanical experience suggests it still looks unusual?"

Katie looked at me with a grin and a shrug. "Well, we can't very well ask her to come out here for every little thing, can we?"

Being a complete novice at this whole clandestine grave thing, I decided for starters to stick with Katie rather than wander off on my own. She handed me the metal detector. "Might as well scan as we walk," she said. "Nothing to lose as long as the batteries hold up."

Amazingly—at least to me—we hadn't walked more than fifty yards when the thing started to beep. I swept the ground back and forth and got a strong signal each time the search coil passed over a spot about six inches square.

I looked at Katie and she looked back. "Guess we better call Rhonda," she said. "You want to do the yelling?"

I did.

Three minutes later Rhonda caught up with us. "Got something?" she said.

"We had a hit with the metal detector. Thought you'd want to take a look."

I moved the search coil over the spot, and then backed off while Rhonda knelt down in the grass. She pulled on a pair of yellow rubber gloves and started digging with her fingers, cautiously pulling aside grass blades and other debris. Katie and I bent down and watched over her shoulder. In a little while her fingers stopped moving.

"Got something," she said. She lifted an object up out of the ground. It was disc-shaped, about four inches in diameter and less than two inches thick. It was caked with dirt, and at first I had no idea what it was. But as Rhonda began to clean it, carefully brushing and blowing off the dirt, at one point it suddenly became familiar.

"That's a fly reel," I said.

Rhonda picked herself up off the ground and held the reel out toward me but not all the way. "You have any gloves?"

"I do," Katie said. She set down her backpack, reached inside, and handed me a pair of clear vinyl gloves.

I pulled on the gloves, then took the reel from Rhonda and turned it over in my hand. "Looks like an old Pflueger. We might be able to get a model number once it's cleaned off."

My mind raced. We knew Sebastian Brophy was a fly fisherman, but what about Rolando Cabrera from El Salvador, the man who'd purchased the Old Town canoe. It didn't seem likely he would have been into fly-fishing, let alone have a vintage Pflueger reel.

"What about a serial number?" Rhonda asked.

As far as I knew, fly reels didn't have serial numbers, but I wasn't sure. "I don't think so. But there is an outside chance the owner of this reel etched his initials into it. I've seen some like that. Maybe if I take it apart—"

Rhonda shook her head. "Not here. We need to get it back to the lab where we can clean it properly."

She asked for the reel back, and started walking away. "You guys keep looking. I'm gonna go put this in an evidence bag."

Katie and I set off in search of a clandestine grave, or maybe another hit with the metal detector. But it all came to nothing. We found no clumps of grass or shrubs or trees that looked taller or greener than any of the rest of them, and the detector never beeped again. After three hours of futility, Katie gave up. "It's humid and buggy, my DEET's worn off, and I just don't see anything out here. Let's pack it in. Maybe the other team has had better luck."

We walked back and joined Rhonda. Mike and Elon were still in the canoe, out in the middle of the lake. "Those guys find anything besides sharks and crocodiles?" I asked Rhonda.

"Maybe," she said to my surprise. "They've marked a spot where the detector lit up. It's just down the shore a ways. I told them to keep searching the rest of the lake until you got back. Then we've got to decide what to do about it. Elon tried pulling whatever it is up off the bottom with his gaff, but he didn't have any luck. Then he wanted to jump into the water, but I told him to hold off. You got any ideas?"

This was the first time Rhonda had asked me for advice instead of telling me what to do. Maybe—just *maybe*—she realized I might know something about the everglades that she didn't.

"You say this thing is close to shore?" I asked.

"Maybe five or six feet out. Why?"

"And how deep is the water there?"

"Uh, not sure. But he could reach the bottom with his detector, so I expect not more than four feet or so."

"Then I think it might be okay for Elon to get in the water if the rest of us protect him with the canoes. I only know of one case where an American crocodile attacked a human. They're much less dangerous than the African and Australian species. Our crocs, along with the sharks, are back here hunting prey items that are smaller than themselves. The trick is for Elon not to splash around."

"Why not?" Rhonda asked.

"Because it's the sound of something flailing around in the water, like a wounded fish, that's likely to attract them." Then I had another thought. "Maybe I should be the one to do this because I've had more experience than Elon working around in the glades."

Rhonda shook her head. "Thanks, but no. Can't risk the liability."

In the end, we formed a triangle around the spot where Elon would get in the water, with two sides being our canoes and the third side being the shoreline. Elon struggled back into his wet suit and put on a pair of swim goggles and a weighted belt. Then he slipped over the side and sank quietly down into the water. I wasn't watching what happened next because I was busy keeping an eye out for any shark fins or crocodile snouts headed our way. But it wasn't more than a minute or two before a gurgling sound caused me to turn around.

The first thing I saw was Elon's head and then his right hand as they came up out of the water. He had hold of something, but—just like the fly reel—it was too caked with mud and debris to tell what it was.

"Got it!" Elon said.

"Good. Now get the hell back in the canoe," Rhonda replied.

Elon dragged the object through the water as he made his way back to the canoe, which had the effect of cleaning off some of the mud and debris. And then, just like with the fly reel, we could all see what it was.

He had found a dog collar.

I expect everybody was puzzled, and for good reason. But I may have been the most puzzled of all. Or maybe the next step beyond puzzled, whatever that might be.

That dog collar looked familiar.

"May I see it?" I asked Elon, as we helped him up into the canoe.

Katie must have noticed that my hands were shaking as I took the collar from Elon. "What is it?" she said.

'I—uh—I think this came from my dog." I turned the collar in my hands, looking for something in particular. And then I found it. Etched into a metal plate riveted to the collar was a name: "Sammy."

Then I knew for certain.

"*Your* dog?" Rhonda said.

"Yeah. Well, not technically. It actually belonged to my uncle Fred. But we got it together from the local animal shelter, and he decided to name it after me."

"What happened to the dog?" Mike asked.

"I don't really know. I used to visit my uncle often in Islamorada, and always looked forward to playing with Sammy. But then I went off to college, and sort of lost track."

"Now wait a minute," Rhonda said, understandably confused. "You're saying a dog belonging to your uncle wore this collar. Are you sure?"

"Yeah, I'm sure. And not just because of the name, though that in itself would be one hell of a coincidence, don't you think? But the collar looks right too. It's a big one with metal plates all around. And Sammy was a big dog. The people at the shelter thought he was a Labrador mix. And one other thing. Sammy loved the water. My uncle took him fishing all the time."

"Then you think it might have been your uncle who came here with that old canoe?" Mike asked.

"I suppose it's possible, but I don't think so. I don't remember him even owning a canoe."

Rhonda asked the question that must have been on everyone's mind except Katie, who knew better. "Is your uncle alive?"

"No, he passed away seven years ago. From a heart attack. At home."

"Then how—?"

"Maybe somebody else took Sammy for a canoe ride. I really have no idea. But Mike, one thing seems certain. I don't think it could have been a farm laborer from El Salvador, do you?"

I realized then that the case of the wrecked Old Town canoe had just gotten a lot closer to home. It was personal and it was haunting. As a young man I *loved* that dog. What sort of awful fate had he met way back here in the glades?

Chapter 9

Our final business for the day, before heading back to Park headquarters, was to patch up the red canoe as best we could and paddle it back out to Ingraham Lake. Somebody once said there were only two things you really needed in a toolbox. One was a can of WD-40 to loosen something that was supposed to move but wouldn't, and a roll of duct tape to stop something from moving that wasn't supposed to. They left out the part about using duct tape to patch up leaky canoes. But I can attest to the fact that it's good for that too.

We covered over the bullet holes with two layers of duct tape just to make sure, and then turned the canoe over and pulled it out into the water. No leaks. I got selected to paddle it back out of the glades. They let me go first, with the idea that if it sank the others would see it in time to rescue me from the crocodiles.

We tied the canoe up to a big mangrove at the edge of Ingraham Lake, and then headed for home. Mike said he would send somebody out later to pick it up.

Once back at Park Headquarters in Flamingo, Rhonda Wilcox requested (demanded?) that we stay for a post-mortem. I didn't blame her, considering what we had found.

We re-assembled in the conference room where the day had begun. Mike provided bottled water and energy bars, and we all dug in except Rhonda Wilcox, who excused herself and went back outside. She came in two minutes later carrying a plastic spoon and two pints of lemon yogurt. I guess energy bars weren't her thing.

Rhonda sat down at the head of the table and popped open one of the yogurts. "Any chance you have a tape recorder, Mike? I didn't bring one, and we should record this meeting. There are complexities and uncertainties to this whole affair, and we need to get things right, including who does what in the future. I'll have it transcribed later and you'll all get copies."

"I think we've got one around here someplace," Mike said.

Once Mike had come back with the recorder and made sure it worked, Rhonda started off by giving the date and the time, and naming everybody in the room. It felt a little bit like some of the criminal interrogations I'd witnessed.

Having dispensed with the introductions, Rhonda got down to business. "Given the slugs Elon Tharpe found, it is reasonable to suspect we may have been at a crime scene today. But whether somebody was wounded or died, and when it happened, remain unknown." She looked around at all of us. "Right?"

Everybody nodded. *And what about Sammy the dog?* I thought to myself.

Rhonda looked at me. "As I understand it, Dr. Sawyer, you and another person were on a fishing trip and discovered a red canoe at the site some days ago. Can you tell me exactly when and whom you were with?"

"Yes. It was six days ago—"

"That would be September 23?"

"Uh, right. And I was with a client, Rashaan Liptan."

"So this Mr. Liptan witnessed the canoe as well?"

"He did."

"Then I'll need his contact information. Does he live in the Keys?"

"Yes, he's a neighbor. He and his family moved to Islamorada after he retired from a career with the Miami *Heat*."

Rhonda looked blank. Apparently basketball was right up there with energy bars. "And what did you do after you discovered the canoe Dr. Sawyer?"

"We wrote down the Hull Identification Number on the canoe and called Mike Nunez to report what we'd found. Then Rashaan and I waited while he came out and joined us at the site."

Rhonda turned her attention to Mike. "What did you see and what did you do once you got there Ranger Nunez?"

"I inspected the canoe and was prepared to tow it back to Flamingo, when I discovered likely bullet holes in the hull. It was then I realized this might be a crime scene and decided it shouldn't be disturbed. So we left and I called you."

"Did you subsequently learn anything about the history of the canoe?"

"I did. I learned that it was an Old Town model manufactured in 1992 and initially sold to a Rolando Cabrera, who apparently was living near Homestead at the time. Or at least the bill of sale had a Homestead address."

"Were you able to contact Mr. Cabrera?"

"No I was not. But Sam Sawyer and I visited the address and spoke to the owner of the property, a Mr. Royce Holland."

Rhonda asked for the spelling for both Cabrera and Holland. "Go on."

"Holland is a farmer who once employed Mr. Cabrera. But apparently Cabrera left a long time ago. Holland claimed he had no idea where his former employee might be, but speculated he might have returned to his native El Salvador. He also remembered that Cabrera had purchased a red canoe, but he said he didn't know what happened to it either."

"Did he give any indication when 'a long time ago' might have been?"

"He guessed maybe around 2001. I asked him if he'd filed a missing persons report and he said no. I suspect Cabrera may have been an illegal employee and Holland didn't want to get in trouble. But I don't know that for a fact."

"I'll need Holland's contact information if you have it, Mike."

"I do."

"If Cabrera actually went back to El Salvador, we may be able to contact him through our embassy down there. Maybe he can tell us if he sold the canoe and who bought it. Assuming that's what happened." Rhonda scooped out the last two spoonfuls of yogurt, and made slurping sounds as she swallowed them. Then she drank some water and partly stifled a small burp. "Now let's turn to what we found today. Dr. Sawyer—uh, Mrs. Sawyer that is—did you find any signs of clandestine graves at the canoe site?"

"No I did not. We did find an old fly-fishing reel using a metal detector. But my husband says there's no way to trace it to any particular individual, at least on a first look. However, it does suggest that the owner of that canoe was a fly fisherman."

Rhonda looked at me. "Is it likely that Rolando Cabrera was a fly fisherman?"

I'd been wondering the same thing. "Possible, but not likely." I hesitated to make the next obvious point because it inevitably would lead us to

Sebastian Brophy. This in turn would lead to Snooks, and I didn't want to get my friend in trouble. But I decided what the hell, it was all going to come out eventually. "It is even more unlikely that Mr. Cabrera somehow ended up with my uncle's dog, don't you think?"

Rhonda nodded. 'Yes, I was coming to that, Dr. Sawyer. For the record, Elon Tharpe discovered a metal object in the water near the spot where you found the canoe. When he retrieved it, you recognized it as a collar from a dog you once knew, correct?"

"Yes, the collar looked familiar, and when I inspected it I found the name 'Sammy' engraved on a metal plate riveted to the leather. That was the name of a Labrador retriever belonging to my uncle, Fred Sawyer."

"And again for the record, your uncle is no longer living, but he died at home, correct?"

"Correct."

"So while it is possible your uncle somehow transported his dog back into the glades, if so it must have escaped and he failed to find it, right?"

"Again, that's possible, but unlikely for several reasons. First, he loved that dog as much as I did. There's no way he would have left it out there. And second, the dog was very loyal. I can't imagine it would have run off. And finally, while my uncle was an enthusiastic fisherman, he preferred the open ocean and—to my knowledge—didn't even own a boat capable of negotiating shallow water, let alone a canoe."

"But didn't you say you'd lost touch with your uncle at some point?"

"I wouldn't say 'lost touch,' but it is true that I no longer visited him in the Keys after I graduated from high school and went off to university."

Rhonda stopped talking and looked around the room. "So the bottom line is, at this point we have no solid leads as to who might have taken that canoe back into the everglades, assuming—which seems likely—it wasn't the man from El Salvador. Correct?"

Now we had come to it. "Actually, there is one possibility," I said.

The room got real quiet. Even Rhonda Wilcox just sat there, fixing me with an unblinking stare.

"It could have been a man named Sebastian Brophy."

More silence.

"Please go on," Rhonda said. "Who is he, and why do you think it might have been him?"

"He was a fly fisherman with a red Old Town canoe, like the one we just found. He lived in the same development as my uncle in Islamorada—where I live now—and they almost certainly knew each other. Brophy disappeared along with his boat and his canoe, back in 1998."

I picked up a "why didn't you tell us this before" look from Rhonda Wilcox. "Did you know Brophy?" she asked.

"No. Never met him."

"Did your uncle tell you about him, or how Brophy might have ended up with the dog?"

"No."

"Then how did you learn about all of this?"

The question was as reasonable as it was inevitable.

"I learned about it from a friend, George Lancaster."

"And how did Mr. Lancaster happen to know about Brophy and your uncle's dog?"

"I don't think he knew about the dog. But I expect everybody knew about Brophy's disappearance. It would have been big news back then."

"I'm gonna need Mr. Lancaster's contact information," Rhonda said.

"Of course," I said, with a mental sigh.

"Alright then," Rhonda continued. "Here's where we go next. Investigative Services will pursue the El Salvadoran angle. But for the Sebastian Brophy case, I'll be in touch with the Monroe County Sheriff's Department. I'm sure they'll want to talk to you Dr. Sawyer, as well as your friend Mr. Lancaster. They're likely to have a missing persons file on Brophy, don't you think?"

Oh yeah, I thought.

Chapter 10

It was early evening by the time Katie and I got back in my skiff for the ride home. The wind had stayed down all day. The angled sunlight was sufficient to pick up hundreds of white pelicans as they made their way to night roosts on Palm Key, but the dark waters gave no clue as to depth or structure. I probably knew the way by heart, but it was reassuring nonetheless to have the route clearly marked on my Garmin GPS.

Katie sat beside me at the console. "Prince must be worried. Or at least pissed. It's getting toward his dinner time."

"Mine too," I said.

"You plan on talking to Snooks?" she asked.

"Got to. Better to hear about it from me instead of the sheriff. He's not gonna be happy." I pulled out my phone. "Still got three bars, but it won't last once we get away from Flamingo. Guess I better try him now."

The call went through, and I made a quick decision while it rang. Better to do this in person. "Hey Snooks, it's me. Any chance Katie and I could pop over later tonight?"

There was a moment's hesitation. "Geez, that would be great. But we're pretty jammed-up right now. The Islamorada Moose are here for an event. The place is full of guys with funny hats."

"What about the Moosettes, or whatever they call themselves?"

"Got them too. Anyway, what about breakfast instead? Flo's just getting that started, and we could use some culinary feedback."

"Culinary" wasn't what came to mind when I thought about food at The Dead Animal Bar, but this didn't seem the right time for a joke. "Sure, that would be fine. Can Prince still come?"

"Natch."

"We'll be early. Katie and I both have things to do."

"That shouldn't be a problem. We open . . ."

The call dropped, just like I knew it would once we got out away from the mainland. I decided not to try again because that would require going back toward Flamingo to have any chance of success. The day had been long enough.

~ ~ ~

Prince, Katie, and I arrived at the Safari Lounge at quarter to seven, and were greeted by the mouth-watering aroma of frying bacon as we walked in. A couple of guides I knew were there already, eating breakfast. I said hello as we made our way into the kitchen. We almost collided with Snooks, who was on the way out with two plates loaded with pancakes, scrambled eggs, and bacon. "Morning guys," he said happily. I knew it wasn't going to last.

Prince was so taken by the breakfast odors that he was reluctant to go downstairs and visit the cats like he was supposed to. Flo muttered something about the health department and how they would feel about finding pets in the kitchen. Then she spoke sternly in what must have been Corgi-speak, because Prince went on ahead. "The last thing we need is another violation," she said, without providing any further details.

Once she had finished shooing Prince into the basement, she turned back to us. "What can I get you guys?"

Katie and I looked at each other. "Just coffee for now," I said. "Actually, we need to talk before we eat."

Flo flipped a couple of pancakes that were ready to turn, and frowned. "What about?" she said.

"It's more Snooks than you."

"Not sure I like the sound of that," she said. "Let me go get him. He's out there blabbing with the customers, instead of coming back for the next order." She went to the door, pushed it open, and stuck her head out. "Hey Snooks, can I see you a second?"

Snooks came back to the kitchen. "What?"

Flo looked at me and didn't say anything, just went back to her grill.

I wasn't sure how to get started, but Katie came to the rescue as she usually did.

"We were over in the Park yesterday at that place where Sam and Rashaan found the canoe. There's something Sam needs to ask you."

60

Snooks' normally upbeat countenance collapsed. "What?"

"We found a dog collar. And of all things I recognized it as belonging to Sammy, my uncle's Labrador. Do you have any idea how it could have gotten there?"

"How the hell would I know?"

"It's just that my uncle never fished the backcountry, so I thought maybe somebody else could have taken the dog with him. Somebody my uncle knew. I was wondering if you might have any ideas about that."

Snooks reached back and fiddled furiously with the rubber band holding up his ponytail. "Well it sure as shit wasn't some guy from El Salvador!" He fiddled some more, then cleared his throat. "What you're really asking is whether your uncle ever loaned his dog to Sebastian Brophy. *Isn't it?*"

"Yeah, Snooks, I guess I am."

He took in a breath and sighed it back out. "God, this is hard. I can't barely stand to think about it. But, yeah, I suppose he could have. Lots of us kept that dog from time to time. You probably know your uncle Fred was a bachelor and he traveled a lot. Somebody had to take care of the dog when he was gone."

"Was the dog with Brophy the day he disappeared?"

"I wouldn't know about that."

"You sure? It seems like it might have come up when they did the search."

"No, godammit! I had *nothing* to do with that search. Come *on*, Sam, give me a break!"

Flo came over beside Snooks and put her arm across his shoulders. "Take it easy, Snooks. Sam's just trying to figure out what might have happened. He knows you had nothing to do with it."

Snooks' face fell and he scuffed a shoe back and forth. "Yeah, sure, I know that. Sorry. It's just this whole thing has me stressed out. You think they're gonna come after me on this?"

"I'm sorry, but it seems likely," I said. "The woman we met with the Park Service yesterday, once we figured out about my dog, she said she was going to contact the Monroe County Sheriff. Of course we don't know for sure that red canoe belonged to Sebastian Brophy, but it's a definite possibility."

"What about your uncle?" Flo asked me. "Did he ever say anything about what happened to his dog?"

It was a good question. "I asked him once about Sammy. All he said was that the dog was gone. And the way he said it, I was scared to push for details. Now I wish I had."

"Do you think Snooks should go to the sheriff?" Flo asked. "Rather than wait for them to come to him? It might look better that way."

"That's one possibility, but I think there's another way to handle this. Have either of you ever met Stella Reynard? She's a detective with the Monroe County Sheriff's Department."

"I might have met her once," Snooks said. "Can't remember for sure. What about her?"

"If it's alright with you I'll go to her with this. Hopefully then she'll arrange to catch the case, assuming the sheriff wants to re-open it. Which I'm guessing he will. She's a good friend of mine and Katie's. We all can trust her to do the right thing."

Snooks and Flo looked at each other. They nodded in unison.

Chapter 11

There were two reasons I was anxious to visit Stella Reynard. The first was to give her a heads-up about the likely reopening of the Sebastian Brophy missing persons case. The second reason had to do with a much more recent event.

A couple of months previously I had helped her track down the killer of a man called Anthony Broom. Or try to at least. Broom had been a member of an exclusive fishing club in Islamorada, until he was found dead on the property in one of their ponds. We'd narrowed down the list of possible suspects in his murder to another club member named Royal O'Doul, a prominent developer of Florida golf courses, along with George "Bud" Light, a bartender who worked for the club. Their motive? In the interests of conservation, Broom had used his money and influence to scuttle development of a golf course on the edge of Everglades National Park, on land owned by Light's family. Before we could solve the case Light himself had ended up dead under very suspicious circumstances. We had strong reason to believe O'Doul had arranged for Light's murder in order to shut him up. But then suddenly O'Doul had moved his whole operation to Texas.

The last time I'd been with Stella Reynard, she and I had gone to Texas in hopes of bringing O'Doul back to the Keys for questioning. But that had gotten nowhere and now I was curious if there had been any further developments in the case.

~ ~ ~

Stella was at her desk when I arrived at the sheriff's substation in Islamorada the next morning. She was in full uniform as usual: regulation forest green pants, a crisply pressed short-sleeved white shirt with a star over the left breast pocket, and sergeant stripes on each arm.

She looked up as I walked in. "Morning Sam. Glad you came by. It saved me a call."

Had the news traveled that fast? "Then you heard about the red canoe?"

Stella frowned. "Red canoe? No, I wanted to bring you up to date about our friend Royal O'Doul. I don't think it has anything to do with a canoe."

Apparently the word had not yet reached the sheriff. Either that or he hadn't thought to contact Stella. "I'm all ears, Stella. Tell me about O'Doul. It's good news, I hope."

"Depends on how you define it. The man may be in even bigger trouble than we imagined. I got word the other day from Sheriff Spivey down in Key West that the Feds have gotten involved. Something about racketeering and lots of suspicious deaths and disappearances. Even some in Europe, apparently. We've been asked to back off. In no uncertain terms."

"So we just sit and wait? Even though we're pretty sure he killed Art Broom, and probably the bartender too?"

"Those are my orders."

"But the sheriff didn't say anything about the Sebastian Brophy case?"

Stella frowned, causing three neat lines of wrinkles to form across her coffee-colored brow. "Who's Sebastian Brophy?"

"I'll fill you in, but this could take a while. Got any coffee?"

"Always. Let me go next door and get you some. I could use a cup myself."

Stella went out into the bullpen where the other deputies had their desks, while I thought about what to tell her and what to leave out.

She came back with our coffees and settled behind her desk. "Okay, shoot. Why might I be interested in a canoe and a man I've never heard of?"

I paused to clear my throat. "A little over a week ago, Rashaan Liptan and I took a fishing trip to a remote area in Everglades National Park. While we were back in there we found an Old Town canoe, obviously long-since abandoned. I got the hull number off it and called Mike Nunez. You know him I think."

"He's their head ranger, right?"

"Correct. Anyway Mike came out to the site and discovered what looked like bullet holes in the hull. When he traced the ID, he learned the canoe had been purchased by a farm worker living near Homestead. He and I visited the place where he'd worked, and learned from his former employer that the man was from El Salvador, but that he'd disappeared decades ago."

"Along with his canoe?"

"The man didn't say, and we can't absolutely rule out that possibility. But for reasons I'm about to explain, I don't think that's what happened."

Stella frowned again. "Okay, tell me what you think *did* happen. And while you're at it, please explain why this should have anything to do with me or with the Monroe County Sheriff. Or with you, for that matter."

"I'm getting to that. Because of the bullet holes, Mike decided to call in Investigative Services. That's the Park Service branch that investigates crimes."

"I know that, Sam." Stella tapped a pencil on her desk and looked out the window. Clearly, she was losing patience, and I didn't blame her.

"Yeah. Well anyway, several days ago Katie and I went back to the canoe site with Mike and a team from Investigative Services to look for forensic evidence. And this is where it gets weird."

"You found a body?"

"No, but we did find two things. First, there were slugs in the ground underneath the canoe. So the holes in the hull almost certainly were from bullets. The other thing we found was a dog collar. And—I told you this was gonna get weird—I actually recognized the collar. It was from a Labrador retriever named Sammy that once belonged to my Uncle Fred. He named it after me."

"You're thinking it was your uncle's canoe? That something might have happened to your uncle back there?"

"There's no evidence of that. And I don't think so. I spent considerable time with him before I went off to college. Mostly we fished together, usually in deep water out in the Atlantic. To my knowledge he didn't even own a canoe. And for sure he didn't die in the glades. He had a heart attack right here in Islamorada. They found him in bed."

"Then how did his dog get way back there, Sam? This isn't making any sense."

"Naturally, I've been thinking about that. I can't imagine a farm-worker from El Salvador ever got hold of the dog. It must have been somebody closer to home. And it sort of fits. My uncle traveled a lot on business and I learned he used to give Sammy to neighbors to look after while he was gone."

"So we're looking for a neighbor who owned that old canoe, who might have bought it from the farm worker, and who was baby-sitting the dog when something bad happened back in the glades? That's your theory?"

"Yup. I know it sounds far-fetched. But here's the deal. My uncle had a neighbor called Sebastian Brophy, a fly fisherman who happened to own a red canoe. And one day he just disappeared."

"Nobody ever found out what happened to him?"

"Nope. It was a real mystery."

"When was this?"

"Twenty-five years ago."

"What about the dog? Didn't your uncle report him missing?"

"I'm not sure. He never got specific about what happened to it. By then I'd gone off to college and I rarely saw him after that."

"Given the deal with the dog, I can see why you feel personally about all of this."

"Actually, there's more."

"You mean there's *another* twist? My head's starting to hurt, Sam!"

"Yeah, well, here it is. You know my friend Snooks?"

"I think we've met. Or maybe I've just heard you talk about him. What about him?"

"Many years ago he got into a very serious fight with Sebastian Brophy. Hurt him so bad Snooks got convicted of assault. And it was right after he was paroled that Brophy disappeared."

I saw a light come on in Stella's dark eyes. "So he was a suspect."

"Had to have been. Of course there was no evidence he was involved, so nothing ever came of it."

Stella tapped a pencil on her desk. "But now with the discovery of Brophy's canoe, along with forensic evidence pointing to murder, the case is likely to get re-opened. And you're worried about your friend."

"I am. He's very upset about all of this."

"But why, Sam? If Snooks didn't have anything to do with whatever happened to Brophy, what's he worried about?"

"I'm not sure. Except we all know innocent people sometimes get arrested for crimes they didn't commit, and sometimes even convicted. Which is why I'm hoping you might call the sheriff."

"And try to catch the case?"

"Right."

"You know if I get involved in this, I'll have to play it by the book. I'll have no choice but to interview Snooks, check for alibis, that sort of thing. Assuming the case gets reopened, that is."

"We both know that's gonna happen, Stella. I'm sure you'll be fair, and that's all either of us is asking for. And I promise to stay out of your way."

"We'll see about that. First, I'd better call the sheriff."

"Let me know how that works out, okay? I won't spill anything to Snooks. I think solving this thing is going to be a challenge. It's a very cold case."

Chapter 12

Two days went by and I hadn't heard anything from Stella Reynard. It ate at me because I was anxious for the Sebastian Brophy thing to work itself out one way or another. I knew she'd called the sheriff by now because she always did what she said she was going to do. Maybe he hadn't yet gotten the details from the Park Service? Or maybe he had, but he hadn't decided whether to reopen the case or who should do the reopening? No way to tell, and there was nothing to do but wait.

Katie had gone off to a three-day forensics conference in Orlando. Prince the Corgi was moping around the house like he always does when one of us is gone. I was doing some moping of my own, missing Katie and—by chance—not having any clients as a distraction.

I was tying flies to pass the time: chartreuse and white Clouser minnows, which were killers for just about anything except bonefish. "If it isn't chartreuse it's no use," somebody once said. Six finished flies lay on the desk in front of me, with a seventh one still in the vice, when my cell went off. It was Rashaan.

"Say, I hear you're batching it for a couple of days, right?"

"Right. Me and Prince." I wondered how he knew Katie was gone.

"Okay then. Julie says why don't you come over for dinner. Nothing complicated, assuming I can get the grill to fire up. Brats and beer, if that suits you."

"Sure does. But can I bring Prince the dog? He's already pissed that Katie's away. If I go off without him, he'll probably head down the street looking for a new owner."

"Uh, sure, I guess it would be okay to bring him. But there might be a problem with the cat."

"You have a cat?"

"Yeah, as of two days ago. Candace and Serena have been after us about getting one, so we went to the shelter and there was this cool-looking long-haired tabby with yellow eyes, and . . . well, now we've got Taylor."

"Taylor?"

"Short for Taylor Swift. The girls are crazy about her, and they heard somewhere she loves cats."

As things turned out, Prince and Taylor the cat had some issues on the occasion of their first meeting, but they paled in comparison to what else happened that evening.

Prince and I decided to walk. It wasn't far and he needed the exercise. When we got there Rashaan was in the backyard fiddling with the gas grill. As we approached an athletic-looking young man popped up out of the canal behind their house and began running toward us. He wore lime green swimming trunks, sported an oversized mop of red curly hair, and had a look of absolute terror on his face.

"What is it, Hardy?" Rashaan asked.

"Serena asked if I could come to dinner and Mrs. Liptan said it was okay—*pant, pant*—and I was on my paddleboard on my way over here, when . . ." Hardy stopped talking, shivered, and hugged himself even though it was a warm sunny afternoon.

"Then what?" Rashaan asked again.

"Then I saw a man back there under the mangroves, and I thought maybe . . ." Hardy trailed off.

"Do you think he was alive?" I asked. "Did you recognize him?"

Hardy held my eyes only briefly, and then turned to Rashaan, a frown on his face.

"It's okay," Rashaan said. "This is Dr. Sawyer. He knows how to deal with things like this. Please tell him what you saw."

"I'm sure it was a man, and he wasn't moving. But I didn't get close enough to tell who it was or if he was alive or dead."

"Can you show me where?"

Hardy pointed across the canal to a thicket of mangroves lining the far shore opposite the house next door to the Liptans. "Just over there. But do I have to go with you? Serena and Candace invited me over to see their new kitty and I'd rather—"

"No, that's fine Hardy," I said. "But please don't go anywhere. Can I use your paddleboard?"

"Sure."

"Rashaan, I'm going over there to check this out. If the guy's still alive we need to act fast. In the meantime I need you to do a couple of things. First, call 9-1-1 and let them know what's happened. Request an ambulance as well as the sheriff's department. And second, could you check to see if your next-door neighbor is home? He's that old guy we fished with the other day, right?"

"Right. Rusty Montrose. Sure hope it's not him."

I walked down to the canal and managed to stand myself up on Hardy's paddleboard. I never have liked those things, but any port in a storm, as they say.

It wasn't hard to find him, bobbing around facedown under a canopy of mangroves. It clearly was a man, rather tall and thin from what I could tell, wearing blue jeans and an off-white t-shirt. I paddled in close and nudged him with my oar. There was no movement, let alone any sign of breathing. There was a big red welt on the back of his head. I got down on my knees on the board, reached out and grabbed the t-shirt, and rolled him over. Dead eyes stared up at nothing. The face was distorted with bloat and the early stages of decay, but from what I remembered of him, it looked like Rusty Montrose. I backed off, not wanting to contaminate what could have been a crime scene.

Rashaan was standing on the patio when I got back to his dock. I could hear sirens in the distance even before we had a chance to speak.

"Was Montrose at home?" I asked.

"Nobody came when I knocked and rang the bell."

"That's not a surprise. I'm pretty sure that's him out in the water."

"Oh shit. He's dead isn't he?"

"Yeah."

It took another ten minutes before help arrived: a sheriff's department cruiser, an ambulance, and a fire truck. I was pleased when Stella Reynard got out of the cruiser. She instructed Oscar Wilson—the other deputy with her—to stay on the street, probably to handle any rubberneckers, and then she caught up with me on the patio.

"What have we got?" she asked.

I told her.

By this time a man and a woman had gotten out of the fire truck and were busy pumping up a yellow raft. Their vehicle had big gold letters on the side: "Islamorada Fire Rescue."

"Any idea who it is?" Stella asked.

"Not for certain, but I think it could be the old man who lives next door. Rashaan rang the bell but nobody answered. His name is Montrose."

"And you think he's dead?"

"Oh yeah."

Stella instructed the EMTs to go across the canal and check on the victim's condition, just in case. "Don't mess with the body beyond what it takes to determine if he's alive or not. If he is alive, get him back here asap. If he's dead, just come back and tell me."

"You know this Montrose?" Stella asked as we both watched the EMT's make their way across the canal in their raft.

"Yeah, but not well. He took Rashaan and me fishing last week. First time I'd ever met the man. He goes by Rusty, but that probably isn't his real first name."

I had a bad feeling in the pit of my stomach. My mind raced toward conclusions that were premature at best but that wouldn't go away. Stella evidently caught a look on my face.

"You know something about all this?" Then she caught herself. "Assuming it's him?"

"Can we wait on that?"

"We can wait."

We watched as the man and woman felt at the man's neck for a pulse, and began mouth-to-mouth resuscitation. It couldn't have been more than half a minute before they backed away and returned to Rashaan's dock without the body.

"Anything?" Stella asked.

They both shook their heads. "No sign of life," the woman EMT replied.

"Any signs of trauma?"

"There's a wound on the back of his skull. No way to tell if it was fatal. Could be he just hit his head when he fell in, and then drowned."

"Okay, thanks," Stella said. "You guys can go now. This obviously is a case for my crime scene folks. They should be here any time."

Stella turned back to me. "Let's assume for the moment that this wasn't an accident, and that the victim is this Mr. Montrose you mentioned. You wanna tell me what you know about this?"

"Sure. This may be nothing, but the other day when we were fishing, the topic of Sebastian Brophy's disappearance happened to come up."

Stella frowned. "You didn't tell him about the abandoned canoe, did you?"

"No, of course not. But he might have guessed something happened. You know, something new about the Brophy disappearance. Because he started asking questions."

"Like what?"

"Like, 'why are you so interested in this guy anyway?' That sort of thing."

"Okay, but what could this have to do with his turning up dead in the canal?"

"Maybe nothing. Probably nothing."

Stella raised an eyebrow. "But?"

"But just suppose he told somebody about our conversation on his boat, and that somebody was really anxious that the Brophy case not get re-opened."

Stella's frown morphed into a scowl. "Come on, Sam. Let's assume there is somebody, maybe even somebody from your neighborhood, who wants the Brophy case to stay buried. Why get everybody's attention by killing Montrose?"

"Yeah, you're probably right. Speaking about the Brophy case getting re-opened, have you had any word from the sheriff?"

"I was gonna call you about that. The sheriff has given me the go-ahead to look into it. But he didn't seem all that excited. He said something about a 25-year-old case without a body, and that I shouldn't make it a priority."

I pointed across the canal to the body. "Maybe now he'll get a little more perked up."

"Maybe. Assuming the two cases have anything to do with each other."

"What about files from the original case?" I asked.

"A deputy is driving them up from Key West tomorrow."

Rashaan Liptan had been sitting on his porch, watching. There was no sign of Julie or the twins, but Hardy was there, looking nervous.

"I'm gonna go talk to the Liptans," Stella said. "And who's that with Rashaan?"

"That's a neighbor boy named Hardy. I think he found the body."

"I'd better talk to him too."

"Mind if I come along?"

"Actually, I was hoping you could stay here until I get back. Just in case one of the neighbors starts to get nosy."

"No problem," I said.

Stella walked up on the porch, spoke briefly to Rashaan, and then followed him and Hardy inside.

Stella was gone about a half hour. She came outside just as a white van pulled up on the street. Anthony Hernandez, the Monroe County Medical Examiner got out, along with Penny McMasters, head of the sheriff's department crime scene unit, along with two of her assistants. I said hello to Anthony and Penny—I'd met both of them before—then left them with Stella and went looking for Rashaan.

He must have seen me coming because he came outside before I got to the door.

"Was it Montrose?" he asked. "Is he dead?"

"Dead for sure. Montrose likely, but I couldn't be certain. We'll know once the crime scene crew is finished." I pointed to a pair of wooden Adirondack chairs. "Can we sit?"

"Of course," he said, easing into one of the chairs. "Can I get you something? Some supper maybe? Julie already fed Hardy and the girls."

"No thanks, I'm fine. But I do want to bring you up to date on things, and then ask you a couple of questions."

"Okay, shoot."

I told Rashaan what the Park Service people had found on our trip into the everglades backcountry, about how we had found bullets along with the collar from my uncle's dog.

"That's all pretty weird," he said. "And now you want to know if I said anything to Rusty Montrose after our fishing trip, right?"

"That, and whether he said anything to you. His turning up dead like this, it seems too much of a coincidence, don't you think?"

"Maybe so, Sam. But to answer your first question: no, I didn't say anything about what we found. And I couldn't have told him about what you discovered the second time you went out there. I didn't even know about it until just now."

"Of course not. I wasn't suggesting—"

"But he did tell me something interesting. I was out working in my yard—I think it was a couple of days after our fishing trip—when he came out of his house and started asking questions about you."

"About me? What about me?"

"He said he'd heard that in addition to being a fishing guide you were some sort of a cop." Rashaan hesitated, then shook his head. "No, that's not right. He said you worked *with* the cops. That you were a cop consultant."

"Those were his exact words?"

"Yeah, that you were a cop consultant."

"And what did you tell him?"

"I told him I didn't know all that much about it, but that you had done some detective work. You and Katie, that is. I hope that was okay."

"Sure. It's the truth. But now I'm wondering—"

"Yeah, me too," Rashaan interrupted. "If Montrose was poking around into your background, is that what got him killed?"

"We don't even know if he was killed. He might have just fallen into the canal, hit his head, and drowned. Or maybe he had a heart attack or something."

I noticed the crime scene people had the body in tow and were on their way back toward Rashaan's dock. "I'm guessing they'll want you to help with the identification. You okay with that?"

"Uh, sure, I suppose so."

Penny McMasters' two assistants had pulled the body up onto the grassy berm beside the canal by the time Rashaan and I had walked down from his patio. Even in the fading light I could tell it was Rusty Montrose. Or had been.

Stella looked at Rashaan and me. "You know who this is?"

We both said yes.

One of the crime scene people handed Penny a plastic bag with a single shoe inside it. "This was in the water next to the body. Other than that, we didn't see anything out of the ordinary."

Penny took the bag and held it up in the fading light. "Looks like some sort of a basketball shoe."

"Let me see that," Rashaan said. He took the bag and turned it over in his hands. "Yep. This is an Air Jordan. They're pretty expensive."

"Is it yours?" Stella asked.

"Nope."

"Maybe it belonged to Montrose. Let's check his feet." She walked over to the corpse and held the Air Jordan against the rather ordinary loafers it was wearing. 'Nope. It's at least two sizes bigger. And you're sure it's not yours Mr. Liptan?"

"Positive."

"Well okay, then. We'll hold onto this as a possible clue in case this turns out to be a murder." Stella sighed, and looked at Anthony Hernandez, who had bent down for a closer look at the man's head. "What do you think?"

"No way to tell at this point. He has a nasty bruise there, but it might not have been fatal. Hopefully we'll know more once I've done the autopsy."

Stella nodded. "I think we'll call this a suspicious death for the time being. Let me know what you find."

"Will do."

We watched as Hernandez and the crime scene crew bagged up the body, loaded it into their van, and drove away.

Stella turned to Rashaan and me. "We'll want written statements from both of you, but I think I have what I need for now. Can you come by my office in the morning?"

We both agreed that we could.

"She seems like a nice lady," Rashaan said after Stella had left.

"And damned good at her job," I said. "She'll get to the bottom of this."

I went inside to collect Prince, while Rashaan stayed on the patio, staring off toward the canal. Julie was in the kitchen, along with her daughters and Hardy. Serena was pulling a rubber mouse attached to a string across the floor, apparently in an attempt to get the attention of Taylor the cat. Hardy had thrown a tennis ball down a hallway that Prince probably was supposed to be chasing. However, neither of these distractions appeared to be working. Instead Prince and Taylor were engaged in a hissing/growling contest underneath the dining room table. They were about three feet apart and neither one was moving. It was a classic cat versus dog standoff.

I broke it up by attaching Prince to his leash and dragging him toward the door. "Maybe we'll try this another time," I said. "And Hardy, thanks for all your help out there. I know it was a tough deal."

"For all of us," Julie replied. "Hope to see you soon, and under better circumstances. And we still owe you a dinner. How about you and Katie come over one of these evenings?"

"That would be nice. I'll tell her."

Rashaan stopped me before I got to the Jeep.

"What?"

"It's about that shoe. Air Jordans are pretty unusual, and I've seen somebody around here wearing a pair just like that one. I just can't remember who. You think this could be important?"

"You bet it could. Maybe you'll remember by the time we meet Stella tomorrow."

"Hope so."

Chapter 13

I asked Rashaan about the shoe as we were driving the next morning to Stella Reynard's office to write our reports about Rusty Montrose. He said he'd worried about it all night, but still couldn't remember who he'd seen wearing Air Jordans.

"But it was around here someplace, not up in Miami. I'm sure about that. I remember thinking at the time it wasn't something you'd necessarily expect to see in the Keys."

Stella was in her office at the Islamorada substation when we got there. She pointed to a pair of chairs opposite her desk, and handed each of us a yellow-lined pad. I noticed an odd expression on her face as soon as we walked in, and it stayed that way the whole time we were there: some sort of mix between sour and glum that I didn't recognize. She made no offer of coffee, which also was unusual for her.

After we finished our reports, she looked through them so quickly that she couldn't possibly have read every word. She thanked us, but she made no comments and asked no questions. Odd.

"Have you heard anything from the medical examiner?" I asked, hoping to melt whatever sort of ice had formed in the room.

"Not yet."

"What about his family? Maybe they'd know if Mr. Montrose had enemies. Assuming, of course, that he was murdered."

Stella rose from behind her desk. "We haven't had a chance to check on that. And now if you'll excuse me, there's something I need to take care of. Thanks for coming in."

Getting the bum's rush from Stella was something brand new. It wasn't like her at all. Even Rashaan picked up on it, despite the fact that he didn't know her nearly as well as I did. "What was that all about?" he asked, as soon as we were back outside getting in my Jeep.

"I really don't know. Something's bugging her, that's for sure."

I was pulling out of the parking lot, looking for an opening in the highway traffic—jammed up as usual—when my cell lit up. It was Stella.

"Sorry about that," she said, without waiting for me to say hello. "Any chance I could come by your place this afternoon? I'd like to talk to both you and Katie."

"Katie's up in Orlando at a conference. It's just me and the dog. But we'd both be happy to see you."

I knew Stella was crazy about Prince, but my attempt to inject a little levity into things fell flat.

"I don't need to speak to your dog. See you about four-thirty?"

She didn't wait for an answer.

~ ~ ~

Stella came up the front stairs and knocked on my door exactly on time. That was usual for her. The unusual part was that she was out of uniform. She had on blue short shorts, a plain white t-shirt, and flip-flops. I'd never seen her dressed anywhere near this casually.

She accepted my offer of iced tea and we took our drinks out on the deck. She took no notice of the pelicans begging entrails from a neighbor who was cleaning fish. But Prince did. He had a thing about pelicans and was barking furiously at them as usual. Stella glared at Prince, and I finally had to escort him back inside so we would talk.

"That damned Mike Spivey," she said as soon as I came back.

I took me a second or two to remember that Michael Spivey was Sheriff of Monroe County. "What about him?"

"He just yanked me off the Brophy case."

So that was it. "Why?"

She snorted. "He said it wasn't all that important, that I should concentrate on other cases."

"Did you tell him about what happened yesterday?"

"You mean the Montrose death? I did afterwards. He said I could continue to look into that, but only if and when the M.E. determines it was murder."

I was incredulous. "You mean he's just dropping the whole Brophy thing?"

"No, not that. Instead he's assigned somebody else. Alvin Beaudry. You know Al? He's a deputy works out of the Marathon office."

I hadn't heard of Beaudry. "Why him?"

Stella shrugged. "Maybe because he's an incompetent asshole?"

Yipes, I thought to myself. This thing has really gotten to her.

"There's one more thing," she said. "The sheriff ordered me to tell you and Katie that your services won't be needed in the Brophy case either."

"Well, hell."

"No kidding. But I have a favor to ask. Could you just keep poking around and let me know if you find out anything? I can't hire you as a consultant, but still I'm hoping—"

"Not sure how we're going to help you with a cold case like this."

"Me neither. But at least you live in the right neighborhood. You might hear something. So are you willing to help?"

"I suppose so. I'll need to talk this over with Katie."

"Good. In that case, I have something for you. Be right back."

Stella went out to her car and returned with a fat manila folder. She handed it to me. "The sheriff made me give the original Brophy case file to Al Beaudry. But here's a copy. Don't tell anybody how you got it."

"I won't. And this could help."

"Sure hope so. There's nothing I'd like more than to stick it to both Spivey and Beaudry by solving the case out from under them. Even if you're the ones who get the credit."

Stella had been sitting across from me, but now she came over and joined me on a padded wooden bench that backed up to the canal. I mentioned earlier what Stella was wearing. I'd missed it before, but now I couldn't help noticing what she was *not* wearing. Her taut bare legs shown like burnished bronze in the afternoon sun. That same sun also made it clear that she had nothing on underneath her t-shirt.

Stella sidled over to me on the bench and put her hand on my knee. We had danced up close to this sort of thing a couple of times before, but never under these circumstances. It had always been at work, with her in uniform, and nothing had ever come of it. But this had the potential of turning into something different. We were in my home alone. She was stressed, clearly in need of comfort, and—frankly—sexy looking as hell. Anybody would have been tempted, including me.

"Thanks for coming over to tell me all this in person," I said. "But—"

"Yeah, I know. Guess I'd better go."

I watched as a lone tear ran down her left cheek.

"I'm good at my job," she said, as she made her way down the stairs to her car.

"I know you are," I said.

~ ~ ~

Later that night I was thinking about what almost happened, when I heard the sound of a motorcycle coming down the street. Most likely it was Nate Sturm on patrol, although I couldn't recall him doing it at night. Then the sound stopped instead of fading into the distance, and thirty seconds later there was a knock on my door. Prince's ears perked up, he let out a solitary "woof," as we both went over to see who had come calling.

It was Nate, dressed in his usual leather garb. I half expected to see the white poodle that usually rode with him, but there was no sign of the dog. Prince sniffed intently at his shoes.

"Mind if I come in?" Nate asked.

"Please," I said. "Anything I can get you?"

"No thanks, but can we talk?"

"Sure. Come on in and have a seat."

Nate chose the kitchen table without asking or being told, so I joined him there. It was quiet for a time while he twisted the ends of his oversized white mustache.

"Got a favor to ask," he finally said. "I heard you might be looking into the disappearance of Bash Brophy."

I knew better than to deny it. Nate seemed to know everything that was going on in our housing development. "A little bit. Why?"

"You know the cops thought Snooks Lancaster killed him, don't you?"

"Yeah, Snooks told me about that."

"You believe he did it?"

"No."

"Well, neither do I."

I couldn't figure out where this was going.

"See the thing is, Bash and me—we were close friends back then. *Real* close, if you get my drift."

Recalling what Snooks had told me about Brophy, I was pretty sure I got the drift.

"Is there something I can help you with, Nate?"

"Yeah. I want you to catch the sonofabitch who actually did away with Bash."

I put up my hands. "Now wait a minute, Nate. You know I'm not an officer of the law."

"I know that. But I also happen to know that both you and Mrs. Sawyer sometimes help solve crimes. And—listen—I'm not looking for any charity here. I may look like a scruffy old guy on a motorcycle, but I have resources. I want to hire your firm."

"Our firm?"

"You know. I think it's called 'Upper Keys' something?"

How the hell did Nate Sturm know about our newly formed LLC? I couldn't recall telling anybody local about it yet except Rashaan, and I couldn't imagine he went around spreading the news. But like I said, Nate had the reputation for being a real newshound.

"We have set up a little company. But it's just getting started. And our only true expertise—actually it's Katie's field, not mine—is forensic botany. I'm not sure how that could help solve a cold case like the disappearance of Mr. Brophy all those years ago."

Nate sighed and looked out the kitchen window, then finally back at me. "I know for a fact that you've helped the Monroe County Sheriff's Department and the National Park Service solve crimes around here. And your wife is highly thought of at the college. You both have good reputations in this part of the world. If you didn't I wouldn't be here. Now, are you going to take this case, or do I have to look someplace else?" He stopped for another mustache fiddle. "Not that I can think of any."

"What about the sheriff's department?"

He shook his head. "Tried that."

"Who?"

"Who what?"

"Who did you talk to in the sheriff's department?"

"Why Sheriff Spivey, of course. We go way back. But he pretty much blew me off."

Where else had I just heard that?

"Alright, Nate, suppose Katie and I do agree to look into this. You have any ideas where we might start?"

Nate slapped the table. "Now we're getting somewhere! Damned right I do! There are two guys I happen to know who had it in for Bash, and there both still around. One is Will Stebbins and the other is Santiago Islava. Goes by Sandy."

I knew Stebbins was a charter fisherman who lived in our neighborhood, but I didn't know Islava. "And their motives were what, exactly?"

"Exactly this. You need to know a little about Bash. First, he was strictly a fly fisherman and he practiced catch and release only. The guy was a serious conservationist back when there weren't that many of us around here. Stebbins is a charter fisherman and Islava is a lobsterman, and Bash was on both their asses."

"For doing what, exactly?"

"He had evidence that Islava was pulling traps that didn't belong to him, and Stebbins was poaching queen conchs. And for all I know he was selling his conchs to Islava, who runs a little fish market at his dock down in Marathon."

"You think Islava could have been selling both conchs and other people's lobsters?"

"Uh huh."

I knew conch harvest in Florida had been illegal since the 1980s, and that stealing other people's lobsters was a major no-no. I heard Snooks joke once that you might be able to get away with murder in the Keys, but if you stole somebody's else's lobsters you were pretty much toast.

"What sort of evidence did Brophy have on these guys?" I asked.

"Not sure about Stebbins. But somehow or another Bash had gotten a spy on board Islava's lobster boat. A crew member who found out they were poaching."

"Do you know who he was?"

"He never told me."

"Didn't you report this to the sheriff's department when Bash disappeared?"

"Of course I did."

"Who did you talk to?"

"Mike Spivey."

"The sheriff?"

"Yeah, but he was only a detective back then."

"And you told him about Stebbins and Islava?"

"Sure. But like I said, they had their sights set on Snooks Lancaster."

"But when they couldn't make that stick, why do you suppose they didn't go after Stebbins or Santiago?"

"Believe me, I asked about that. Spivey said they looked into it, but couldn't find any evidence." Nate paused for another mustache adjustment. "So, you gonna take the case?"

"I'm thinking yes, but let me talk to Katie about this. It needs to be as much her decision as mine."

"Can I give you some sort of a retainer? You know, to sort of seal the deal?"

"Not yet. Katie's away at a meeting. She should be back tomorrow, and she needs to be in on this decision. Give me your cell number and I'll be in touch."

Then I remembered something. "One more thing before you go, Nate. You heard about Rusty Montrose?"

"Yeah. Too bad about that. Me and him were buddies from clear back in high school. Do they know what happened to him?"

"Not for sure. So you and Brophy and Montrose all went to school together?"

"Yep. And we all were on the football team. Along with your uncle Fred."

Small world.

As soon as I showed Nate Sturm out the door, Prince came over and nosed my leg, hinting it was time for his evening walk. I leashed him up and we went downstairs. I heard the rumble of Nate's Indian motorcycle fading in the distance as we set off up the street. We walked together, Prince sniffing and peeing, me staring into the dark and thinking, hard.

What had I just gotten us into? How did one go about solving a case that was better than a quarter century old? Would Katie agree to working for Nate Sturm? Just that afternoon, Stella Reynard had asked if we could poke around in the matter of Sebastian Brophy and his mysterious disappearance all those years ago. Maybe she'd be thrilled. Either way, I had the feeling we were about to get involved in something as big as it was elusive.

Chapter 14

I had clients the next day, but only for six hours. Katie wasn't due home until later that night, so after I finished cleaning up the boat and stowing my gear, I decided to go over to the Safari Lounge. Partly it was for a beer, but my real motive was to have another talk with Snooks.

He was mixing a couple of margaritas as I walked in, but he waved me to my usual stool. "Be right back." He picked up the drinks and carried them to a couple sitting at a table on the deck outside.

"What'll it be?" he asked, once he was back behind the bar.

"I'll take a *Modelo* and some of your popcorn."

"Sure thing. Where's Katie and the dog?"

"She's at a forensics conference up in Orlando. I can't stay all that long, so I decided to leave Prince at home."

Snooks grinned. "Pouting and moping, no doubt."

"Yeah, probably."

Snooks brought over my beer and a bowl of popcorn. I took a sip, set the glass down on the bar, and ate a handful of popcorn. "I had a surprise visit last night. You know Nathaniel Sturm? Rides a vintage Indian bike?"

"Nate? Sure. He's kind of a busybody, but an okay guy I think. He went to high school with my brother. What did he want?"

"He wants to hire me and Katie to help figure out who killed Sebastian Brophy. I guess they were old friends."

Snooks had been wiping down the bar. This stopped him in mid-wipe. "Does he think I did it?"

"Nope. And from what I could tell, I don't think he ever did. He gave me the names of a couple other suspects, and he seemed pretty sure it was one of them. Will Stebbins and Santiago Islava. You know them?"

Snooks shrugged. "Depends on what you mean by 'know them.' They drink pretty regularly here in the Safari, but I wouldn't say we're friends or anything. Did Nate say why he thought one of them might have done it?"

"He said Brophy had caught them poaching and threatened to turn them in to Fish and Wildlife, or maybe the Park Service."

Snooks nodded. "That fits, I suppose. Neither of those guys has what you'd call a stellar reputation. Anyway, you gonna help?"

"I haven't had a chance to talk to Katie yet about it. But yeah, I'm thinking we might."

Snooks tugged at his ponytail and favored me with a knowing smile. Or was it a smirk?

He pointed to my glass. "And that beer you're not drinking. That's just a prop while you pick my brain, right? Or maybe ask for my help?"

I threw up my hands. "Okay, ya got me. But seriously—"

"But seriously, from what I've heard about those two guys—and what I remember about Bash Brophy—it's a possibility."

I took another swallow of beer. "Could you elaborate?"

"Yep."

Two guys on the other side of the bar waved their empty glasses at Snooks.

"Maker's, rocks, with a splash?" Snooks asked.

Both men nodded.

"Coming up." Then to me: "Betcha can't wait for my special elaboration."

Snooks came back from delivering the drinks. "Okay, what do you have?" I asked.

"Maybe not much, and only about Stebbins. He was in here a couple of days ago with Islava, and they were talking about how they were going to take care of somebody."

I thought immediately about Rusty Montrose. "Did they say who?"

"Nope. Or at least I didn't hear it."

"Did I hear somebody mention Sandy Islava?" I turned to see Flora Delaney standing outside the kitchen door, carrying a big paper bag.

"Yeah. You know him?"

"From way back."

That sounded interesting. "What can you tell me about him?"

Flora shrugged. "Let me deliver this food first." Then she disappeared out the door.

"You do carry-out?" I asked Snooks.

"Not usually. It's for a friend."

Flora was back in less than two minutes. "Why don't you come into the kitchen? We can talk there." She disappeared through the swinging door without waiting for me to answer.

"You know anything about this?" I asked Snooks.

He shook his head. "But Flora isn't into idle gossip. You'd better check it out."

"Why are you interested in Sandy Islava?" Flora asked as soon as I had joined her in the kitchen.

I told her about my visit from Nate Sturm, and how he suspected that either Islava or Will Stebbins had murdered Sebastian Brophy.

"Well, I wouldn't know anything about that," she said. "And I don't know Stebbins at all, except that I've seen him in here occasionally."

"But you do know Islava?"

"Sure. We went to school together down in Marathon. I knew his whole family. They were lobster fishermen, and they ran a little fish market next to their dock." She paused, seeming to reflect on something. "Good people, except for Sandy."

"What about Sandy?"

"He was always in trouble. It started out as simple kid stuff, like spraying graffiti around. But it got more serious once he reached high school. He actually killed a classmate in the parking lot one day after school. Something to do with a girlfriend."

"Was he convicted?"

"Nope. Not even tried. The cops decided it was an accident. A lot of us felt otherwise."

"You ever hear of him poaching lobsters?"

"Nope. I'm sure his family wouldn't stand for it when he was working with them. Like I said, they were good people. But now that he's out on his own—which I guess he is—I wouldn't put it past him."

"But you haven't heard of any particular instance?"

"No, but then why would I?"

~ ~ ~

Back home, waiting for Katie, with Prince on my lap, I thought about what I had learned from Snooks and Flo. Neither had any sort of evidence that Stebbins or Islava could have had anything to do with Sebastian Brophy's disappearance. But it sounded like either of them might do such a thing if he'd threatened their livelihoods. And I really had to wonder about Stebbins' threat to 'take care of somebody,' and whether that somebody could have been Rusty Montrose.

But what would have been the motive, and what—if anything—could it have to do with the Brophy case?

I was deep in these thoughts when the sound of tires on gravel brought me back to the present. It was Katie, back home at last. I almost beat Prince to the door.

Katie came inside and dropped her travel bag on the floor. We kissed and then hugged while Prince growled for attention at our feet.

"Wonderful to see you," I said while Katie bent down and gave Prince a scratch behind his ears. "And I have some interesting news."

"Good, I hope."

"Not exactly. Just interesting. Why don't I get you something and we can talk."

"Some tea would be great. Let me unpack."

Ten minutes later we were seated in the living room with Prince wedged in between us. I was just about to bring Katie up to speed on the Montrose death and my visit from Nate Sturm, when my cell phone lit up.

I hurried across the room to the kitchen table where I'd left it. The caller ID said "U.S. Government."

"Hello, this is Sam Sawyer."

"Hey Sam, it's Mike Nunez."

"Hey Mike, what's up?"

"We just found another abandoned boat back in the everglades."

"Wow. Talk about déjà vu."

"Yeah, but this time there's a body. Or what's left of it."

"Huh. You think it could be Brophy?"

"Seems likely. The registration links to a white Hells Bay he owned."

"Was it near the canoe?"

"Nope. It's in a backcountry area west of Flamingo that's been closed since the last hurricane. I was doing a reconnaissance before we open up the place for non-motorized access."

"Huh."

"You keep saying that. Anyway, Rhonda Wilcox is coming down day after tomorrow and we're gonna do a search of the area. Thought you might want to come along. You and Katie that is."

"She's right here. Let me check."

"It's Mike Nunez from Everglades Park," I said to Katie. "Looks like they've found Sebastian Brophy's flats boat, apparently with his body in it. They're gonna do another search and we're invited. Can you go along? It's day after tomorrow."

"I had a couple of appointments, but nothing I can't re-schedule."

I got back to Mike. "We can be there. Where and what time?"

"Nine-thirty at Flamingo. Shouldn't take us more than 45 minutes or so to reach the wreck site. Oh, and you won't need to bring your canoe. My outboard can easily get in there and we'll all fit."

"So I won't need to bring a boat?"

"Nope. You can drive if you want to, though it might take longer than coming by water. Your choice. And thanks for coming. I'm probably gonna need some backup."

"Backup?"

"Yeah, from Rhonda. I think she's kinda pissed."

Based on previous interactions, my feeling was that Rhonda was always kind of pissed about something. "Any particular reason?"

"Just before she hung up on me, she muttered something about 'how could we miss two wrecked boats that had been right there in our backyard for twenty-five years?' Or something to that effect."

"Well, it's a pretty big backyard, but I guess she had a point. I can see it with the canoe, but a white Hell's Bay should be pretty conspicuous. You do aerial surveys from time to time, don't you?"

"Sure we do, and I wondered the same thing. Either the boat wasn't there until recently, which seems unlikely, or—and this is what I think—it only got exposed after the latest hurricane."

"Yeah, that sounds reasonable. Anyway, thanks for the invite. Katie and I will see you in a couple days."

"Here we go again," Katie said as soon as I got off the phone with Mike.

"Yeah, but this time we might be getting paid."

"How's that?"

I spent the next half hour telling Katie about all of the things she'd missed while she was up in Orlando, including the death of Rusty Montrose, Nate Sturm's request that we help track down Sebastian Brophy's killer, and his two possible suspects.

"You think we should do it?" Katie asked. "This is an awfully cold case."

"Well, we've got this new LLC. It seems like as good a place to start as any, don't you think? After all, we're already involved. And there's one other thing I forgot to tell you."

"What's that?"

"The sheriff pulled Stella off the case and assigned it to somebody else."

"Who?"

"Somebody named Beaudry who works out of the Marathon substation. I don't think Stella likes him very much." I left out the details about when and where Stella had given me this news. "She did manage to get me a copy of the Brophy case file, so we won't be operating totally in the dark."

Katie gave me a knowing look. "But the fact that she's off the case means your usual consulting fee is out the window. Now I see where you're headed with this. I guess we should get together with Nate and sign some papers, maybe ask for a retainer. You think he's got the resources?"

"He says he does."

"Well okay then. Why don't you give him a call?"

"I'll do that right now."

"Good," Katie said. "In the meantime I'll put together a contract for him to look over and sign in the morning. I'm anxious to get a look at that old case file, but not tonight. I'm beat."

And that was how Upper Keys Investigations got its first official job.

Chapter 15

The next morning about nine-thirty I heard the familiar rumble of Nate Sturm's Indian coming to a halt in our front yard. I went to the door and watched as he bounded up the stairs, a look of excitement on his face. He introduced himself to Katie and accepted the offer of coffee. "Just black, thanks. So I guess you're gonna let me hire you, huh? That's great!"

At this point Katie took charge of things. She knew a whole lot more about private investigations than I did.

"You do understand we can't guarantee anything Mr. Sturm," she said.

"Oh sure, sure. But at least you're willing to take a look at things. That's more than anybody else has been willing to do."

"And while we're as anxious as you to find out what happened to Mr. Brophy, you also must understand that we don't work for free. We can't actually, since whatever time and resources we put in on this case will be at the expense of our other activities."

Nate twirled the ends of his mustache and looked at me with a twinkle in his eye. "Understood. After all, instead of raking in the big bucks taking rich clients fishing, you'll be poking around trying to figure out what happened to my friend."

I was about to return the banter with a crack about how my clients usually weren't all that rich, but Katie put up a hand.

"Ours will be a professional, not a personal, relationship," she said. "We have some paperwork to do, and then we need to talk about money." She went over to her desk and came back with a sheaf of papers. She passed it over to Nate.

"What's this?" he asked.

"It's a contract, specifying that our fees will include $100 an hour for full-time work on the case, plus reasonable expenses, and asking for a $500 retainer to begin with. This will make our relationship legal and binding."

"I don't have a problem with that," Nate said.

"And there's one other thing. This contract states that we are working only for you, that we will keep our relationship confidential, and that we will provide you with any and all information we discover about the disappearance and possible death of Sebastian Brophy. But you must understand something. If we find evidence of a crime, we are ethically bound to turn it over to the appropriate authorities."

"Wouldn't want it any other way," Nate replied. "And I don't care who knows that I'm hiring you, either."

Katie shook her head. "We'll keep it confidential, Nate. If this case involves a murder, you could be at risk."

"Yeah, okay. I guess I can see that." He reached into his hip pocket and pulled out a checkbook. "You said $500? And where do I sign?"

"You sign once at the bottom of the last page, plus there are several places I have marked where we need your initials. You will see that Sam and I have already signed."

Nate wrote out his check, signed and initialed the contract, and took a big slug of coffee. "When do you start?" he asked.

"First thing tomorrow," I said. "And we already have some news about the case to share with you. I had a call yesterday from a friend with the Park Service. They just found a Hell's Bay flats boat that apparently belonged to Brophy."

Nate's face lit up. "Where?"

"In a remote part of Everglades National Park. And there's one more thing. They found a body in the boat."

Nate's happy countenance collapsed. "Is it him?"

"We don't know for sure, although that certainly seems likely. We'll be joining a search team up there tomorrow, looking for evidence."

"What sort of evidence?" Nate asked.

"Anything we can find," Katie said. "But the most important thing will be to determine if the body is actually Brophy's. It may not be all that simple, and we might be able to use your help."

"Of course, anything I can do. What do you need?"

I knew this was going to be hard for Nate, if he and Brophy were as close as he'd said they were. "See here's the thing. After all these years the only thing left is a skeleton, and not even all of that. You know, animals may have hauled off—"

"Okay, okay, I get that. But what can I do?"

"Any chance you remember the name of Mr. Brophy's dentist? There may be old records for dental work and x-rays that can be useful in missing persons cases. Assuming there are enough teeth remaining in the skull."

Nate nodded. "Back then there was only one dentist in the upper Keys. His name was Dr. Mathews. I remember he took x-rays and I'd bet he kept good records. I heard his grandson inherited his practice and continues to work out of Marathon."

"That could help," Katie said. "And a couple more things. Do you know if Mr. Brophy wore a distinctive watch or any sort of identifiable jewelry?"

A vacant faraway look came into Sturm's eyes, like he'd gone to a different time and place. Then he snapped back to the present. "He had a belt buckle that I gave him. It was engraved with the image of a jumping tarpon. He's—he was—a passionate fisherman."

"Anything else?"

"He always wore two rings. One was a high school graduation ring." Nate held up his right hand. "Just like this one. We all had 'em. All members of the football team, that is."

"And the other ring?" Katie asked.

There was just the briefest hesitation. "It was one I gave him. It had an enamel replica of a conch on it. The setting was gold."

"Thanks. This could be a big help," Katie said.

"You said there were a couple of things?" Nate said.

"Another has to do with DNA," she replied. "It may be hard to get any off an old skeleton like that, but even if we can, there's the problem with identifying it as Brophy's. The most likely way would be to compare it with samples from his closest relatives. Can you tell us anything about his family?"

Nate Sturm sighed. "I know he had a brother named William, but I don't know where he is or even if he's alive. I don't think they were close." Then he snapped his fingers. "But now I remember something, and it could be important. William had a son named Tyler, and he spent a summer with Bash the year before he disappeared. Bash told me once Tyler was helping him 'track down the bad guys.' Those were his exact words. 'Track down the bad guys.' Guess that might be important, huh?"

"Sure could be. We probably could use his DNA if nothing else. Any idea where this Tyler might be today?"

"No idea."

Katie had been taking notes. She stopped and looked up at Nate. "Did Bash say just what Tyler was doing to help him track down the bad guys?"

"No, he was real vague about that. Said he didn't want to get his nephew in any trouble."

"You mean like he might be doing something illegal?"

"Maybe. Like I said, Bash wouldn't give me any details."

"Well thanks, Nate. This could be important. We'll look into it."

It occurred to me there might be something about Tyler in the case file that Stella had copied for me. I made a mental note to check it out later.

Katie took the contract papers, walked over to her desk and used her printer to make a copy. She handed it to Nate. "We'll keep the original, but you be sure to hang on to this duplicate. We'll let you know if we find anything tomorrow."

Nate drained the last of his coffee, declined the offer of a second cup, and stood up to leave. "Thanks for doing this. Now I'll get out of your hair. It's time for my rounds."

"There's just one last thing," Katie said. "Would you happen to have a photograph of Sebastian we could borrow? We'll be sure to get it back to you."

Sturm hesitated for a bit. Then he pulled out his wallet, extracted a small photo, and handed it to Katie. "This one's pretty old, but it's all I've got." He pointed to the picture. "That's me and Brophy in our high school football outfits." Then he was out the door and down the stairs.

"Interesting," Katie said after Nate had left. "You remember Nate telling us Brophy had arranged to have a spy on Santiago Islava's lobster boat?"

"Uh huh."

"And just now he told us Brophy's nephew Tyler was down here in 1998 helping him track down the bad guys?"

"Yes."

"Don't you suppose Tyler was the spy?"

"Damn, that's right! We need to find this Tyler."

"Nate's really hurting, isn't he?" Katie said. "You'd think by now it might have worn off a bit."

"Hope we can bring him some sort of closure," I said. "Though I think there's zero chance Brophy's still alive."

"I agree."

"Brophy must have meant a lot to him, if he's kept that picture in his wallet for all these years."

"Yeah. I think it kind of embarrassed him when you asked. Why do we need a picture?"

"We probably won't. But suppose we find a witness who saw something. It's standard procedure in any investigation to have a picture of the victim."

She would know, just like she was the one who figured out that Tyler Brophy must have been the spy on Santiago Islava's lobster boat. Not for the first time, I realized who the real detective was in this outfit.

Chapter 16

Katie began gathering up some papers and books off her desk and stuffing them into a tote bag. "Got a lecture before lunch, and then a lab that'll take up most of the afternoon. But we should talk strategy about all this when I get back. Are you fishing today?"

"Nope."

"Then I have a suggestion. We probably should make contact with the detective who's handling the Brophy case, and explain how we're going to be involved."

"That's a good idea. I'll call down there as soon as you leave and try to set up an appointment. Do you want to be in on it?"

Katie thought about that for a bit, and then shook her head. "That's probably not necessary at this point. But if and when you do get to see this guy, don't give away too much."

"You mean like the fact that we already have a copy of the Brophy case file?"

"For sure, along with the fact that the Park Service may have discovered his body, and that we're going to be in on a search tomorrow."

"He may already know about it."

"Maybe. You should try to find out, but only indirectly."

Katie must have caught the puzzled look on my face. "See, here's the deal. In my experience law enforcement is very reluctant to give away what they know about a case to private citizens, including investigators, unless they get something back."

"So we don't volunteer any information about the case until we need something in return?"

"Exactly. Unless we have solid incriminating evidence of who likely killed Brophy. Then we're obliged."

As soon as Katie left I put in a call to the sheriff's office in Marathon, and eventually got through to Al Beaudry. I explained who I was and what I wanted to see him about. He didn't sound enthused, but agreed to see me at three that afternoon.

The Marathon substation of the Monroe County Sheriff's Department was a one story cream-colored building with a red tile roof. I parked in front and walked inside. A sergeant at the front desk directed me down the hall to a windowless cubbyhole. The door was open. A pudgy man sat behind a desk cluttered with piles of paper. He had a burr haircut that made his jowly face look even fatter than it might have otherwise. He wore a white short-sleeved shirt and a pale yellow tie with a coffee stain in the middle.

"Deputy Beaudry?" I asked.

"It's Detective Beaudry," he replied with a scowl. "Are you Sawyer?"

I said I was.

He pointed to a metal chair. "Sit," he said. "You say you're involved with the Brophy case?" He began shuffling through one of the taller piles of paper on his desk, eventually pulling out a manila folder about two inches thick. It was about the same size as the one Stella Reynard had given me two days earlier. "What can I do for you?"

"My wife and I are private investigators. We've been retained by an individual interested in determining what might have happened to a man named Sebastian Brophy when he disappeared 25 years ago."

"What individual?"

"I'm sorry but that's confidential."

"Doesn't have to be. Just between us, that is."

"I'm sorry."

"Yeah well, anyway, what do you want?"

"Anything about the case that could help our client. Any suspects you might be checking out. That sort of thing."

"What suspects? This is just a missing persons case, isn't it?"

Now I knew two things. He hadn't heard about the discovery of Brophy's boat and it didn't seem likely he'd even read the case file that probably had been sitting on his desk since Stella gave it to him.

I had to be careful with my next move. Revealing that I knew some things already in the case file seemed safe, since he probably would learn about them anyway once he got around to reading it. "I believe the original investigator considered it likely that Mr. Brophy had been murdered, and in fact had come up with at least one suspect: a man named George Lancaster."

Beaudry grunted but said nothing.

"And then just recently a friend and I found a canoe back in the everglades that we discovered belonged to Brophy, and there was evidence of foul play associated with it." I pointed to the file in front of Beaudry. "But perhaps I'm telling you things you already know."

Zing.

Beaudry's jowly face got a shade redder, and then he let something slip. "Mike—uh, that's Sheriff Spivey—told me about you. Told me you sometimes work with Detective Reynard up in Islamorada. Then he made it clear I wasn't to have anything to do with you." He stopped to shuffle some papers on his desk. "So I guess we're done here."

I probably should have walked out at that point. Katie would have, no doubt about it. But I just couldn't help myself. "I'm sorry you feel that way, Detective. I really thought we might be able to help each other on this. And in that spirit I'm going to give you two names: Will Stebbins and Santiago Islava. What do you know about them?"

"Could you spell those names for me?" Beaudry said as he took a pen from an empty coffee cup sitting on his desk.

I gave him the spellings, and he wrote the names down. I expected him to probe further, like asking where they lived and what their relationship might have been with Brophy. Instead he just dropped his pen noisily back into the coffee cup and looked bored.

"You are anxious to solve this case, aren't you?"

I didn't wait for an answer.

Since I already was in Marathon, I decided to pay a visit to Islava's fish market. No particular reason, except a sense it would be a good idea to know what the man looked like. It was late afternoon. I hoped he'd be back from pulling lobster traps, and that he'd be available to sell me a couple of tails. I did a search on my phone, and learned that a place called "Santiago's Fish Market" was in a small marina on the bay side, not all that far from the sheriff's substation. It seemed likely this was the place, so I made the quick drive over there.

The "market" was little more than a glorified Tuff Shed with grimy four-paneled windows on three sides, and a door in the front. The door was ajar, which I took as a good sign. That and the fact that there was a mid-sized lobster boat tied up to the dock gave me reason to hope I was about to get my first look at Islava himself.

I pulled off the road into a graveled yard, and parked next to an older model Ford Econoline van. Rust had broken through the white paint around the tire wells and below the driver's side door. Behind the van were stacks of lobster and crab traps, many of which were in obvious need of repair. The whole scene was a classic mishmash of marine clutter, including coils of algae-encrusted rope and a rusted anchor propped up against one of the traps.

I got out of the Jeep, walked over to the shed, and knocked on the door. A man appeared out of the gloom, holding a cigarette in his left hand and lobster in his right. The lobster's legs were flailing around, which I took to mean he'd probably just brought it in as part of the day's catch.

He took a drag on the cigarette and spit a bit of ash off his tongue. "Can I help you?"

"Mr. Islava?" I asked.

Islava stood about three inches short of my six feet, with a thick mop of curly black hair that was graying at the temples. He tossed the remains of the cigarette into a bucket next to the doorway. "That's me."

"It looks like you've got some fresh lobsters. I'd like to buy a couple for my dinner."

"Yep. Had a pretty good day. Come on in."

One wall of Santiago's Fish Market included a wooden countertop with a built-in sink. A fifty-gallon aquarium sat next to the sink with a half-dozen live lobsters in it. He dropped the lobster he'd been carrying into the aquarium with the others, and wiped his hands on a dirty apron that probably had been white in its infancy but was no longer.

"How many would you like? They're fifteen bucks apiece."

"That seems a little steep."

"They're big and they're fresh." He paused and scratched at a day's stubble. "I can give you the two buck discount for locals. If you are one, that is."

"I live in Islamorada year-round."

"Well, okay." He pointed to the aquarium. "You wanna pick 'em out?"

"No, just any two are good."

"You want me to pull off their heads, or do you want to do that when you get home?"

"Uh, I'd appreciate it if you'd do that."

Islava reached into the aquarium, loaded two lobsters into a bucket, and started walking out toward the canal. "Be right back."

While he was out at the dock decapitating my lobsters (actually de-thoraxing them as well), I took the opportunity to look around inside the shed. There was a calendar on one wall, advertising a local hardware store. It had not yet been turned to the current month. But it was an old faded photo taped to one of the refrigerators that got my attention. Three men were standing in front of a big sailfish suspended by its tail from a heavy beam. The fish was at least two feet longer than any of the men, one of whom was holding a big fly rod. I walked in for a closer look.

The man on the left was a much younger Santiago Islava. But it was the man in the middle that got my attention. It was my uncle Fred. What had he been doing with Islava, and when?

The third man in the photo looked familiar, but I couldn't place him. He was the one holding the fly rod.

Islava came back inside with two lobster tails and put them along with some ice in a plastic zip-lock bag. I asked him about the photograph.

"That was back when I did a little guiding. Helluva fish, huh?"

"It sure is. Who were these other people and when was this taken?"

"I don't remember their names. It would have been in late spring or summer, when lobster season was over, because that was the only time I guided. Gave me something to do in the off-season. But I can't remember the year. Why?"

"I'm pretty sure the man in the middle is my uncle, Fred Sawyer, but I don't recognize the other man besides you."

"Like I said, I don't remember their names."

"Did you fish with them often?"

"Don't think so, or I might remember 'em. Which I don't." He reached into his shirt pocket and pulled out a lighter and a pack of cigarettes. He fired up and took one puff. "You say the man in the middle is your uncle?"

"Was. He's dead now." I pointed to the old photograph. "You mind if I take a picture of that?"

I thought I detected a brief look of suspicion in his eyes, but it could have been my imagination. He shrugged. "No, I suppose not."

I pulled out my phone, clicked on the camera icon, and held it up close to the photo on the refrigerator. I took three images and checked to make sure they had what I needed. The original photo was old and faded, and my phone could only do so much, but I thought it was going to be enough.

I paid for the lobsters and got back in my Jeep, thinking that maybe I'd told Santiago Islava more about myself than I should have. But it wasn't until I was about halfway home that it hit me. He looked a lot different out of his football uniform, and of course I'd never seen the man himself, just in another old photo. But I was almost certain the third man was Sebastian Brophy.

Chapter 17

As soon as I got home I put the lobsters in the refrigerator and said hi to Prince and Katie.

"How did it go with Beaudry?" she asked.

"Interesting. Let me check something and then we can talk about it."

I walked over to Katie's desk, where I knew she kept our files on the Brophy case. I searched until I found the photo of Sebastian Brophy in his football uniform that Nate Sturm had given us. Then I opened up my phone and compared the images. There was no doubt.

Katie was in the kitchen slicing up a lemon. "Come over here and look at this," I said.

She came into the living room and peered down over my shoulder. I held up my phone and pointed to the man on the right in the image. "Doesn't that look like Sebastian Brophy holding the fly rod?"

She glanced back and forth between the two images. "Neither photo is much good, but I think it does. Where did you take that?"

"In Santiago Islava's fish market down in Marathon."

"I thought you were going there to talk with Al Beaudry."

"I did, but then I decided it might be a good idea to get a look at Islava. I bought two lobster tails from him." I pointed to the old photo. "He's the one on the left. The man in the middle is my uncle Fred."

"What the hell?"

"My reaction exactly."

"Did you ask him about it?"

"He said he couldn't remember who the people were or when it was taken. Just that he'd been a fishing guide at the time."

"Seems odd."

"More than odd. I was tempted to push him some more, but then I thought better of it. He seemed a little suspicious as it was."

"You probably should show that to Nate. See if he remembers anything about it."

"That's a good idea."

Later, after our lobster dinner, Katie and I sat in the living room while I told her the details about my interview with Al Beaudry and my visit to Santiago Islava's fish market.

"Sounds like you got the bum's rush from Beaudry," she said. "Any idea why?"

"Not really. If Stella has it right, the sheriff put him on the Brophy case because he doesn't think it's that important. And I got the same impression from Beaudry. When I told him about Islava and Stebbins being possible suspects, it was all he could do to bother writing down their names, let alone ask me any questions."

"Huh."

At this point Prince had a barking fit. A few seconds later there was a knock at the door. I went to answer it, with Prince shoving his way in front of me. We'd tried to teach him not to get pushy with visitors, but so far it hadn't had any noticeable effect.

I opened the door. Prince dashed out from between my legs and jumped up to greet the man facing me. It was Hank Simpson, the neighborhood developer and sometime fishing client. He ignored Prince. "Mind if I come in?" he asked.

I stood aside. "Sorry about the dog. He gets a little excited when we have guests."

"No, no, it's fine," he said as he walked into the room. I got the distinct impression it wasn't fine.

I wasn't sure Katie had ever met our neighbor, so I introduced them and then invited Simpson to sit. "Can I get you something to drink?"

"I'd take a soft drink. A diet brand if you have it."

I looked at Katie. "Can I get you anything?"

"No thanks."

I went to the kitchen, added ice to a glass, and then filled it up with a cola that proclaimed in big letters right on the can that it had no calories and no caffeine. Katie must have gotten it somewhere in a fit of virtue. Why drink a soda that was little more than colored water?

I went back to the living room where Hank Simpson was in the midst of telling Katie about himself: his history of building homes in our development, his involvement in various civic activities, and our history of fishing the backcountry together. He seemed quite chatty.

I assumed Simpson was here to set up a fishing date, but that wasn't it. Or at least that wasn't all of it.

Simpson took a swallow of his drink and then set it down on the coffee table in front of him. "I understand you teach at the local college. Something to do with criminology? I myself am a member of their Board of Trustees. My fellow board members tell me we're lucky to have you."

"Thank you," Katie said. Then she shot me a look that said: "What is this guy doing here?"

It didn't take long to find out.

"Anyway," he continued. "The reason for my being here is to ask you a question. Have you ever considered selling your house?"

To say this came from out of nowhere would be an understatement. Katie and I looked at each other. "Uh, not really," I said. "Why?"

"As you may know, our development is completely built out. There are no vacant lots remaining. And even if there were, getting a building permit can be a pain in the neck, even for an experienced developer such as myself. But for an established dwelling I can do a remodel without all of that red tape." He paused to take another sip of his drink. "Or at least most of it."

I realized where Patrick Henry ("call me Hank") Simpson was coming from. The modest wood house my uncle had built back in the 70s wasn't much, even back then. And by today's standards, embedded as it was in a neighborhood full of glass and concrete mansions, it was even less.

Apparently Katie also got the message, and she never has been as tactful as I am when dealing with people like Simpson. "You don't really want to remodel this, do you? You're just after the lot."

Simpson vigorously shook his head. "No, no, it would have to be a remodel, even if we only left a small—"

Katie put up a hand. "Perhaps you could just get to the bottom line?"

"Well now, um, such things are negotiable. But, um, I was thinking about one, or maybe one and a half."

"One and half what?" Katie asked, although I think she had a pretty good idea.

"Million," he said.

"Just for a *lot*?" she said.

Simpson didn't quite roll his eyes, but it got close. He turned to me. "I understand you became the owner of this property after you inherited it from your uncle, is that right?"

"It is."

"Then I put it to you, Mr. Sawyer: would *you* be interested in selling me this house? I can make you a cash offer right now."

"My inclination is to say no, Mr. Simpson, but in any event I would never make such a decision alone. Katie and I are partners in every sense of the word."

"I understand, and I'm delighted you are considering my offer. But I must warn you. There are others in the neighborhood who also have— um—*older* homes. Their locations are not as desirable as yours, but I'm not in a position to wait all that much longer before turning to them."

"You'll hear from us very soon," Katie said. She didn't say "and in the meantime you can drop dead," but I could hear it in her tone.

Hank Simpson chugged the remains of his soda, thanked us for our time, and ignored Prince as he went outside and started down the stairs. He stopped halfway down. "Oh, one other thing. Any chance we could fish some time? It's been a while."

"Sure. When would you like to go?"

"I don't know. I'll need to check my schedule. I'll get back to you."

He went on down the stairs, got in a high-end Mercedes SUV I hadn't seen before, and left.

I came back inside and joined Katie at the kitchen table.

"If he's good for it, a million and a half is a hell of a lot of money," I said. "We could even retire."

"And do what, exactly?"

"I don't know. Whatever we wanted."

"For you, it would have to involve fishing, right?"

"Sure, I suppose so, but—"

"And you're already fishing, Sam."

I started to point out that fishing in retirement would be different from getting paid to take other people out, but she interrupted before I could say it.

"We can always sell this house—*you* can sell this house—at some point in the future. And probably for even more money, unless something weird happens to the market."

"Which it has done in the past, Katie. I understand there were people down here back in the 80's who invested heavily in local real estate and then got killed when the market crashed."

"Yeah, and maybe Hank Simpson was one of them." She stopped and shook her head. "No. Sorry. It's your house and your decision. I should stay out of it."

"I meant what I said to him, Katie. There's no way I'm deciding this alone."

I put both hands on the table and stood up. "I'll call him tomorrow and tell him it's no deal, if that's alright with you."

"You know it is."

Chapter 18

Because Katie had been planning a visit to the Robert Is Here fruit stand, we decided to drive to Flamingo rather than use the boat, even though it might take a little longer. We left the house just before seven the next morning, after having given Prince a dawn walk and an early breakfast. As usual, he wasn't amused by our abrupt departure. He was still barking grumpily as we drove off.

Katie decided to bring along the Brophy case file to read along the way, since neither of us had yet found time to give it more than a brief perusal. There was little traffic on the Overseas Highway as we made our way up toward the Florida mainland. She gave me the highlights as she read. The top sheets in the file had been written by Stella Reynard, summarizing our discovery of the abandoned red canoe and its contents. The last entries before then went back to 2003, five years after Brophy's disappearance. Nobody had added anything to the file in the intervening twenty years.

"Who wrote up the early stuff?" I asked.

"That's the interesting part. It was Michael Spivey."

"The sheriff?"

"The very same. But I believe he was just a detective back then."

I remembered Nate Sturm telling me it was Spivey he'd talked to when Brophy first disappeared.

Katie went back to reading, and we had nearly reached the mainland when she finally closed the file.

"Can you summarize?" I asked.

"Sure, but there isn't much we don't already know. Our client Mr. Sturm reported Brophy and his boat missing on the first of July, 1998. Evidently Nate had started out with the sheriff himself, a man named Griscom, but he was quickly handed off to Spivey. The first thing they did was search Brophy's home, which turned up nothing. Then there was contact made with Brophy's brother William. But the brother hadn't heard from him in over a year, and had no idea where he might have gone."

"Was there an address or phone number for William?"

"Just a phone number, and a note to the fact that he lived in Orlando."

"And no other contact with William?"

"Apparently not."

"What about William's son Tyler, the one who stayed with Brophy the summer before he disappeared?"

"There's no mention of a Tyler."

"That's odd. So what happened next?"

"It was a week or two after the disappearance when Snooks' name first comes up. I guess by then Spivey was thinking foul play, and Snooks was suspect number one because of his earlier fight with Brophy. There are records of several interrogations, but then nothing."

"Because Snooks didn't do it," I said.

"We hope."

"It's more than a hope, Katie."

"Sure, I suppose so."

Was Katie less convinced than I was about Snooks' innocence? I decided not to push it. "What happened next?"

"Besides a few comments about the fact Brophy was still missing, the next thing is a write-up of a visit by Nate Sturm, where the names of Santiago Islava and Will Stebbins appear for the first time. We know about that from our talk with Nate."

"Did Spivey follow up on this?"

"He did, but apparently to no avail. He did some digging and found out that both Islava and Stebbins had been in trouble for illegal fishing activities, and that Islava was arrested on an assault charge that later was dropped."

"Did he talk to either one of them?"

"Yes. I'll need to go back and read his summary of those interrogations in more detail, but it seems both men proclaimed they had no idea what had happened to Brophy. Though did admit they didn't like the man. One of them—I think it was Stebbins—referred to him as a 'goddam tree hugger,' to quote Spivey's report."

"There's nothing more about those two guys?"

"Nope. At least none that I can find."

"What about Brophy's co-workers at the building department?"

"No mention of them either."

"It's odd Spivey didn't check on that."

"Maybe we should," Katie suggested.

"Good idea, but it's unlikely anybody's still around from 25 years ago."

We'd been cruising steadily along, making good time, when suddenly everything came to a dead stop about four miles south of the mainland. Nobody was coming in the other direction either, which was an ominous sign. For most of its length the Overseas Highway was only two-lanes. This meant even a little fender-bender could tie up traffic until the roadway got cleared. Apparently we'd hit one of those occasions. I got on the phone to Mike Nunez and told him we'd probably be late. In the meantime, idling in place with nothing else to do, I got back to Katie and the Brophy file.

"What's your overall impression?" I asked her.

"I need to read this thing again just to make sure, and you should as well. But overall I think it's pretty skimpy. Either Spivey did a lot of investigating that didn't get included in the files, or he pretty much blew it off once the case against Snooks went nowhere."

"Maybe he was just a lazy cop, or maybe somebody wanted the whole thing to go away."

Katie seemed skeptical. "But you gotta remember this was nothing more than a missing persons case."

"Until Rashaan and I found his canoe. And if they've just found his body—"

"Then it's a whole new ballgame, and we're playing in it."

I liked her analogy.

After about a half hour traffic started to move again, and we continued north on the Old Dixie Highway into Florida City, passing two smashed-in pickups by the side of the road about a mile from the mainland. I turned left on 344th Street and drove west until we came to the Robert Is Here fruit stand; then left again and followed the signs to Everglades National Park. Our plan was to hit Robert's place on the way back. It was 9:45 by the time we got to Flamingo and met up with the Park Service crew. Mike Nunez waived as Katie and I got out of the Jeep, but all that Rhonda Wilcox could manage was a scowl.

"You're fifteen minutes late," she said as we walked up. Same old Rhonda.

Moored at the dock was a 22-foot Pathfinder bay boat with a t-top and center console and a 300-horse Mercury outboard. It had a pale green hull with the Park Service logo on the side. I thought it might be a little big to get into the everglades backcountry.

"Can this thing make it to the wreck site?" I asked Mike.

"Hope so. I want to try to pull the thing out of there, and we're gonna need some oomph. The wreck is truly stuck, as you'll see. Let's load up and move."

Rhonda and her assistant Elon Tharpe were already in the boat. I wondered how much longer Mike could have waited for us before she gave the order to leave without us. Likely it was a close call.

Our gear for the day included a backpack containing Katie's forensic supplies, phones with cameras, my binoculars, plus water and some energy bars. We'd also brought our metal detector. We climbed on board. Mike fired up the motor, while I shoved us off from the dock.

Mike headed east out of Flamingo, past Snake Bight channel, Rankin Key, and Big Key, and then turned left into a bay I'd never fished. A creek draining the everglades emptied into the north end of the bay. Mike drove into it. We all had to duck down under a low canopy. The creek was narrow but surprisingly deep, giving the Pathfinder sufficient draft. We hadn't gone more than 500 yards when we came to an old white skiff, wedged sideways between the roots of two massive red mangroves.

"This is it," Mike said. "What are your first impressions?"

"Looks like a Hell's Bay, alright," I said.

"But this doesn't make any sense," Katie volunteered.

Mike got a knowing look on his face, as if this was the response he'd been looking for. "Why not?" he asked, almost rhetorically.

"Because somebody would have found it here a long time ago."

"Not if it wasn't here until recently."

Katie frowned. "You mean somebody brought it here so it would be found? Who would have done that?"

"Maybe it was a what and not a who," Mike said.

"What?" I asked.

"I said—"

"I know what you said, Mike. What I mean is, what sort of "what" could have done this?"

"I'm just speculating here, Sam. But like I suggested the other day, suppose somebody stashed Brophy's boat way back in the glades where it wouldn't be found, even from the sky, but then hurricane Irma dislodged it and it ended up here. This place has been closed since that storm. Nobody's been back here. At least not legally."

"Were Irma's winds that strong up here?" I asked, knowing the center of the hurricane had been much farther down the Keys.

"Pretty damned strong," Mike replied. "I saw boats around here bigger than this one, lodged upside down in trees that were nowhere near the water."

Katie raised an eyebrow. "So that boat blew in here with a body inside it?"

Mike shrugged. "I know it's a stretch, but can you think of a better explanation?"

"Only if we go back to the 'who' notion rather than the 'what' explanation."

"But why would anybody do that?" he asked.

At this point Rhonda Wilcox jumped into the conversation. "Alright everybody, that's enough speculation. We can do that later, and believe me I'm planning to. But for now let's get on with the job at hand. Katie, you and Elon take your metal detectors and work that clearing over there behind those mangroves. Mike and Sam, you guys search the boat and deal with the corpse, assuming it's still in there. I'll be taking notes." She turned to Elon. "You brought a body bag, right?"

"I did. It's in the bow compartment."

We set about our assigned tasks, ultimately with varying success. Katie and Elon had no luck at all with their detectors, which lent credence to Mike's theory that the boat had blown in here only recently. But there definitely were some interesting things in the Hell's Bay, not least of which—of course—were the remains of a human body. It was wedged in between the center console and the port side hull, which may have explained why it had stayed in place as the boat was being tossed about by the hurricane—assuming Mike's theory was correct.

Little was left of what once had been a whole human, except for a skeleton with bits of dried flesh and clothing here and there.

"Looks like predators have been at this," Katie said. "No surprise there. What sorts do you suppose?"

"Crocodiles, most likely," I said. "Or maybe even a panther, though there aren't many around anymore. And of course the bugs and bacteria and fungi would have added their finishing touches."

In retrospect, we were lucky to have found much of anything left of the body. But there was enough. First, there was a neat round hole in the back of the skull. Further forensics would determine whether or not it had been made by a bullet. Maybe we'd even get lucky and find a slug inside. But second, there was a class ring on the third finger of the left hand, and a leather belt with a buckle attached to it that was engraved with the image of a jumping tarpon: two items that Nate Sturm had told us Sebastian Brophy regularly wore.

I explained to Rhonda about the jewelry. "Looks like it's Brophy, alright," I said. "Plus, we might be able to use dental records. That skull appears to have a nearly complete set of teeth, and we were given the name of a dentist that Brophy probably used."

"Good," Rhonda said. "Be sure and give the M. E. the name of that dentist."

"Of course."

"Okay, let's bag him," Rhonda said. "And then take a look at the rest of the boat."

Katie and Elon had by this time returned to the Pathfinder. Both were swatting and scratching and grumbling about the bugs, even though we had all lathered up with DEET before entering the creek.

The holds in the Hell's Bay contained an assortment of fishing gear, but since I had no idea what particular brands Brophy had used, they weren't going to be all that helpful in identifying the body. Given the ring and the belt buckle, it probably didn't much matter. What did end up mattering—a whole lot—was one other thing we found. In a starboard side hold, up near the bow, I found a tin box that looked like the sort of lunch pail I used to take to elementary school. It was corroded shut, but I managed to pry it open with a screwdriver Katie had in her tote bag.

Inside the box were about a dozen plastic labels, each about one by two inches in size. I recognized them immediately as tags the Florida Fish and Wildlife Conservation Commission required all commercial lobster fishermen attach to their traps. Each tag had a year, and what I knew was a certificate number and an individual tag number. The years were from the late nineties, which fit the timing of Brophy's disappearance. But the certificate numbers were what interested me the most. They weren't all the same. I didn't think Brophy had been a lobster fisherman, but even if he had, why would the tags have different certificate numbers?

What I was looking at were an assortment of trap tags, most likely from a number of different fishermen. Assuming the records went back that far—and I was pretty sure they did—we could trace those certificates to the individuals holding the licenses. What might this tell us about who killed Sebastian Brophy? I had no idea, but it certainly brought to mind one of the suspects Nate Sturm had singled out: a lobsterman named Santiago Islava.

~ ~ ~

Towing Sebastian Brophy's flats boat back to Flamingo proved an easy task. This time, unlike the last, Rhonda Wilcox asked for only the briefest of post-mortems. She would contact Anthony Hernandez, the Monroe County Medical Examiner, to take charge of the body. This meant Detective Al Beaudry would find out soon enough that he had a murder on his hands, even if Rhonda didn't contact him directly, which I suspected she would. I agreed to trace the lobster trap tags, although Rhonda insisted on keeping them herself and instead gave me photocopies.

Katie and I made it back to Robert Is Here in time for a milkshake, and she bought three kinds of orange marmalade and a bag of mangos to take home. Prince was glad to see us when we got there, although at first he refused to make eye contact, letting us know he was hurt we'd deserted him for the whole day. Corgis are like that.

Chapter 19

There were two phone calls I needed to make as soon as we got home. Katie agreed. She volunteered to take Prince for his constitutional. He appeared to have quit his mini-pout, and he eagerly followed her out the door.

My first call was to Nate Sturm. He was our client and he deserved to learn what we had found today. He must have realized by now there was almost no chance Sebastian Brophy was still alive. Nevertheless our discovery was bound to be painful.

His phone went straight to message. "Sorry I missed your call. I'm probably out on my bike. Tell me what's up and I'll probably get back to you."

Sounded like him. "Hi Nate, it's Sam Sawyer. Katie and I went to the wreck site today with the Park Service people. We found what we're pretty sure is Sebastian Brophy's body. Both the ring and the belt buckle you described were with him. Give me a call and we'll talk about what happens next. Sorry about this."

My second call was to Dave Ackerman, a good friend and a wildlife officer for the Florida Fish and Wildlife Commission. Unlike with Nate Sturm, he was right there.

"Hey Sam. What's up? I was about to call you."

"Hi Dave. There's a case where Katie and I could use your help. But it could take me a while to describe it. You go first."

"Okay, here's the deal. I've got a day off tomorrow, and I was hoping we might go fly-fishing and look for bonefish. It's about the only species I haven't caught since I moved to Florida."

At least he didn't say something about bonefish being on his "bucket list," which in my opinion had become an overused cliché, and not relevant in any event for somebody fifteen years younger than me. "Yeah, well, there's a reason for that, Dave. You must know bonefish are pretty scarce around here. You'd be better off going to someplace like Belize or one of the islands."

"Sure, sure. But I got a tip. A couple of warden buddies were on patrol yesterday out by Indian Key, and they spotted a trio of them working the shallows. Good-sized ones too, apparently. And the place is practically in your backyard. What do you say we give it a shot?"

I knew the Indian Key area had produced some world-class bonefish over the years, though not recently in my experience. "I've got nobody booked tomorrow, so—"

"Great! I'll see you at your dock at—oh, sorry, you said you need my help with something?"

"I can give you more details tomorrow while we're fishing. But this has to do with a cold case—a *very* cold case actually—involving the disappearance of a man called Sebastian Brophy back in 1998. We just found his body, along with his flats boat, in a remote part of Everglades National Park. Katie and I have a client who has some ideas about who might have killed him way back then, and why. You ever dealt with a lobsterman named Santiago Islava or a charter boat captain called Will Stebbins?"

Dave's phone went silent for a second or two, and I thought maybe we'd lost connection. "Never heard of Stebbins, but Islava is another matter. He's a lobster fisherman, and one bad dude. He has a habit of taking lobsters out of other people's traps. We've caught him a couple of times. We tried to yank his commercial license, but the judge wouldn't go for it. Just big fines."

"You mean the guy's still at it? Poaching, I mean?"

"Seems likely. But why would he have killed this Brophy fella?"

"Not sure he did. But our client says Brophy was a passionate conservationist who sometimes took it upon himself to go after scofflaws."

"You mean he was some sort of vigilante?"

"Maybe. I'm not really sure."

"And you want me to go after Islava for something he might have done twenty-five years ago?"

"No, nothing like that. But we found some items in Brophy's boat today that you might be able to help us with."

"What?"

"I'll show you tomorrow. Be at the dock by seven."

114

Katie came back in with Prince, followed closely by Nate Sturm, who was carrying his helmet under one arm and his poodle under the other. The poodle and Prince circled each other in the living room, and then apparently decided they liked each other because there wasn't any trouble. They mostly just ignored each other.

"Got your message," Nate said. "Thought maybe we should talk in person. You sure it was him?"

"Pretty sure. Like I said, with the jewelry and it being his boat—"

"What about DNA?"

"I'm sure the medical examiner will try to get some, but then we'll need a relative or two for comparison."

"There's that cousin I mentioned, Tyler. Maybe you can find him."

"I'm gonna try."

Nate sighed, picked up his helmet from the kitchen counter where he'd laid it, and called to his dog. "Okay, then, I'll leave you to it. Thanks for letting me know. Now, go find the sonofabitch who did this!"

"We're gonna try."

Katie made Prince his dinner, then joined me in the living room with two glasses of red wine. "I gather you're taking Dave Ackerman fishing tomorrow. For bonefish?"

"That's what he wants to do. At least it will give me a chance to show him copies of those lobster trap tags we found on Brophy's boat. What are your plans?"

"I've got a lecture in the morning. Then I thought in the afternoon maybe I'd drop by the Islamorada Building Department. See if anybody remembers Brophy, though it's unlikely after all these years."

"Still worth a shot. What's for dinner?"

"It's your night, remember?"

"Oh yeah, that's right. I'll put a pizza in the oven."

"I'm not sure that counts, but okay."

~ ~ ~

Dave showed up at quarter to seven the next morning. Bonefish feed most actively on a rising tide. I'd checked the night before and learned we wouldn't be having one until about nine thirty or so, which gave us time to talk about the case before we went out.

He accepted my offer of coffee, and we walked out on the deck to catch the morning sun. I handed him a photocopy of the tags.

"What's this?" he asked.

"Yesterday when we searched Sebastian Brophy's boat I found a tin box full of old lobster tags. You're looking at copies. The Park Service people kept the tags themselves. Anything you can find out about them could help us with the case."

"You mean like were they tags belonging to Santiago Islava?" He held the eight by eleven inch sheet up close. "But these are all different."

"Exactly."

Dave looked puzzled. "Then how do you think Brophy got them, and why were they so important he stashed them on his boat?"

"This could be way off the mark, Dave. But let's suppose Islava was poaching other people's lobsters. You said he's been suspected of doing that. And suppose Brophy found out exactly whose lobsters he was poaching by getting his hands on their trap tags."

"And how would he do that?"

"We have a source who says Brophy had a spy on board Islava's boat, posing as a crew member."

"Do you know who it was?"

"We think so. All I'm asking you to do right now is figure out which lobstermen had those tags, and whether some of them might still be around that I could talk to."

"I can certainly do that, assuming our records go back that far. Oh, and one other thing. I sniffed around about that man Stebbins you mentioned the other day. We have nothing on him, except that one of his crew members got busted poaching conchs a couple of years back."

"And let me guess. Stebbins himself said he had no knowledge of it. That the crew member had just borrowed his boat for a fishing trip."

Dave grinned. "How did you guess?"

"Thanks, Dave. You can keep that paper with the lobster tag info. Now let's go fishing."

We got in my skiff for the short ride over to Indian Key. The tide had begun to rise, and there were abundant shallows where bonefish likely would be hunting. We worked hard and finally spotted one tailing fish. Dave made a good cast with a shrimp fly but the fish spooked anyway, and that was it.

Typical bonefish day.

Chapter 20

Prince was helping me stow the fishing gear and clean up the boat, when his ears perked up. Of course Corgi ears are always perked up, but I'd learned the difference between standard perkiness and a 'somebody's here' version. A minute later Katie came out on the deck, holding a bowl of kibble in one hand and a glass of red wine in the other. Prince immediately lost all interest in whatever I was doing that obviously didn't have anything to do with food or being scratched. He bounded up the stairs. I finished my work and followed.

"Have a good day?" I asked.

"Interesting. How about you?"

"Likewise. Let me get something and then we can catch up."

I went inside, poured myself a shot of Maker's Mark, and joined Katie back outside. It was a warm afternoon with no wind. We touched glasses without saying anything, and watched as a snowy egret made its way up the canal, its white plumage lit by the afternoon sun.

Katie had a little grin on her face. "I gather you didn't catch a bonefish or I would have heard about it by now."

"We had a shot at one, but nope, you're right."

"Did Dave say he could help indentify those lobster tags?"

"He thinks so. What about your visit with the city fathers? Any luck there?"

"Actually, it was mostly mothers, and they probably weren't even born when Sebastian Brophy worked there. But there was one man who remembered him, a guy named Wallace Burke. They were building inspectors together. Burke's the head guy now."

"Did he have any ideas about what might have happened to Brophy?"

"That was a little tricky because I decided not to tell him we knew Brophy was dead."

"Why not?"

"Remember my number one private eye rule?"

"Uh, no."

"Never give anything away unless you can get something in return."

"Oh yeah, that's right. But he must have assumed Brophy was dead after all these years."

"Yeah, he said as much. And then we got to the interesting part, as far as it went. Apparently Brophy was as passionate about building codes as he was about conservation."

"Maybe more than Burke?"

"That was the impression I got. He kept talking about how back in the old days things were a lot more relaxed than they are now."

"But not for Brophy?"

"Right."

"Did Burke mention anybody in particular? Some developer, say, who got his pet project scuttled?"

"No he didn't. And believe me, I pushed him on that. But the man's no fool, and it didn't take him any time to figure out what I was after. He asked me right out: 'You want to know if Brophy could have gotten himself killed because of a building permit?' Those were his exact words."

"And what did you say?"

"I said 'Well could he?' And then Burke shrugged and said maybe."

"But he couldn't give you any names."

"Or wouldn't."

"I wonder if their records go back that far? Maybe we could find out the names of people Brophy crossed."

"Naturally I asked about that. But there's bad news. They kept records of course, but it was all paper back then, and hurricane Wilma flooded their storage room in 2005. Or so Burke claimed."

"You think he's covering something?"

"No way to tell, but I didn't much like the man, and it's easy to imagine money changing hands, especially 'back in the old days,' as he put it."

Later that night, after dinner, I fired up my computer and searched for somebody named Tyler Brophy. There were three hits. Two of them were obituaries for guys who had lived in Ohio in one case and South Dakota in the other. Based on their ages, it was extremely unlikely either of them was Sebastian Brophy's nephew. The third hit was an odd one: a website for a business called A-One Outfitters, in a Georgia town I'd never heard of. I clicked it open, and read that they offered guided hunts for deer, turkey, quail, and especially wild hogs. I also learned that a Tyler Brophy was the owner and head guide, or maybe the only guide from what I could tell. Martha Brophy was listed as the office manager. There was a phone number.

Jackpot?

I told Katie what I had found and asked if she wanted me to put my phone on speaker. She said yes. I dialed, and got lucky.

A man answered. "A-One Outfitters. How can I help you?"

"Yes. This is Sam Sawyer calling. I'm a private investigator down here in the Florida Keys, and I'm looking for information about a Sebastian Brophy. Would you by any chance be his nephew Tyler?"

"*Damn* that woman! She and her website! I told her not to . . . uh, Mr. Brophy's not here."

"Then would you take a message to have him call me?"

"What is this about?"

"Sebastian Brophy disappeared back in 1998. We understand that his nephew Tyler spent the summer with Mr. Brophy that year, and that he might know something about the circumstances."

"I have no idea what you're talking about."

"Well now, you wouldn't know what I'm talking about if you're not Tyler, right?"

Nothing.

"Hello?"

The line was dead, so I dialed again. It rang six or eight times, then went to message. I couldn't think of one, other than to leave my number and ask that Tyler Brophy please call back. Fat chance, I thought to myself.

I looked at Katie. "What do you think?"

"I think that was Tyler, and I think you scared the hell out of him."

"Me too. I wonder why."

"Seems likely he's hiding something."

"Yeah, but what? We can't make him talk to us, but the law can. I believe I'll tell Detective Beaudry about this. If he's willing to take my call."

"Good idea."

Chapter 21

Early the next morning I was finishing up the breakfast dishes when there was a knock on the door. I opened it and there stood the man himself.

"Detective Beaudry from the Monroe County Sheriff's Department," he said, flashing a badge. "We met a couple of days ago. Is it alright if I come in?"

Talk about a coincidence. "Uh, sure. Can I get you a cup of coffee?"

He nodded. "Thanks. Black."

Prince eyed Beaudry suspiciously, then went off to the living room and curled up on the couch. It wasn't like him. He usually was super-friendly with strangers.

Katie had been putting finishing touches on herself before heading out for a full day at the college. She came out from the bedroom just as we were sitting down at the kitchen table. I introduced the two of them.

Beaudry fidgeted with his cup and looked back and forth between Katie and me.

"It's okay, Detective. Katie and I are partners in crime. You can speak freely."

He looked puzzled.

"We do our private investigating together."

"Oh."

"So what can we do for you?"

"When you came to my office the other day, you mentioned two people . . ." He stopped to consult a little spiral-bound notebook. "Islava and Stebbins, that you thought might have had something to do with the disappearance of Sebastian Brophy?"

"That's right."

"Well, I've been doing a little digging, and I think you may be on to something. Both men have records, mostly just fish and game violations for Stebbins, but Islava also has a violent streak. What I'd like to know is how did you come up with their names in the first place?"

I looked at Katie, who gave me just a hint of a nod. "They were given to us by our client."

"That's what I thought. I'd like his name so I can talk to him directly. Uh, or her, depending."

This time Katie gave me the opposite of a nod, but it wasn't necessary. "No, Detective, I'm sorry, but we cannot reveal his name."

"Why not?"

"Because it could put his life in danger," Katie said. "We have reason to believe Brophy was murdered, and that the killer might still be out there. Would you excuse us for a minute? I'd like to talk to my husband in private. We'll be right back."

Beaudry shrugged and slurped some coffee. "Sure."

Katie led me out onto the deck. "Didn't you say this guy pretty much blew you off the other day?'

"Uh, huh. Makes me wonder what changed. All of a sudden he's borderline charming."

"I wouldn't go that far, Sam. But we decided last night to tell him about Tyler Sebastian, and now he's here. So I say let's do it."

"And maybe tell him why Islava or Stebbins might have been involved?"

"Sure. Just don't tell him about Nate Sturm."

Once back inside we both got coffees and I offered Beaudry a refill, which he accepted.

"Our client was a close friend to Sebastian Brophy. He told us Brophy's passion was for the conservation of wildlife in the Florida Keys, most especially its marine creatures. Brophy had evidence that both men had been breaking game and fish regulations, and he was planning to turn them in."

"Our client suspects that's what got Brophy killed," Katie added.

Beaudry had been jotting things down in his little notebook. He laid the pencil down and caught my eye. "Speaking of getting killed. When you came to see me three days ago, you failed to tell me they'd found his body in some boat back in the everglades. Why not?"

"Because we didn't know for sure it was him. Still don't for absolutely certain. Has the Park Service been in touch with you?"

"Only indirectly. Our medical examiner, Dr. Hernandez, called yesterday and told me about getting Brophy's—or somebody's—body for autopsy."

"Has he made any determination about cause of death?" Katie asked. "Has he been able to identify the body?"

"He said there was a bullet hole in the back of the guy's skull. He found a slug inside the skull cavity that likely killed him. As to identity, Hernandez said he was able to compare the teeth with dental records from an office in Marathon, and it's an apparent match, so most likely it's Brophy. He's still trying to get some DNA from the bone marrow, but it's proving difficult, likely because of the long time the body spent in salt water. And then, of course, he would need to find a relative for comparison."

"We might be able to help out there," Katie said.

Beaudry looked up from his notebook. "How's that?"

"Our client mentioned that Brophy had a nephew named Tyler," I said. "Not only could he provide DNA, but apparently this Tyler spent time with his uncle the summer before he disappeared and might know something about what happened. Last night I made contact with Tyler, or at least I think it was him. He's a hunting guide in Georgia."

"What do you mean, you think it was him?"

"He wouldn't identify himself, but his name is on the website as owner of the guide business."

"This person you talked to, whoever he was, did he tell you anything useful?"

"Not a thing. We don't have the authority to go after a reluctant witness, but—"

"But I sure as hell do," Beaudry interrupted. "Can you give me his contact information?"

"Glad to. But there is a favor we'd like in return. Two, actually."

"What are they?"

"First, we'd appreciate having access to the original case file, all the way back to when Brophy disappeared."

Beaudry frowned. "Well, I don't know . . ."

"And second, we'd like the criminal records for Will Stebbins and Santiago Islava."

Beaudry traced an index finger around the rim of his coffee cup. "I guess that could be arranged. Given that you've shared information with me and all." He stood up to leave. "I'll be in touch."

~ ~ ~

"Why did you ask him for the case file, when we already have a copy?" Katie asked me as soon as the detective had left.

"Because otherwise he'd wonder why we didn't ask for it. And that could get Stella Reynard in trouble."

Katie drained the last of her coffee. "Well, I'm outta here. Got a lecture that starts in fifteen minutes and I haven't even had a chance to look at my notes. What are your plans for the day?"

"I think it is time to get everybody on the same page and tie up some loose ends. There's a lot of balloons in the air in the case."

"And maybe dot some i's and cross some t's, as long as you're mixing metaphors," Katie said, with a half grin. "Which reminds me of my grandmother's all-time favorite: we need to grab the bull by the tail and look the matter straight in the eye."

I put up my hands. "Okay, okay. What I *really* think we should do is arrange a meeting with all the players at the same time and place. It worked before on the Mabel Schwimley case, remember?" Then I snapped my fingers. "Oh that's right. You were still up in Lauderdale then."

"That's right. But I'm here now, and a meeting sounds like a good idea. Where you gonna start?"

"With the Feds, of course. They'll want to be in charge anyway. I'll call Mike Nunez right now and fill him in on the details, including who should be at the meeting and why. What's your schedule for the next few days?"

"Nothing I can't work around."

Chapter 22

It took three days to get things organized, but Mike Nunez persuaded Rhonda Wilcox to host a gathering of all interested parties. The meeting was set for ten in the morning in the headquarters building of Everglades National Park. Dave Ackerman would be there representing Florida fish and game. Dr. Anthony Hernandez from the Monroe County medical examiner's office would attend, along with detectives Stella Reynard and Al Beaudry from the sheriff's department. I had a little trouble persuading Stella to come since she'd been "kicked off the case," as she put it. But she was still in charge of the Rusty Montrose death, which I reminded her could be related to the Brophy case. Rounding things out would be Katie and me, along with our hosts, Mike Nunez and Rhonda Wilcox.

We met in a conference room in Park headquarters. It was a bright airy place, with windows that looked out onto a good-sized freshwater pond. I could see alligators in the pond and a variety of wading birds along the shoreline. It was tempting to walk out for a closer look. Katie and I had arrived fifteen minutes early. But Rhonda already was at her place at the head of the long table, looking very official, and—since the meeting was my idea—skipping off to watch the wildlife didn't seem like such a good idea.

There were eight of us in the room, including Rhonda. Sitting along the side of the table to her left were Mike Nunez, Anthony Hernandez, then Katie and me. To her right sat Al Beaudry, Dave Ackerman, and Stella Reynard. I couldn't help but notice that Al and Stella had arrived separately and had chosen not to sit next to each other.

Rhonda punched a recorder and called the meeting to order promptly at ten. She began by having everybody introduce themselves and explain briefly why they were there. She also passed around a yellow-lined tablet and asked each of us to write down our names and contact information. Then she got down to business.

"As many of you know, this case first came to our attention last September 24th, when Dr. Sawyer and a fishing client discovered the partial remains of an abandoned red canoe in a remote part of the everglades. Subsequent investigation suggested the canoe might have belonged to a Mr. Sebastian Brophy, a Florida Keys fisherman who had disappeared back in 1998. More recently a second vessel was discovered, also in a remote area of the Park, with a decomposed body inside it. That boat definitely belonged to Mr. Brophy, and two personal items found on the body strongly suggest it is, or was, Mr. Brophy's as well."

Clearly, Rhonda Wilcox had done her homework. I had to give her credit.

She stopped and looked around the room. "Do we all agree with these facts?"

Everybody agreed.

"Good," she said. "Now to start things off, I'm requesting that Everglades Park Head Ranger Michael Nunez share his theories as to why the two abandoned vessels in question remained undetected for better than two decades. He and I have discussed this in private, but I would like to have his opinions on the record."

Did Mike squirm like a butterfly on a pinning board, or was it just my imagination? "Well," he said. "I naturally have given this issue considerable thought. As for the canoe, it's easy to imagine how we missed it. It was in a remote area of the Park rarely visited by anybody, and covered in debris. It would scarcely have been visible from the air." He stopped to clear his throat. "However, the Hell's Bay flats boat is more problematic because it's larger and white and relatively exposed. One possibility is that someone moved it to that area only recently, though it is hard to imagine where it would have been all this time, especially with a decayed body on board." Mutters from around the room suggested general agreement that this scenario made little sense. "A much more likely possibility is that the boat had been deliberately well-hidden by Mr. Brophy's killer or killers, and that it became visible only recently after having been dislodged from its hiding place by Hurricane Irma."

Rhonda stared at Mike in silence, evidently waiting for him to say more. "So that's it?" she finally said.

"That's all I can think of," he replied.

"Then I suppose we'll have to go with your theory, unless somebody else here has another idea?"

Nobody said anything.

"What I would suggest, then," Rhonda continued, "is that staff of Everglades National Park become more vigilant about goings-on inside its boundaries, including more regular aerial surveys. Frankly, I can understand how you missed that old canoe, but an intact brightly colored boat? I believe you should be able to do better in the future."

Having thoroughly chastised Mike Nunez, Rhonda Wilcox proceeded to change the subject. "I would now like to ask Dr. Anthony Hernandez, the medical examiner for Monroe County to whom we gave the body, to tell us results of his autopsy. Assuming it has been completed. Dr. Hernandez?"

Anthony cleared his throat and consulted his notes. "Given the advanced state of decomposition, there are many aspects of a typical autopsy that were not possible in this case, including anything having to do with soft tissues. However, from an examination of the skeletal remains, I have determined the body likely is that of a male in his mid-thirties to late forties. I was able to obtain dental records, including x-rays, for Mr. Brophy from a dentist in Marathon, and there is a close match with teeth in the skull. Between that and some jewelry items associated with the body, I have little doubt the deceased is Sebastian Brophy. There were no obvious signs of trauma such as healed bones, although that was hard to determine with certainty, as there is evidence that predators gnawed on some of them. Fortunately—if that is an appropriate term—we have good evidence for a probable cause of death. I discovered a hole in the base of the skull, and a bullet inside. Therefore, I have concluded that the individual almost certainly was the victim of a lethal gunshot."

"Could it have been suicide?" Rhonda asked.

"Extremely unlikely," Hernandez replied. "The shot was fired into the base of the skull and exited through his right eye socket."

"Have you been able to compare the bullet with those recovered at the site of the abandoned canoe?" Rhonda asked.

Anthony shook his head. "I have not. I did bring it with me, but I'm not sure an exact detailed comparison can be done. There were both distortions and fracturing of the slug, probably caused by interaction with the skull bones. One possibility would be to loan it to the FBI lab in D.C. They have experts on this sort of thing."

"Any idea about caliber?" Mike asked. "The bullets we recovered at the canoe site were 38s."

"That sounds right," Anthony replied. He reached into a satchel and handed Mike a small paper envelope. "Here it is. We should do a chain-of-custody form before I leave today."

"Of course," Mike said. "And thank you for bringing it."

"Actually, I'll take that with me back to our lab in Atlanta," Rhonda interrupted. "We'll let you know what we find. Anything else Dr. Hernandez, before we move on?"

"I have been able to extract some DNA from the bones. Most likely it is from the victim rather than the perpetrator. I have not yet been able to obtain DNA samples from any relatives for comparison. But frankly, given all the other evidence, that may not be necessary."

Rhonda nodded in agreement. "But if you are able to obtain the necessary DNA, our lab in Atlanta can do the comparisons. And now I'd like to turn to Mr. Ackerman from the Florida fish and game. I understand you have examined photocopies of certain items recovered from the abandoned boat that may have a bearing on this case?"

"Yes ma'am, I have," Dave replied. "Dr. Sawyer tells me that you all found a box filled with lobster trap tags on the derelict boat. He gave me a photocopy of those tags and asked if I could identify the original owners. As you may know, each commercial lobsterman must attach a tag to each of his or her traps identifying it as theirs."

"And what did you find?" Rhonda asked.

"Those tags belonged to five different individuals. By checking our records I was able to determine the identity of each of them. None of the tags belonged to a lobsterman named Santiago Islava."

"And for the record, why do you think that is significant Mr. Ackerman?" Rhonda asked, pointing to her recorder. "For the transcript that is."

"I understand from Dr. Sawyer that Islava is a possible suspect in the murder of Sebastian Brophy."

"We'll get to the Drs. Sawyer next, Mr. Ackerman. Thank you. But before we move on, was there anything unusual about any of the five other lobstermen?"

"Yes, ma'am, there was." Dave stopped to consult his notes. "One of them, Rudy Valdez, disappeared along with his crewman in 1997."

"What do you mean, 'disappeared'?"

"Just that, ma'am. The Coast Guard found his boat adrift outside the Channel Five Bridge, with nobody on board. They searched extensively, but neither man was ever heard from again."

"Never?"

"Never."

"And why do you think the disappearance of Valdez might be related to the Brophy case?" Rhonda asked.

"At the academy we were taught to be suspicious of apparent coincidences. The fact that lobster tags belonging to one dead person ended up in the possession of another dead person seems like one of those."

"I agree." Rhonda then turned to Stella and Al Beaudry. "Are either of you familiar with the Valdez case?" she asked.

Both shook their heads.

"Then I suggest you become so."

Typical Rhonda, issuing orders to people not under her command. But it was a good suggestion.

"Thank you, Mr. Ackerman. And now I'd like to ask—uh—the *Doctors* Sawyer [at least she got that right] about their involvement in the case, and what they might know about possible suspects and their motives."

Katie and I had already agreed that I'd speak for both of us, at least to start things off.

"This all began when a fishing friend and I discovered pieces of a red canoe, which led—as you know—to the discovery at the site of a dog collar from a pet that once belonged to my uncle. We also learned that Sebastian Brophy regularly kept this dog when my uncle was away. In addition, we knew that Brophy had owned an identical Old Town canoe. Subsequently an individual close to Sebastian Brophy engaged our—that's Katie's and my—services in an attempt to find what happened to his friend, including who might have been responsible for his death."

"Can you give me the name of your client?" Rhonda asked. "I'll keep it confidential."

"We'd rather not," Katie said.

Rhonda frowned and muttered something I didn't catch. "Can you at least tell us what you've learned so far, working for this anonymous person?"

"Of course," I said. "The client gave us the names of two individuals he had reason to believe would have had motive to kill Brophy. One was the lobsterman named Santiago Islava, while the other was a charter boat captain called Will Stebbins."

"Why did your client believe they might have been responsible?"

"It turns out Brophy was a passionate conservationist. Apparently he had learned that both Islava and Stebbins were scofflaws when it came to fishing regulations, and he was in the process of gathering information that could lead to their prosecution."

"What did Brophy think they were doing?"

"According to our client, Islava was stealing lobsters out of other people's traps, while Stebbins was poaching conchs."

Rhonda frowned. "Isn't murder a bit of an overreaction? I mean, just because—"

"Not necessarily," Dave Ackerman interrupted. "Depending on the severity of their crimes, either of these two individuals could have lost their livelihoods permanently if convicted."

"I see," Rhonda said, turning back to me. "In any event, what evidence have you found that suggests either of these individuals could have killed Mr. Brophy?"

"For Will Stebbins, nothing definitive so far. But in the case of Mr. Islava, we have discovered that Sebastian Brophy's nephew, Tyler Brophy, spent the summer of Sebastian's death in the Florida Keys, probably working as a deck hand on Islava's boat. We suspect Brophy asked Tyler to gather evidence that Islava was robbing traps belonging to other lobstermen."

"Have you spoken to Tyler Brophy about this?"

"Yes and no. We recently traced him to a hunting guide service in Georgia. When I called the number listed on their website a man answered. He claimed not to be Brophy, but he was generally uncooperative and we suspect it was him."

"Oh it was him, alright," said Al Beaudry. Seven heads simultaneously turned in his direction. "Tyler Brophy currently is in a county jail in Georgia, awaiting extradition to our jurisdiction."

"Please explain," Rhonda said, perhaps unnecessarily.

"Three days ago the Sawyers told me about this Tyler Brophy, and that they had traced him to a hunting guide service up in Georgia somewhere. I subsequently did an in-house search on Tyler and discovered we have an outstanding warrant for his arrest on drug-related charges here in Monroe County. Serious charges, I might add. Our sheriff contacted local officials and made the arrangements. I'm to pick him as soon as possible."

"How did we lose this guy in the first place?" Stella asked. It was the first time she had spoken. "The Sawyers had no trouble finding him."

"I'm not sure."

I had no particular desire to rescue Beaudry from his embarrassment. But there did seem to be an explanation, and I felt a duty to offer it. "When I searched on line for a Tyler Brophy, the only hit was a link to his guide service. Based on his reaction when I called, I had the distinct impression that his wife—or girlfriend or whatever—only recently developed the website and included his name and a telephone number. Before then he could well have been off the radar."

Beaudry didn't say anything, but he nodded in my direction and looked relieved. Perhaps I'd just earned some bonus points that would prove useful later.

"Have you had a chance to interview Mr. Islava?" Rhonda asked Beaudry.

"Yes we did, ma'am. He claimed he didn't know anything about somebody named Sebastian Brophy. We'll see how that goes once we have Mr. Tyler Brophy's testimony to throw at him."

I felt more than heard a buzzing in my shirt pocket. I pulled out my phone and saw that I had a message from Stella: "Can we meet afterwards? Someplace without what's-his-name?"

I replied: "What about Robert is Here for a milkshake?"

"Deal," she answered back.

"So is it your intention to interrogate Tyler Brophy?" Rhonda asked Al Beaudry. "Not only about his drug charges, but also for what he might know about the death of his uncle, right?"

"Right. Just as soon as I can get out of here and go pick him up."

Rhonda frowned at that, and he got it. "Uh, what I mean is, as soon as we have finished this meeting. Which has been very helpful."

"I believe we can wrap things up pretty quickly," Rhonda said. She looked down at her notes and then back up to Katie. "Is there anything you can to add to what your husband has told us, Dr. Sawyer?"

"Yes. There is one aspect to Sebastian Brophy's life we have not discussed. He was a passionate fisherman and conservationist, but actually he made his living working for the Village of Islamorada as a building inspector. It may have had nothing to do with his death, but I'm sure you know that these inspectors have considerable power and sometimes find themselves in conflict with individuals in the housing business."

"Are you aware of any such conflicts in his case?"

"I am not. I'm just saying it's something we should keep in mind as things develop."

Al Beaudry squirmed in his chair. What little relief had spread on his face when I let him off the hook about Tyler Brophy had just disappeared.

Rhonda went back to her notes. "There is one final item we need to consider before we adjourn. "Detective Reynard, I understand you are investigating the death of a Mr. Rusty Montrose. Can you explain, for the record, any possible connections with the Brophy case?"

"There may be none, ma'am, but I am happy to tell you what we have learned. Mr. Wilford Montrose, who went by 'Rusty,' was found dead in the canal behind his house. We know he was acquainted with Sebastian Brophy, and had been for most of his life. I learned from Dr. Sam Sawyer that Montrose seemed particularly anxious to learn the details of Mr. Brophy's death, or at least his disappearance. Sam admitted to me that he may have told Mr. Montrose more of those details than he should have."

"That seems a bit tenuous, Ms. Reynard," Rhonda replied.

"I agree. And in fact, Dr. Hernandez tells me he cannot rule out the possibility that Mr. Montrose died from accidental drowning."

Rhonda turned to Anthony. "Is that right Dr. Hernandez?"

"That's correct. He had a nasty bruise on the back of his skull, but no fracture and no major damage to the brain itself. During the autopsy I found water in his lungs and foaming around the mouth and throat, but no other signs of trauma besides the bruise, and no evidence of a stroke or heart attack. I am confident he drowned, but the question remains whether it was an accident or not."

"Do either of you see this case as being resolved one way or another?" Rhonda asked.

Stella and Anthony looked at each other. "Doesn't seem likely until we find additional evidence," she said. Stella did not mention the Air Jordan shoe found next to Montrose's body, probably because we had no evidence about the owner of the shoe. If and when Rashaan Liptan remembered whom he'd seen wearing a pair, then maybe this would turn out to be an important clue.

Rhonda looked around the room. "Does anybody have anything else they'd like to add before I summarize?"

Nobody said anything.

"Alright then, here is where I think things should go from here. Dr. Hernandez, thank you for unearthing Mr. Brophy's dental records, and also for extracting some DNA from the corpse. And Mr. Beaudry, as part of your interrogation of Tyler Brophy, please do get a DNA sample for possible comparison. It seems almost certain to me that the body in Sebastian Brophy's boat was Brophy himself, but we need to make certain in all possible ways. And also, Mr. Beaudry, please keep us informed about the results of your pending interrogation of Tyler Brophy concerning what he knows about the activities of Santiago Islava."

"Of course, ma'am," Beaudry replied.

At this point Rhonda Wilcox actually sighed, which to me was a brand new emotion coming from her. "I'll compare the slug from Brophy's skull with those we found at the canoe site, of course. But even if they match, unless we can find the weapon that fired them, I don't see where this is going to get us." She stopped and looked around the room. "Frankly, ladies and gentlemen, this whole thing is looking pretty bleak to me. As long as I've been with Investigative Services, I can't recall a case with fewer solid leads. It's possible this is a cold case that will never be solved."

Katie and I exchanged glances. I couldn't say we disagreed.

As Katie and I were making our way to my Jeep in the parking lot, Dave Ackerman caught up with us. "Sam? Katie? Got a minute?"

"Sure, Dave. What is it?" I said. The three of us turned at the sound of a big splash coming from the pond next to Park headquarters.

"Looks like a gator heading out for an evening hunt," Dave said. "Uh, anyway, you remember my telling you that one of Will Stebbins' crew got busted for conch poaching a few years ago?"

"Yes."

"A couple of days ago I mentioned to my bosses that Stebbins could be a suspect in a cold case murder. Then I suggested maybe some heightened surveillance of Stebbins could be warranted, and they agreed."

"Good idea," I said. "Maybe if you can bust him we might learn something during an interrogation just like we hope to do with Tyler Brophy."

"Yeah, well, I've got an idea, Sam. Snooping around after Stebbins in my boat with a big departmental logo on the side might not be as productive as doing it under cover, so to speak."

"So you want to borrow my boat?" I asked.

"That and more. I also was hoping to borrow you and your fishing gear. That way we'll look like a couple of regular guys out on the water. When can you start?"

"Tomorrow, I guess."

Katie laughed. "Gosh, fellas, that seems like a fine idea. What you really need to do is disguise yourselves as a couple of innocent fishermen. Shouldn't be too hard, should it?"

Chapter 23

Katie was still giggling about our "so-called surveillance" when we pulled into the parking lot at Robert Is Here. I protested, but only mildly. "It could work, you know. And even if Stebbins had nothing to do with the murder of Sebastian Brophy, catching a conch poacher would be a reward in itself, don't you think?"

Stella already was standing in the milkshake line. She waived us over and we cut in, explaining to the people behind her that we were old friends. Nobody grumbled. Maybe it had to do with the fact that Stella was in uniform.

"What are you in the mood for?" she asked. "I checked the blackboard and the special of the day is dragon fruit with key lime."

"I think I'll try that," Katie said. "It costs extra compared to their ordinary shakes, but Nate's paying, right?"

Stella raised a quizzical eyebrow. "What?"

"The client we're working for is a neighbor, Nate Sturm," Katie said. "He's agreed to cover our expenses. But I was only kidding about the shake."

We all settled on the special. I offered to pay for Stella's, but she declined. "The department has pretty strict rules about deputies not accepting favors from the general public."

"Even a free milkshake?" I asked.

"Even that." She pointed to the badge pinned on her shirt. "At least not when I'm wearing this."

Once we'd been served, we took our shakes out to one of the picnic tables behind the fruit stand where we could talk in private. There were families around with children dashing back and forth between their parents and a little zoo featuring goats and pigs and tortoises. Nobody paid much attention to us.

Stella took a drink of her shake. "How's it going with Al Beaudry?"

"It started out just like you warned me," I said. "At first he wouldn't give me the time of day. He practically threw me out of his office. Then three days later he shows up at our house, out of the blue, suddenly all interested in talking about the case."

"What changed, do you think?"

"I can't be certain, but he says he did background checks on Santiago Islava and Will Stebbins after I gave him their names. He seemed particularly interested in learning more about Islava, who apparently has a record for violence."

"Huh."

"As you heard at the meeting just now, I also gave him information that led to Sebastian Brophy's nephew, Tyler."

"And now they're about to bring him in for questioning." Stella scratched at an ear lobe. "Interesting. I still don't trust the guy." She shook her head. "No, that's not right. It's the sheriff I don't trust. Beaudry's just his flunky."

"Don't you think that's a little harsh?" Katie said.

Stella sighed and shrugged. "Yeah, I suppose you're right. It's just that I don't like being taken off a case for no reason."

"I agree, but I have a favor to ask."

"Sure, Sam. Anything."

"I'd like to be there when they interview Tyler Brophy."

Stella frowned. "I don't see how I can arrange that. It's not my case, and Beaudry probably won't give me the time of day anyway."

"But won't somebody from the State Attorney's office be in on it?"

Stella snapped her fingers. "You know that might work, at least if Walt Stone catches the case. He owes me a couple of favors."

"So you'll check it out?"

"Sure. I'll let you know what luck I have."

"Good. At least you can tell me when they plan to interview Tyler."

The time seemed right to change the subject. "Have you gotten anywhere with the Montrose death? Beyond what you just told us at the meeting, that is?"

"I wish there was more," Stella said. "We went through the man's house, but we didn't find anything useful. That Air Jordan shoe we found seemed like a good lead at the time, but not unless we can figure out where it came from."

"What about family?" Katie asked.

"He has two sons. Both live on the west coast. Apparently they weren't all that close to their father. When I raised the possibility that Mr. Montrose might have been the victim of foul play, they couldn't think of anybody who might have a grudge against him. In fact it was odd. Neither son seemed particularly interested in what happened to their father. All they wanted to know was when they could put his house on the market."

"What about his body?' I asked.

"That was another odd thing. They never even asked about it. I volunteered they could have it once we were finished with the autopsy."

"What are your next steps?" Katie asked.

Stella shrugged. "As I said in the meeting, there don't seem to be any."

It wasn't like Stella. In my experience she hung on like an attack dog once she'd sunk her teeth into a case.

"Odd about Stella," Katie said, once we were back in the Jeep. "What do you think is going on with her?"

"I don't know. It's probably the job. She doesn't have much else going on in her life."

"You mean like a boyfriend or something?"

Was Katie circling around the possibility that something could be going on between Stella and me? There wasn't, of course, but was she that perceptive?

"Or something. I'm pretty sure Stella will get back on track. Speaking of getting on track, what do you think our next steps should be?"

"For me?" Katie asked. "I think maybe while you're busy fishing with Dave Ackerman, I might sniff around the city building department a bit more."

"You have anything specific in mind?"

"No, just that I got the impression their head guy—Wallace Burke— wasn't telling me everything he might have known about Sebastian Brophy. There were a couple of women working in the office with him that day who spent most of their time avoiding eye contact."

"With you or with him?"

"Both. So I thought I might pop in there when the boss isn't around and see what they might have to say."

"How are you going to arrange that?"

"Do a stakeout I suppose. When he leaves, I go in."

"Worth a shot. Did you happen to notice Al Beaudry's reaction when you brought up the subject of the Islamorada Building Department during our meeting back there at Park headquarters?"

Katie frowned. "No. Why?"

"He seemed unhappy about it."

"About what?"

"Maybe like why would we be looking at anybody for the Brophy murder except Islava? Or maybe Stebbins. But definitely not anybody associated with the building department."

"Guess I missed that."

"And I may have been reading too much into it."

We drove a while in silence. Finally Katie spoke up. "Let me try you out on something about the Brophy case. It's something that's been bothering me."

"Okay, shoot."

"Let's assume whoever killed Sebastian Brophy did it back where we found his canoe."

"Okay. The slugs under the canoe suggest that was the case."

"But the killer or killers for some reason didn't leave the body there. Instead they hauled it out to his Hell's Bay skiff."

"Yeah, that must have been the case."

"But here's what's bothering me. Why then did they take his boat and his body way back into the glades like that?"

"As opposed to what?" I asked.

"Why not just drive it somewhere out into the Atlantic and sink it, along with his body? Wouldn't that have been easier? And wouldn't that make it even less likely anybody would ever find it?"

She had a point. "There must have been a reason because that's obviously not what happened."

"Then what did happen? We're missing something here, Sam. Something important."

I had to agree.

Chapter 24

Will Stebbins drove a 25-foot center console Yellowfin fishing boat, with a gray hull, a flying bridge, outriggers, and two Yamaha 300 horsepower outboards. It was a good-sized vessel, built for ocean fishing and not ideal for poaching conchs in shallow water. But maybe that was the point. After all, Stebbins was supposed to be a deep-sea charter fisherman. At the very least his Yellowfin had plenty of speed to run away should anybody come snooping around. Like me and Dave Ackerman, for example, in my little Maverick skiff.

I knew that Stebbins lived on a canal near me, and there was only one way out into Florida Bay from his dock. Our plan was to anchor where his canal opened to the bay, and pretend to be fishing while we waited for Stebbins to come out. I'd brought along two pieces of equipment left over from my birding days, in case we caught Stebbins doing something that looked like conch fishing: a spotting telescope and a camera fitted with a big telephoto lens.

In the first couple of days, Stebbins took clients out beyond the continental shelf, presumably after sailfish or mahi mahi. He didn't even slow down anyplace there might have been reachable conchs. Dave and I quickly gave up the chase when we realized what he was doing, and—"as long as we're out here" as Dave put it—we went fishing instead. We caught porgies for dinner, using live shrimp for bait. On the second day we got into a school of cero mackerel that hammered our Clouser minnow flies. It was fun, but unproductive in terms of crime fighting.

The third day was different. Our first clue was that Stebbins didn't seem to have anybody on board except one crewman when he came out into the bay. Our second was that, instead of heading under the Channel Five Bridge and out into the Atlantic, he went north toward Rabbit Key Basin. This was prime conch habitat according to Dave. We followed, but stayed back a good 300 yards. When Stebbins anchored up near a small key, we did the same. Dave fished—just to keep up appearances of course—while I set up the spotting telescope on the bow platform and began to watch. It was easy to figure out what he was doing. Stebbins was throwing a cast net. I could see the splash every time his net hit the water. This was standard practice for blue water fishermen: catching live bait such as mullet in preparation for an ocean run that afternoon or the next day.

"That's it? He's just catching bait?" Dave asked.

"As far as I can tell." I bent down and looked through the scope one more time. "No, wait! Somebody in a wet suit just went over the side!"

Dave stopped fishing and reeled up, ready to roll. "What's he doing?" he asked.

"The diver came up and handed Stebbins something."

"Was it a trap?"

"No, it was something smaller. He held it in one hand."

"Like maybe a conch?"

"Maybe. You might want to pull up the anchor."

Dave did that while I fired up the outboard and began following a course about thirty degrees left of Stebbins' location. When we got even with him, maybe 150 yards off, Dave said to stop, which I did.

But Stebbins was no dummy. This time when the diver surfaced, he pulled himself on board empty-handed. Stebbins started his twin engines right away, spun the Yellowfin around, and headed back the way he had come. There was no way we were going to catch him. Even if we had, the only proof Dave had of any wrongdoing was that Stebbins churned up a lot of bottom as he sped off. If he'd even suspected anything, all he had to do was dump his conchs overboard.

"Damn, that was close," Dave said. "And there might not be a next time, at least in your Maverick. From the way he was acting, I think he must have spotted us."

"Seems likely," I said. "For one thing, we live near one another and belong to the same homeowners association. So he knows what I look like, and probably even knows what sort of boat I drive. But I've got a backup."

"Another boat?"

"Uh huh. My friend Snooks Lancaster has a cute little Mako I'm sure we can borrow."

"Sounds like a plan," Dave said, with a sigh. "And now as long as we're out here, that little key over there has a moat around it that's probably full of mangrove snappers. Might as well bring home dinner."

It was and we did.

One the way home, I got a call from Stella Reynard.

"Good news, Sam," she said. "Walt Stone plans to interrogate Tyler Brophy tomorrow down at the Marathon Detention Center, and you're invited. Hope you can make it."

"Oh I definitely can make it. Will you be there?"

"Nope, just you and Walt. Oh, and Al Beaudry of course."

"I know he'll be thrilled to see me. But thanks. I owe you one."

"No you don't. Just catch the bad guys, okay?" She hung up.

"Who was that?" Dave asked.

"That was Stella Reynard with the sheriff's department. She says I'm invited to an interrogation of Tyler Brophy. It's tomorrow, so I guess our conch watch will have to go on hold for a day, or maybe two. At least if you want me along."

"That's okay. Probably good to leave Stebbins alone for a while, anyway. I think we spooked him today."

Chapter 25

The next morning I met Assistant State's Attorney Walter Stone in the lobby of the Marathon Detention Center. Stone was a bespectacled man, probably in his mid-thirties, with neatly combed straight black hair and blue eyes. He was about my height. He had on a short-sleeved white shirt with a pale blue tie, and the same khaki chinos I think he was wearing the last time I'd seen him. Al Beaudry was there as well. Unlike the last two times I'd seen Al, today he was in uniform. Maybe the idea was to intimidate the prisoner?

"Good to see you," Walt said, extending his hand for a shake. "Thanks for coming."

"Thanks for inviting me," I said.

Beaudry glowered and didn't say anything. Perhaps now that he had Tyler Brophy in custody, I was no longer interesting or useful.

Walt pointed to a conference room adjacent to the lobby. "Let's go in there and talk. Then I'll let you into the booth next to the room where we're planning to interview Brophy."

"Does he have a lawyer?" I asked.

"Uh huh. Alden Jones, one of our regular public defenders. He shouldn't be a problem."

I wasn't sure what that meant.

I sat across the table from Stone and Beaudry, and watched as Walt opened a file folder. He read for a while, then looked up and cleared his throat. "Tyler Brophy is charged with possession with intent to sell significant amounts of marijuana. From what I can see, he began his career in the drug business in the early 2000's if not before. We busted him several times over the years, but only for small amounts that never resulted in jail time. Then, in 2019, we caught him with a whole boatload of the stuff. He was arrested but made bail, which he subsequently jumped and disappeared." Stone paused and looked at me. "Until you tracked him down five days ago up in Georgia, right?"

"That's right. Of course I wasn't positive it was him until the sheriff's department confirmed it."

Stone turned to Beaudry. "And how did you do that?"

"Uh, well, Mr. Sawyer here gave us a tip, and we followed up once we determined he had an outstanding arrest warrant."

"Just for the marijuana. No other drugs?"

"Not that we're aware of," Beaudry replied.

Because I knew Walt Stone had talked to Stella, I was pretty sure he knew why it had taken the sheriff's department so long to track down Tyler Brophy. But rather than follow-up on that, he changed the subject.

"I have been instructed by my boss that as part of our forthcoming interrogation we are to explore the possibility of a plea bargain with Mr. Brophy, in return for his testimony regarding another case. Because the charges against him are serious, any such plea would have to be for something very substantial. I think I know the general issue, but it's important that I understand the whole picture before we sit down with the man. Would either of you gentlemen care to elaborate?"

Beaudry and I looked at each other. I was prepared to let him do the talking, since he was the law and I had no official reason for even being here. But Beaudry surprised me. "Mr. Sawyer here can fill you in."

And so I did.

"A man named Sebastian Brophy, who lived in Islamorada, disappeared along with his boat back in 1998. Recently we found both his canoe and his boat abandoned in remote parts of Everglades National Park. A body in the boat almost certainly was his. This much is fact. But we—Katie Sawyer and I—have a client who strongly suspects a lobsterman named Santiago Islava may have murdered Brophy. This is where the whole thing gets a little speculative."

"What was Islava's possible motive?" Stone asked.

"According to our client, Brophy had evidence that Santiago was poaching other people's lobster traps, and he planned to turn over his evidence to the fish and game people."

"And where does Tyler Brophy fit in?"

"Our client believes that Sebastian Brophy arranged to have his nephew Tyler work on Islava's boat and gather the incriminating evidence. We do not know this for a fact, but it is possible that Tyler may well know something about his uncle's disappearance and probable murder."

"But if Tyler knew something, why didn't he come forward?"

"I wondered that too, at first. But a likely explanation has to do with his own criminal behavior, don't you think?"

Stone raised an eyebrow. "Isn't it equally probable that, if Tyler knew something about his uncle's murder, he would have used it as a bargaining chip to get out of his earlier drug charges?"

I hadn't thought of that. "That's a possibility, I suppose."

Stone sucked on his ballpoint pen and rattled it between his teeth. "Frankly, gentlemen, this whole thing seems pretty speculative. But Sam, I've worked with you before on other cases, and I've found your instincts are pretty good. So I think we can go ahead with Tyler Brophy's interrogation and see what develops." Stone gathered up his papers and pushed back his chair. "Oh, before we go, I have one more question. Does Tyler know any of the details about the discovery of Sebastian Brophy's boats or his body?"

"If so, he didn't learn them from me," Beaudry said.

"And you, Sam?" Stone asked.

"I've only spoken to him that one time, over the phone, assuming it was him. And all he learned was that I was a private investigator looking into the disappearance of his Uncle Sebastian."

Walter Stone took me down the hall and put me in a booth connected by one-way glass and a speaker to an interrogation room. I sat and watched as he and Al Beaudry came into the room and took seats on one side of a small wooden table. Five minutes later a guard came in with a man in handcuffs and an orange jumpsuit that had to be Tyler. He was of average height and probably somewhere in his mid-forties. His brown hair was tied up in a loose ponytail. He had wrinkled skin on his face and neck, likely the result of smoking too much for too long, and spending too much time outdoors without sunscreen. Accompanying Brophy was a shorter balding man in a crisp gray suit.

Stone pushed the button on a recorder and began. "This is a recording of an interview between me, Assistant State's Attorney Walter Stone, and Mr. Tyler Brophy. Mr. Brophy is being represented by a public defender, Alden Jones. With me is Detective Allen Beaudry of the Monroe County Sheriff's Department." Stone stopped to look at some paperwork on the desk in front of him. "Mr. Brophy, you have been charged with possession with intent to sell of more than one thousand pounds of marijuana. I understand you have pled not guilty to these charges. Is that still your position?"

Tyler looked at Jones and said nothing. "My client maintains his innocence," Jones replied.

"Alright then, I would like now to explain to Mr. Brophy the following facts. First, you were caught red-handed with a boat full of marijuana, and there are multiple witnesses to that fact."

"But I—"

"And in light of both the quantity of drugs seized and the fact that you are a repeat offender on drug-related charges, you could be facing up to 15 years in prison if convicted."

Brophy folded his arms across his chest, and sat back in his chair. "Yeah? Well I guess I'll just have to take my chances in court."

"There is, however, the possibility that we might be able to reduce the severity of your sentence, if you can help us in another matter."

Brophy sat forward. "What matter?"

"We understand that you may have worked in the summer of 1998 on a lobster boat belonging to Santiago Islava. Is that correct?"

"I might have done that, why?"

"And while you were pretending to be a simple crew member on that boat, your actual purpose was to help your uncle Sebastian Brophy gather information proving that Islava was poaching other people's lobsters. Is that also correct?"

Tyler leaned over and whispered something in Alden Jones' ear. The public defender nodded and whispered something back. "My client would like to know if his proof that Santiago Islava was poaching lobsters would extricate him from his present, uh, situation."

Stone did not hesitate. "No, it certainly would not. Trading hearsay information on a fishing violation for leniency on a major drug charge? No way."

"What if I had solid proof?" Tyler said.

"That probably wouldn't work either. But just for the record, what sort of proof?"

"I have photographs."

This was a revelation.

144

"Please explain," Stone said. "Perhaps this could help your case."

"Okay, then. You're right about my Uncle Sebastian. He got me a job on Islava's lobster boat—I'm not sure how—and then he paid me to do two things. First, I was to lift the little tags off the traps we were bringing in illegally. And second, he gave me a camera. It was one of those Kodak Instamatic things everybody was using back then. He asked me to take pictures of the poaching activities, and to make sure they included Islava and his boat."

"What happened to the tags and the photos?" Al Beaudry asked.

"I gave my uncle the tags, and most of the photos. But I kept some for myself."

"Why would you do that?" Stone asked.

Tyler turned again and whispered something to Jones.

"I need to have a word with my client in private, Mr. Stone, before we can proceed."

"Agreed," Stone said. He pushed back in his chair, which made a loud scraping noise on the concrete floor. "Detective Beaudry and I will leave you in this room. You have my word we will neither record nor listen to your conversation."

Stone and Beaudry left and joined me in the booth. "What do you think so far?" he asked me.

"Sounds like you've got Islava nailed for the lobsters. But—"

"Yeah, but that doesn't get us anywhere on the murder, does it?"

"In other words, so far we've got shit," Beaudry said.

"Not necessarily," I said. "Don't you wonder why Tyler kept some of the photographs for himself?"

Beaudry looked blank, but I saw the light come on in Stone's eyes.

"Because he wanted to have something on Islava. Something personal. But what?"

"Maybe you're about to find out," I said.

Once the four of them got back together in the interrogation room, Alden Jones started reading from a yellow pad. "In return for leniency, including no jail time, my client agrees to provide you with photographic evidence that not only was Santiago Islava poaching lobsters, he also was involved in the import and sale of marijuana. The reason Mr. Brophy kept the photographs was because he got tangled up in the drug business himself, and thought he might need them for protection. A sort of mutual blackmail, if you will. Furthermore—"

"That sonofabitch got me hooked into the drug business!" Tyler screamed.

Jones put his hand on Tyler's arm. "Don't say anything more."

But the man would have none of it. "If it wasn't for Islava, I wouldn't even be here! And now, by God, I'm gonna nail that bastard. I'm gonna nail him good!"

Stone stayed calm, naturally, but I could read the anticipation on his face. "Tell us about your relationship with Islava in the drug business."

"Will this help my case?" Tyler asked.

"It could."

"We'd take his boat out into the Atlantic and meet up with somebody running drugs up from—I don't know—Cuba or Haiti or somewhere. Then we'd bring them in to the dock. We'd unload 'em and I would drive the stuff up north, usually to Philly, sometimes to the D.C. area. So I was the—what do you call it?—the mule."

"And you have photos of these operations?"

"I do."

"But we arrested you about five years ago, and you made no mention of Islava. Why was that, Mr. Brophy?" Stone asked.

"Because by then we weren't in business anymore. By then I had my own boat and my own contacts. I got tired of sharing the money with that bastard."

"Excuse me, gentlemen," Alden Jones said. "There is more to Mr. Brophy's statement, which I was about to read before he . . . before I was interrupted."

"Go ahead," Stone said.

Jones glanced back down at his yellow-lined sheet. "In addition to providing testimony and evidence concerning Santiago Islava's lobster poaching and drug activities, my client also is prepared to testify to the fact that Islava committed two murders. In exchange for his evidence and testimony on these matters, we suggest that Mr. Brophy's sentence be reduced such that he does no jail time."

Stone fiddled with his tie, probably giving himself time to come up with the right answer. "Before we get to that, Mr. Jones, we need to talk about these two murders your client claims to have witnessed."

"You saw him kill Sebastian Brophy, didn't you!" Beaudry blurted out. It wasn't a question.

Up until this point Tyler's face had held a look of wild-eyed glee. He probably thought he'd just gotten a get-out-of-jail free card while sticking it to his old partner at the same time. But now his look morphed to one of puzzlement. "My uncle Sebastian? I don't know anything about what happened to him. You say he was murdered?"

"You saw a murder but it wasn't your uncle? Is that your testimony?" Stone asked.

"Hell no. It was that other lobsterman, Rudy somebody-or-other. Him and his mate. They caught Islava taking their lobsters, and there was this big confrontation."

"What happened?" Stone asked.

"It was fuckin' awful. Islava tied Rudy and the other guy to a couple of their traps, and sank 'em out in the Atlantic."

"Why didn't you report this?" Stone asked, although I think he knew the answer.

Tyler looked down at his hands and spoke quietly. "Because I knew it could get me in trouble. Not that I was involved in it, but with the drugs and all—" He trailed off.

I remembered Dave Ackerman telling me about how one of the lobstermen whose tags ended up in Sebastian's boat was a man named Rudy Valdez. Suddenly it all began to make sense, but not in a good way in terms of solving Brophy's murder.

Beaudry, for his part, wasn't having it. "Are you telling me Islava didn't murder Sebastian Brophy? Come on, Tyler. You must have seen what was happening after you gave your uncle those trap tags and the photographs. He went after Islava, didn't he, and he got caught."

Tyler put his head in his hands. "No, no, I don't know what you're talking about." He turned and looked at his attorney. "They're still gonna let me off, aren't they? For Christ sake, I've given them Islava for poaching and drugs and murder. Ain't that enough?"

In the end it was enough, or nearly so. Stone agreed to a reduced sentence of two to three years, with time off for good behavior, in return for Tyler Brophy's evidence and testimony.

But Beaudry still wasn't buying it. "Wait until we get Islava in that little room back there," he said, as we were leaving the Detention Center together. "We'll get him on the Brophy murder too. Take my word for it."

I don't know about Walt Stone, but I wasn't taking Al Beaudry's word for much of anything.

Chapter 26

Katie was out walking Prince when I got home, but I could see that they'd reached the end of our block and had turned around. There would be time for me to fix us something to drink and munch on, which turned out to be a bowl of pretzels and two rum-and-cokes for us, and a handful of mini dog biscuits for Prince. I was waiting outside on the deck when they came upstairs, Prince predictably excited because he knew snacks were about to happen.

They joined me on the deck, but Katie walked to the railing and stared out at the water instead of sitting down beside me.

"What is it?" I asked.

"Just a thought. Do you suppose we could take a cocktail cruise and watch the sunset? It's been ages since we did that, and I miss it."

"Sure. Let me get the keys while you load up Prince and the refreshments."

In less than five minutes we were anchored up out in the bay. We had calm water and a cloudless sky: a prefect opportunity to watch for the fabled green flash as the sun disappeared below the horizon. I claimed to have seen it three or four times, but Katie never had, even when she was in the boat with me. She was skeptical the flash was anything but imagination. I estimated we had about an hour and a half to go.

"You're gonna look for it, aren't you?" Katie was smiling, no doubt remembering all the other times when I said we were going to see it and then we hadn't.

"Uh huh."

"Well be sure and keep me posted."

A group of five large black birds flew overhead. They had long wings, and two of them had bright red-orange throats.

"Those are frigatebirds, aren't they?" Katie asked.

"They are."

"You're the ornithologist here. Why are they called that?"

"A frigate is a fast and agile warship."

"But why the comparison? I still don't get it."

"Frigatebirds have exceptionally long and narrow wings, which provide lift but little drag. This allows them to soar effortlessly over the water for long periods without expending any calories, and then they can dive with great speed on their prey. Frigatebirds never land on the water. I expect it's their speed and maneuverability that draws the comparison with those warships. I've heard some fishermen refer to them as warbirds."

"Then how do they eat?"

"They search for fish and other marine prey that have been driven to the surface by bigger fish, and then they use their long hooked beaks to scoop them up off the water. Fishermen have learned to use soaring frigatebirds as indicators of the presence of things like tuna and marlin."

Katie and I watched the frigatebirds until they disappeared down toward the Channel Five Bridge. "As long as you're in the mood to lecture, Professor Sawyer, perhaps you can also explain what this green flash is supposed to be all about?"

"Speaking as an ornithologist, I don't have a clue." I munched on a pretzel and drank from my rum and cola.

"But as an all-purpose know-it-all, maybe you do?"

I faked a big sigh. "Oh, alright. What I've read is that the atmosphere acts like a prism, bending the sun's rays and separating them into different colors. Sometimes—rarely—the one we see just as the sun falls below the horizon is green. But it only lasts for a second or two and then it's gone."

"I guess maybe I can buy that," Katie said, as she popped a pretzel into her mouth and chewed. "Anyway, how did your day go?"

I told her about the interrogation of Tyler Brophy.

Katie tossed Prince a treat. "Sounds like this Islava is a pretty bad guy."

"Yeah, but Tyler couldn't—or at least wouldn't—tie him to the murder of his uncle. Only to those other lobstermen."

"But Walt Stone still wants Islava brought in, right?"

"You bet. I expect Al Beaudry is out looking for him right now."

Katie looked across the bay and shook her head.

"What?"

"I still don't understand why the sheriff pulled Stella Reynard off the case."

"Me neither. But it is what it is. Nothing we can do about it."

"Are you sure?"

"What can I do?"

Katie gave me a look. "You?" she said. "Maybe nothing. But I'm tight with some of the forensics people in Monroe County. We get together often in my office at the college. You know, to talk over the latest techniques and the like. Maybe I can find out from them what's going on with Stella and Sheriff Spivey."

"That would be great. But tell me about your day. Any luck with your stakeout at the building inspector's department?"

"Some. I sat outside all morning, watching for their head guy, Wallace Burke, to come out. It finally happened around lunchtime, so I hurried in before anybody else had a chance to leave. The two women I'd met before were still at their desks. One of them was eating something that looked like leftovers."

"What did you say to them? I mean, they must have wondered why you'd come back."

"I introduced myself and explained that when I was here before I'd forgotten to ask if they knew anything about Sebastian Brophy's employment history with the department."

"Did it result in anything?"

"Nope. They claimed it was before their time and I would have to come back later, when their boss had returned from lunch. It was after that, out in the parking lot, that I got lucky. An old man caught up with me as I was getting in the Prius. He said he was a custodian in the building, and that he'd overhead my conversation with the women in the office. Then he said he'd been around since back when Brophy and Burke had first started out in the department. He said they hated each other, right from the start."

"Wow. Did he say why?"

"Yep. He said Brophy was a stickler for the rules and for following protocol, while Burke had a more casual attitude."

"Casual, as in maybe looking the other way? As in maybe being on the take?"

"The custodian didn't say that in so many words, but that was the impression I got."

I thought about what I'd just learned. Did we have another suspect in Sebastian Brophy's murder? If he had evidence that Wallace Burke was taking bribes, and threatened to turn him in, that would be plenty of motive.

I was curious about something. "Why do you suppose this janitor fellow went to the trouble of tracking you down in the parking lot? Just being a good Samaritan?"

"Maybe. But I got the clear impression he doesn't like his boss."

"I hope you got that janitor's name."

"Of course. And he was glad to give it. Andy Simms. He also gave me another name: Pete Robinson. He said Robinson was head of the department back when Brophy disappeared, that maybe I should talk to him." Katie stopped to give Prince another treat, and we both watched him crunch it down.

"Anything else?"

"Yes. I asked Simms about the records that Burke had said were destroyed in Hurricane Wilma, and was it true."

"What did he say?"

"He said he wasn't sure. That there was plenty of damage to the building, but he didn't know anything about the records. He suggested Robinson might know something."

"Did he know where Robinson lived?"

"He said he didn't even know if Robinson was still alive."

"Too bad."

"Yeah, especially now that we know about the issues between Burke and Brophy."

"We need to keep after this. We should try to find Robinson, don't you think?"

Katie caught my eye. "That and a whole lot of other things. You know the problem with this case?"

"Too many suspects?"

"Exactly. But let's start with Robinson. I'll make some calls, while you cook dinner."

"What are we having?"

"That's up to you, being the cook and all."

We drank and ate pretzels and watched as the sun and the horizon approached each another. At the last minute the sky lit up in a fan of orange and yellow streaks. But there was no green flash.

Chapter 27

Katie had many more contacts in the Monroe County Sheriff's Department than I did, mostly related to her work. When we got back from our booze cruise with Prince, I went to work on dinner—which turned out to be spaghetti and meatballs with a Caesar salad—while she got on the phone. I kept an ear out while slaving away in the kitchen. After a couple of tries I could tell that she found somebody who—even after hours—was willing and able to do a search for Peter Robinson.

"Good news," she said, as she made her way to the kitchen table. "A Pete Robinson who used to run the Islamorada Building Department is still alive and lives in Key West. I have an address and a phone number."

After dinner I made the call while Katie cleaned up. Those were our house rules: whoever cooked, the other person did the dishes.

I dialed the number and a man answered. "Is this Peter Robinson?"

"This is Pete. Who are you? I'm in the middle of dinner. If you're selling something—"

"No sir, it's nothing like that. My name is Sam Sawyer. I'm a private investigator from up here in Islamorada. We—that's my wife and I—have a client who has hired us to look into the disappearance of Sebastian Brophy. We understand that he once worked for you, and we were hoping you might be able to help us with some questions."

There was no response at first, and I thought maybe he'd hung up or we'd lost connection. "What sort of questions?"

"Would it be possible to do this in person?"

"You mean tonight? My wife and I go to bed pretty early."

"We'd been thinking about tomorrow. If it's convenient, that is."

Again, there was a moment's hesitation. "Yeah, I guess that would be okay. What time?"

I knew it was a good hour's drive from our place to the edge of Key West, and then at least a half hour more fighting inevitable traffic to reach the street where Robinson lived. "How about nine-thirty?"

"Okay. But I've got Rotary lunch tomorrow, so you'll need to be gone by noon."

"That should work. And thanks for seeing us."

Peter Robinson lived in a one-story conch house on Elizabeth Street in Key West, It was painted bright yellow, with white window trim and green shutters. The small yard was richly landscaped in palms and other tropical vegetation. By some miracle we were able to find a place to park only three houses away.

A woman answered the door and identified herself as Magda. She must have been expecting us. "He's outside. Come on through." She pointed toward the back yard, and then went off into a bedroom and closed the door. There was no offer of refreshments.

We found Robinson standing next to a small pond with a circulating fountain. He was a small man, with a fringe of white hair and deeply veined hands. He was carrying a plastic bucket and tossing pellets out of it into the pond. There were good-sized goldfish in the pond, perhaps eight or ten inches. He finished feeding the fish and then pointed to chairs and a bench next to the pond. "Sit," he said, while looking at his watch. "I don't have a lot of time. You're late."

"Yes, sorry about that," I said. "The traffic was bad, due to some unexpected road construction."

He grunted. "Around here road construction is something you can count on. Seems like it never ends. You should have planned for it instead of being surprised."

Peter Robinson was a blunt man, if not outright rude.

"We're sorry," Katie said. "And thanks for seeing us."

We took our seats, he in a white Adirondack chair, Katie and I on a bench on the opposite side of a low glass-topped table between us.

"What is it you need?" mister blunt said.

I explained about the recent discovery of Sebastian Brophy's body on a derelict boat back in the everglades, and about how our client suspected he had been the victim of foul play.

"We're attempting to learn who might have had reason to do him harm, and thought you might be able to help," Katie said. "We understand he

154

used to work for you in the Islamorada Building Department, and that another member of your staff was Mr. Wallace Burke, who currently has your old job. We have learned from other sources that Mr. Brophy and Mr. Burke did not get along. Can you tell us anything about that?"

Robinson sat back farther in his chair, and glanced briefly out into the yard. When he looked back at us, something had changed. "Burke is a nasty man," he said. "That's all I can tell you."

"You think he might have done something to Brophy?" I asked.

"I really have no idea, but like I said, he's a nasty man."

"Nasty how?" Katie asked.

Robinson took in a deep breath and let it out, long and slow. "We—I— suspected he was on the take."

"What does that mean?" she said.

Robinson barked a short laugh. "What do you think it means, lady? Look, the department I ran had the power to make or break people in the business of building things in Islamorada. I took the job seriously, always tried to be firm but fair. I long suspected Wallace Burke had other ideas, that for him the job was about using his authority for personal gain. But I never could catch him at it."

"You think he might still be doing that?" I asked.

"How the hell would I know?"

"What about Sebastian Brophy?" Katie asked.

Robinson shook his head. "Brophy was just the opposite. If anything, he was too much of a fussbudget, always suspecting people of doing bad things. He would issue a stop work order if a builder made even the slightest violation of one of our codes. I wish I could have made the two of them meet somewhere in the middle. But that didn't happen. And they went at it so much I thought I was going to have to let one of them go. Would have, but then Brophy disappeared."

"And you had no idea what happened to him?" I said.

"Nope. Nobody did, as far as I know. But now you say they've found his body?"

"They have."

"What happened to him? Did somebody kill him?"

"We're not at liberty to say. The sheriff's department controls release of any information like that. You'd have to ask them."

Robinson gave us an unmistakable "yeah right" look but said nothing.

He followed us back into the house and we thanked him for his time. Katie was halfway out the door when Robinson reached out and put a hand on her shoulder. "You do know I would have kept Brophy and fired Burke's ass if they'd have let me."

"Who?" she said.

"The Village Council. They had charge of all the hiring and firing. And really, it didn't matter all that much after Brophy was gone. Anyway, right after that I took the inspector's job down here in Key West. Held it for fifteen years, until I retired."

"What do you think? I asked Katie as we drove home.

"What I think and what we can prove aren't the same. I think Burke could easily have killed Brophy."

"But in his boat or in his canoe, or whatever, way back in the everglades? I'm still putting my money on either Islava or Stebbins. They have boats and make their living on the water."

"I guess we need to find out if Wallace Burke is a fisherman," Katie said.

Chapter 28

I had a longstanding date to fish with Marshall White the next day. Given the current frenzy related to the Brophy case, it was tempting to cancel. But Marshall was a generous longstanding client, and an expert fisherman, so I decided to keep it. A banker from the Boston area, Marshall always flew down to Islamorada only to fish with me. I know I could have talked him out of it on this occasion, but like I said . . .

Marshall showed up at my dock promptly at 7 AM. We took time for coffee, then said goodbye to Katie and Prince and headed out. It was a clear morning, with a light wind out of the southwest. Marshall was an absolute master with the fly rod. I assumed we would be chasing tarpon or bonefish or permit that day because those were the species usually targeted by fly fishermen. We had an incoming tide, ideal for hunting bonefish or permit as they moved up into the flats to prey on crabs as they emerged from their hidey-holes. In anticipation that this would be our plan for the day, I'd tied up a dozen of my special crab flies the night before.

But it turned out Marshall had other plans. "You know what I'd like to do?" he asked as soon as we left the dock. "I'd like to go after those big mangrove snappers that hang out around those smaller keys out in the bay."

"Really?" I said. "They're great eating fish, but we'd probably do better with bait than with flies. I didn't even put spinning rods in the boat. You should have told me this before we set out. I suppose we could go back and pick up a couple of rods, along with some live shrimp."

"No. No. I want to do it with flies. Then assuming we have luck, we can keep two or three big ones and I'll take you and Katie to dinner at one of those places that cook your catch. Okay?"

"Sure. You're the client. And believe me, Katie and I would never turn down a mangrove snapper dinner. They're among the very best."

"Where are we gonna start?" he asked.

"I'm thinking about Cameron Key. The last time I was out there the place was loaded with snappers. But the biggest ones were tucked up under the mangrove canopy, and they wouldn't come out very far to chase even live bait. So fly casting will be a challenge."

Marshall cracked a grin that matched the twinkle in his blue eyes. "Oh darn," he said.

We motored out past the Peterson Keys and then made our way into the Rabbit Key Basin. From there it was only a short trip north to Cameron Key. There didn't seem to be any other boats around, which was good news. It looked like we were going to have the place to ourselves, at least to start.

I approached the key within fifty yards, then cut the outboard and switched to my trolling motor.

"Goin' in stealthy?" Marshall asked.

"Uh huh. Snappers can be as spooky as any game fish."

Our quiet approach turned out to have consequences beyond angling success, some good and some not so good.

The shoreline of Cameron Key was an alternation of points and pockets, with the biggest mangrove overhang usually in the pockets. I followed the contour of the shoreline, with the goal of keeping Marshall about thirty feet out from shore. He would have to make his casts side-arm, keeping the fly low to the water so that it could skid back under the canopy where I knew the bigger fish lurked. Thirty feet seemed the best compromise in order to reach the fish without spooking them, and I knew Marshall could cast at least that far.

We worked our way along the western and then the southern shore of the key, with Marshall making four or five casts into each of the best spots. It took about an hour, by which time he had hooked and landed ten snappers, all between nine and sixteen inches. He opted to keep the three largest individuals and release the other seven.

A sharp point jutted out into the bay at the southeastern corner of Cameron Key. I asked Marshall if he wanted to go around it and try the other side of the island.

"Is it any good?" he asked.

"In my experience maybe not quite as good as where we just fished, but not bad."

"Then let's go for it."

I throttled up the trolling motor, rounded the corner, and damned near ran into another boat.

And not just any boat. It was a familiar gray Yellowfin, with an equally familiar captain. Will Stebbins was at the helm. It must have taken some careful navigation to get a boat of this size in to Cameron Key without running aground. But there he was.

"Sorry," I yelled across to Stebbins. "Didn't know anybody else was back here."

"Like hell you didn't, Sawyer. I saw you out here the last time, you and some other guy, obviously tailing me. What's with you, anyway?"

Just then a diver popped up beside his boat and tossed a big queen conch over the transom. I hadn't been expecting to run into Stebbins, and so I didn't have my phone out and ready to collect the photographic proof of what we'd just seen.

Stebbins took one look at the shell his diver had thrown on board, then reached down and held it up. "Manuel, you damn fool!" he said. "This is a *queen*, not a helmet conch. Don't you know the difference?" Then he tossed it back into the water.

I had no doubt this little show of outrage was for me and not for his crewman, but either way it had been a big mistake on his part. If he'd just thrown it overboard instead of holding it up, I might not have had time to pull out my phone and snap a picture. As it was, I had at least three images. I couldn't wait to show them to Dave Ackerman. The two conch species were easy to tell apart, and my photos would make it clear Stebbins had been holding a queen.

The question was: what to do next? I was pretty sure if I could get on Stebbins' boat I would find a bunch more conchs. But I also had every reason to suspect that he was capable of violence. Doing something to provoke him right there and then might have been a possibility if I'd been on my own. But to risk the safety of a client? No way.

"Glad you caught the mistake," was all I said. "If you'd kept that queen conch, as a licensed guide I would have been required to report it."

Stebbins put his hands on his hips and glared at me. "Yeah, yeah. Now would you mind fishing someplace else so we can get back to our *legal* collecting? I've got a big contract with one of those shell stores, and I'm behind on my deliveries."

"Bullshit," Marshall White said as we were leaving. "What's with that guy anyway?"

I filled him in about what we knew, or at least suspected, as we made our way to another fishing spot.

"If you need a witness, all you have to do is ask," he said. "Plus you got photos, right?"

I put the skiff in idle, pulled out my phone, and took a look at the three most recent images. "Bingo. Looks like we got him. I gotta make a call."

It was a familiar number, already stored in my phone, and Dave Ackerman answered on the first ring. I told him what we'd seen. "I'm sending you some photos. And you might want to meet Stebbins at the dock when he gets back. I'm guessing he has a boat full."

"We've already tried that a number of times in the past, and always come up empty. He must have another place he drops off his catch before he returns home. But you say he's at Cameron Key. That's inside Everglades Park, right?"

"Right."

"I'm gonna call Mike Nunez and then head out that way myself. Maybe we'll get lucky and catch him before he has a chance to unload."

"You want me to follow him?"

There was a moment's hesitation. "I'm guessing you're with a client, so I don't think so. Too risky. I don't trust that guy at all."

"Me neither. But keep me posted, okay?"

"Will do."

~ ~ ~

Marshall and I fished three more keys that day and caught lots more snappers. There was no call from either Mike or Dave. At our last stop Marshall opted to keep two more fish. "That makes five nice ones," he said. "Just right for our dinner. I'll bet you know some good places that'll cook 'em up for us."

"There's lots, but it gives me an idea. Have I ever taken you to the Safari Lounge?"

"No, I don't think so. Does it specialize in seafood?"

"No, not really. Mostly it's just a burger and drinks place. But the owners are friends of mine, and I know they've been thinking of adding 'cook your catch' to their menu. Maybe we can give them a trial run."

"Sounds like a plan," Marshall said.

And that's what happened.

Katie was home by the time Marshall and I got back to the dock, and she was all for it. I called the Safari. Snooks answered and I told him what we had in mind.

"Let me check with Flo," he said. "She's the one who'll be doing the cooking." He got back to me in about thirty seconds. "Flo's all for it, but she has a favor to ask."

"Sure. Anything."

"She thinks it would be a good idea if you didn't bring Prince tonight. One of our cats is under the weather and she doesn't want it disturbed."

"Nothing serious, I hope."

"Probably not. The vet thinks it was something he ate."

"Well no problem then. We'll have a client, Marshall White, with us. See you shortly."

I cleaned the fish and packed the filets in ice, while Marshall cleaned up the boat. It wasn't really the client's job to do it, but he was that kind of a guy. Marshall and I both had quick showers and changed out of our smelly fishing outfits, and then the three of us took the short drive down to the Safari. On the way my cell phone chirped. It was Dave Ackerman.

"No luck," he said.

"What happened?"

"We caught up with Stebbins just outside of your neighborhood, and boarded his Yellowfin. But it was empty except for a bucket full of other kinds of shells."

"Damn. He must have dumped his catch."

"Yeah, or passed it off to somebody before we found him."

"I guess we're back to square one."

"At least we know he's still in the business."

When we got to the Safari Lounge, Snooks showed Katie and Mike to a table, while I went straight to the kitchen and gave the fish to Flo.

"Hope your cat is okay," I said. "Which one is it?"

"It's Honky. I'm sure he'll be alright, but I didn't think it would be a good idea to have Prince dashing around downstairs. Hope you understand."

"Of course."

Flo picked up the bag of filets. "What are these?"

"Mangrove snappers."

"Good. They're among the best eating of anything around here. If I can't make them edible, then we probably shouldn't even think about adding 'cook your catch' to the menu."

"I'm sure they'll be great, Flo."

I joined Marshall and Katie at a table with a fine view of the Atlantic. A breeze had come up, putting a light ripple on the water. Thousands of small waves reflected the last the of the sun's rays.

"The ocean looks jeweled," Marshall said. "As if it's encrusted in diamonds."

"You sound more like a poet than a banker," Katie said, with a smile.

"Perhaps both?" he replied. "Sort of a Bostonian T. S. Eliot?"

Maybe there was more to Marshall White than I realized, but before I had a chance to pursue the subject, Snooks came over with our drinks: his special margaritas all around.

"I gather you had a good day on the water," Snooks said.

"We did," I replied. "And an interesting one."

"Interesting how?" he asked, as he sat down in the fourth chair at our table.

I told him about our encounter with Will Stebbins.

"Well I'll be damned," Snooks said. "There's been rumors about that guy for years. Now it sounds like you've got the goods on him. What are you gonna do about it?"

"First thing tomorrow, or maybe even tonight, we'll have a talk with Nate Sturm. Will Stebbins is one of the people he thinks might have murdered Sebastian Brophy."

"Yeah, I think I remember you telling me that. But even if fish and game nails him for poaching conchs, how does that get you closer to tying him to Brophy?"

"It doesn't, but you never know what might happen when the interrogations start."

Snooks looked puzzled. "Did you say interrogations, plural?"

"Uh huh. There was another man on board Stebbin's boat today. He was doing the diving. If the man's been around long enough—"

"Ah, the old 'rats leaving the sinking ship' ploy, huh?" Marshall said.

"You never know," I said. Then I had an idea. "I've got a favor to ask, Snooks."

"What is it?"

"Dave Ackerman and I have been tailing Stebbins in my boat, trying to catch him poaching conchs. Dave thought it would work better than using his Fish and Wildlife vessel. But now that he knows I'm in on this, and he recognizes my skiff, that isn't going to work anymore. But if we used your boat and disguised ourselves, we might still have a chance."

"You're more than welcome," Snooks replied. "But I've been having a little trouble with the throttle. It needs tweaking a bit. Shouldn't be a problem, though. Let me get back to you in a couple of days."

"Thanks. I really appreciate this. I owe you one."

"No you don't. Catching that clown before he does any more damage to the conch population is all the thanks I need."

Just then Flo walked up with a big platter of snapper filets. We all dug in, while Snooks went back to bartending. Not surprisingly, the food was delicious.

Chapter 29

We dropped Marshall off at his motel and headed home. Katie and I went upstairs, fully expecting Prince to greet us at the door like he usually did. But he wasn't there.

"Hey Prince, we're back," Katie called out.

"Prince? Where are you, boy?" I said in a louder voice.

No Prince. This wasn't like him at all. He frequently gave us a look when we'd gone off without him. But he never just hid. We searched the whole house, including under the bed, in the closets, and even on the deck in case we'd accidentally left him outside. Still no Prince.

The fear in Katie's eyes was palpable. "We gotta do something fast, Sam! We need to go looking for him. I'll go down the road along the canal. You go the other way. He can't have gone far. Corgis are real homebodies." She rubbed a hand across her cheek, brushing away a tear. "Maybe somebody stole him. Oh my God!"

"I'm sure he's right around here someplace," I said, without really believing it.

We took our phones and set off in different directions. Katie went toward the bay, while I went toward US-1 and the Atlantic. I pushed away a vision of Prince being hit by a car out on the highway. No, that's just not possible, I said to myself.

I walked all the way out to the little mom and pop convenience store at the end of our street. Still no Prince, and nobody in the store had seen him. I was on my way back when Katie called and my hopes rose. "Any luck?" I asked.

"No." Her voice quavered. "Where *is* he, Sam? I'm really scared!"

"Let's go back. I'm gonna get in the Jeep and look farther away."

"Should I go with you?" she said.

"No. I think you should stay home in case he comes back."

I could see that Katie had been crying when we met back at the house. She sniffed and blew her nose. "Really?" she said. "No sign at all?"

"No."

Katie went upstairs, while I began to drive the neighborhood. I worked outwards from the closest streets to the farthest in the development, stopping to peer into likely places and to call his name.

Nothing.

I was about to drive out to the highway and expand my search when Katie called. "He's back," she said.

"Thank God. Where was he?"

"I don't know. He just showed up at the door and barked. But there's something else. You need to get back here."

"I'm on my way."

Prince greeted me at the door, jumping up to lick my hand. We'd tried training him not to jump on people, but it didn't seem to be working, with us or anybody else.

I went to give Katie a hug, but she stopped me and instead held up two plastic bags. There was an envelope inside one of the bags, and a single sheet of white paper in the other. The paper had writing on it. "This was attached to his collar. The paper was inside the envelope."

She handed me the bag with the piece of paper. I held it up close and read what was typed on it in big block letters: "YOU NEED TO BACK OFF. THE NEXT TIME YOUR DOG WILL BE GONE FOR GOOD."

"Nothing on the envelope to indicate who did this?" I asked.

"Nope. Nothing. And the way the note's printed, almost any computer or laptop could have done that. I don't think there's any way it can be traced."

"I'll bet it was Stebbins. This is too much of a coincidence after what happened today. I think that guy just moved way up on our suspect list, don't you?"

"You mean for the Brophy murder?"

"Uh huh."

Katie frowned. "Not necessarily, Sam, but you could be right."

"I'm gonna call Stella. Maybe there's prints on the note or the envelope."

"It's a long shot, but I agree. That's why I put them in those plastic bags. I did touch the envelope and the note before I saw what they were."

I made the call and told Stella what had happened.

"I'll be right over," she said.

We sat on the couch in the living room while we waited for Stella. Prince wedged himself in between us. I thought once he was back that Katie would feel a sense of relief, as did I. But instead, she suddenly bolted upright and erupted in anger.

"I want that guy's balls on a platter!" she screamed. Her face turned bright red and there was a wild look in her eyes I'd never seen before. "I wish I could kill him."

"We don't even know if it was a man, Katie."

"Like hell we don't! What kind of a fucking *monster* would do something like that? Damn!"

I put my hand on her arm. "It's okay, Katie. It's okay. Prince is back and safe. Stella will be here soon. Maybe she can figure out who did this."

But Katie was having none of it. "And just how the *hell* is Stella gonna do that?"

I decided not to interrupt, and instead just give her time to vent. There was a knock on the door, and Stella came in without waiting for a response. Prince rushed over and she bent down to give him a scratch behind the ears. Instead, he rolled over on his back in hopes she would give him a belly rub.

Stella knelt down and obliged. "Good boy. Glad to see you're okay." She stood back up. "That must have been scary as hell. You say somebody took him while you were out? And then he just showed up back here by himself?"

"That's right," Katie said. "I was waiting here just in case while Sam was driving around looking for him. I heard a 'woof' and a scratch at the door, and there he was."

"Did you see or hear anybody outside when he came back?"

"You mean like a vehicle or somebody walking around? No, nothing like that. He was just there. I called Sam and then he called you."

"And thanks for coming," I said. "I know it's late, and no doubt you were off duty."

Stella left Prince and joined us in the living room. "You think there's any way he could have gotten out by himself?"

Katie and I both shook our heads. Katie handed Stella the note and the envelope it had come in. "And even if he did leave on his own—which Corgis would never do by the way—how do you explain this?"

Stella held up the bag and read the note. "And there was no sign of a forced entry when you got back from dinner?"

We shook our heads again.

"Then how do you suppose the kidnapper—or is it dognapper?—got inside? Does anybody else have a key?"

"I'm afraid the answer to that is simple," I said. "We didn't lock the door. We hardly ever do."

Stella rolled her eyes. "I strongly suggest you do so from now on. I also recommend you purchase one of those camera thingies that keeps an eye on your place when you're gone. It looks like somebody has a serious issue with one or both of you. Any idea who that might be?"

I told Stella about my encounter with Will Stebbins earlier that day, and also reminded her about our suspicion that Stebbins might have been the one who murdered Sebastian Brophy. "So, yeah, I suppose he might have a motive to tell us to back off or else."

Stella thought for a minute and then shook her head. "I can see that for conch poaching—maybe. But if he thinks you've got something on him for murder, wouldn't he do more than just borrow your dog?"

I hadn't thought of that. If Stebbins was the one who took Prince, did that eliminate him as a suspect in Brophy's killing? Not necessarily, but it did make me wonder. It also made me think about the other possible suspects.

"Have they interviewed Santiago Islava yet?" I asked Stella.

"I was going to bring that up. There's an arrest warrant out for him, based on Tyler Brophy's testimony. For some reason, the sheriff asked me to accompany Al Beaudry when we went to his house to serve the warrant."

"How did it go?"

"It was the shits. Beaudry, bless his feeble little brain, he goes up to the door and knocks. When nothing happens he yells 'Come on out, Islava, we've got an arrest warrant for murder!' It's quiet for a while, until Islava's wife shows up, claiming she had no idea where he was."

"Which means now Islava knows you're after him. His wife must have called him as soon as you'd left."

"You got it. After that we went straight to his dock, but—big surprise— he's not there and neither is his lobster boat."

"You mean he actually fled in the boat?"

"Doesn't seem likely, does it?" Stella said. "I'm guessing he already was fishing when his wife called, and now he's out there somewhere, afraid to come back to his dock where we'll be waiting for him."

"I'll bet Beaudry's thrilled his prime suspect is missing."

"Couldn't happen to a nicer fella," Stella said. Then she must have thought better of it. "Of course I hope we catch him. I heard the sheriff is mad as hell about this."

"Which puts Beaudry in an even tighter spot, doesn't it?"

"Yeah, but like I said—" She trailed off. She was holding the plastic bags with the note and envelope. "I'll have these checked for any prints or partials. Would you like me to send somebody around to dust the doorknob and maybe other things in the house? They could also dust Prince's dog tag."

"That would be a good idea," Katie said. "Prince doesn't like anybody taking off his collar, but it shouldn't be for long. And they could get my prints at the same time. I touched both the note and the envelope before I knew what we were dealing with."

"Won't need to do that," she said. "We've already got yours and Sam's on file."

Stella stood up to go, but I stopped her with a question. "Any developments on the Rusty Montrose case? It's been a couple of weeks, hasn't it?" I still had a bad feeling I might have been at least partly responsible for what had happened to him. Assuming his drowning wasn't accidental.

"I'm glad you asked, Sam. I wasn't going to bring this up tonight, given what you've just been through. But there is something I wanted to ask you about."

"No problem. We're okay, now that Prince is safe." I looked at Katie. "Well, we're better anyway."

"You remember that shoe we found in the canal along with the Montrose corpse?"

"Sure. It was a big Air Jordan. Rashaan remembered seeing somebody wearing a pair, but he couldn't recall who it was."

"Well guess what? Rashaan called a couple of days ago. He remembered who it was: a man named Patrick Simpson that he met at your homeowners meeting. Do you know him?"

This was interesting. "Uh huh. He's a neighbor and a fishing client. I introduced him to Rashaan at that meeting, and we learned he'd actually built the house Rashaan just bought. Have you talked to Simpson about this?"

Stella nodded. "Of course I did. He acknowledged he has a pair of Air Jordans, but claimed he still has both of them. He said he could show me if he had to."

"Did you take him up on it?"

"Sure. And he showed me a pair."

"Did you ask him if he knew Rusty Montrose?"

"He said he did, and that he had hoped to buy the man's house, but Montrose turned him down."

"That's interesting," Katie said. "Simpson came around here a while back and asked us the same question."

"What did you tell him?" Stella asked.

"Same thing as Montrose. Nope."

Stella sighed and put her hands on her knees, ready to stand up. "The M.E. still has the Montrose death listed as a 'suspicious,' but unless we can get some sort of evidence that somebody pushed him into the water, he might eventually change that to 'accidental.' And that would be the end of it."

"What about DNA?" I asked.

"The M.E. didn't find any on the body or on the shoe. Apparently he didn't expect to, since DNA tends to degrade pretty quickly in water."

"You think it could have been Simpson?" I asked.

"It would explain his shoe being in the water."

"Except he claims it isn't his shoe, and there's no way to prove otherwise is there?"

"Not unless we can prove he had two pairs of Air Jordans. And even then—"

"What about a phone? Montrose must have had one. Maybe the two talked."

"We looked, but never found one. Montrose had a Verizon account, and I got his records. But there was nothing unusual. No calls to or from Simpson, for example."

~ ~ ~

"I don't usually drink after dinner," Katie said as soon as Stella had left. "But tonight I need to make an exception. This thing with Prince really shook me to the core, Sam."

"Maker's on the rocks?"

"Sounds good. With a splash."

We took our drinks outside on the deck. It was warm, with almost no breeze. We settled on a wooden bench next to the railing, with Prince in between us as usual. A night bird called somewhere down the canal.

"What was that?" Katie asked.

"Probably a yellow-crowned night heron, if my somewhat rusty ornithological memory still works."

Katie sipped some bourbon. "I suppose we should do something about security. I couldn't bear the idea of something happening to Prince. Tonight was bad enough."

"Probably a good idea. Stella's right. There's somebody out there who doesn't like us."

"Are you sorry we got into this crime fighting thing, Sam? I'm thinking maybe you just did it as a favor to me."

"No, I'm not sorry at all. Are you?"

"I hadn't been until tonight. Now I'm not so sure. My forensics work has always been pretty much removed from any personal danger. But this is different."

"We could always sell this house to Mr. Simpson. It's worth a lot of money."

"And then do what?" she said, with a scowl. "By the time we paid for another place down here that was at all livable, there'd be nothing left. "

"We'd have to move somewhere cheaper."

"Oh sure, like a place with *winter*. You really want to do that?"

"No, Katie, I'm just thinking out loud here."

"Well think of something else, okay?"

"Are you scared?"

"Maybe a little bit, right now." She stopped and shook her head, just once. "But you know what? Mostly I'm just *mad*."

"Me too. Maybe after this is all over, we can decide if we want to keep going with Upper Keys Investigations. But first—"

"But first we're gonna catch the *monster* that took Prince!"

Prince had been asleep, but he sat up at the mention of his name. He looked back and forth at the two of us, then cocked his head to one side like he does when he's trying to figure out if we've said anything important to dogs.

Chapter 30

"Maybe he's hiding on a houseboat," Flo said.

"What?"

Katie and I had driven over to Flo and Snooks' place in the Safety Harbor development because he'd called to say his Mako was ready for me and Dave Ackerman to borrow. We were having coffee out on their deck, and I had told them about Santiago Islava being missing.

"He has a houseboat?" I asked Flo.

"Uh huh. Or at least the family had one. A bunch of us from Marathon High used to go out there and party." She glanced over at Snooks. "Of course that was a long time ago."

Snooks fiddled with the rubber band holding up his ponytail and raised an eyebrow. "What sort of parties?"

"Oh you know, the usual kid stuff. We'd sneak beers and maybe a little pot. Nothing serious."

Snooks fiddled again. "Yeah. I'll bet that wasn't all that happened out there."

Snooks being jealous of something that happened to Flo way back then didn't seem like him. It wasn't as if he'd led all that pure a life before they'd met each other.

"You're absolutely right," Flo said. "That's not all we did. We also dove for lobsters and conchs. It was a great spot for both, and taking conchs was legal back then."

"Where was this houseboat?" Katie asked.

"Behind Channel Key, on the bay side out from the Hawks Cay Resort. It was painted a sort of turquoise color."

"I thought Channel Key was down by Stock Island?" I said.

"That's another one. Confusing, huh?"

171

"Yeah, it is."

"But I'm sure about the one where his family kept the houseboat."

"So it's still there?"

"Last time I looked. Of course I'd have no way of knowing if it still belongs to Islava, or what's left of his family. It was a sorry boat even back then."

"Seems like a long shot he'd be there," Snooks said.

"Maybe," Katie said. "But I think we should tell the detective in charge of this case. I guess that's still Beaudry and not Stella, right Sam?"

"As far as I know."

We thanked Snooks and Flo for the coffee. I walked Katie out to the Jeep. She would take it back to the house while I drove Snooks' boat from his dock to ours, a trip of no more than thirty minutes.

"Will I see you at home, or do you need to get to school?"

"I'll stick around until you get home. I have a lab to teach this afternoon, but nothing critical until then. You going fishing today?"

"Nope. Dave Ackerman will want to start tailing Stebbins again, but that won't be until tomorrow at the earliest. Our plan is to get out early and watch for Stebbins leaving his dock, and then follow him."

"What happens if Stebbins goes into Everglades Park like he did before? Florida Fish and Wildlife doesn't have authority there, does it?"

"Not unless they've made some sort of special arrangement. I expect Dave would call Mike Nunez if we see Stebbins taking conchs inside Park boundaries."

I said goodbye to Katie and went back to help Snooks splash his Mako. It was a trim little flats boat more than capable of following Will Stebbins anywhere he'd likely be diving for conchs.

I drove to our dock and tied Snooks' boat next to mine. I looked up, half expecting to see Katie and Prince watching from the deck like they usually did when I came home. But there was no sign of them. I was worried something might have happened. "What now" I thought to myself.

"Katie?" I called. There was no answer. I called again. Still nothing.

I climbed the back stairs with growing alarm, especially in light of what had just happened the night before. But when I got up on the deck I was relieved to see Katie at her desk. She had her back to me and she was busy sorting through some papers. She didn't turn around as I came in the door, but Prince came bouncing over to get his usual rub behind the ears.

"Hi."

"Oh hi," Katie said, without turning around. "You need to see this."

"What is it?"

"When I got home from Safety Harbor there was a shopping bag leaning against the front door." She pointed to the pile of papers on her desk. "These were inside. Come take a look."

The papers appeared to be photocopies of originals, some typed and some handwritten. Most of them had the words "Islamorada Building Department" printed across the top.

"I'm just getting started on this. They're copies of building permits or the results of building inspections."

"Any idea how they got here?'

"No. Like I said, they were here when I got home. But it must have been somebody from the department."

"You think it was their head guy, Wallace Burke? He'd be the one most likely to have access to those documents."

"Burke?" Katie shook her head. "Doesn't seem likely, given the icy response I got from him when I visited there. More likely one of the women in the office, or perhaps that custodian Andy Simms." Katie tapped a pencil on the desk. "I'll bet it was him because he made it clear he didn't like Burke. And—this is interesting—he told me that Burke and Sebastian Brophy had it in for each other when they both worked for the department back in the 1990s."

I had another thought. "Or could it have been Pete Robinson, the former head of the department? Maybe he kept a copy of those records when he moved to Key West. He made it clear when we visited him that he suspected something was going on between Brophy and Burke, but he never could prove it."

"And now he hopes maybe we can. Good point, Sam. Anyway, I've gotta get to class." She pointed to the pile of papers on her desk. "Why don't you have a look at all this, and we'll talk about it when I get back."

Before getting down to that business, I had two calls to make, one to Al Beaudry and the other to Dave Ackerman. Beaudry's phone went straight to message, so I left one: "We have a possible tip that Santiago Islava might be hiding out on a houseboat next to Channel Key. That's the one near

Hawks Cay Resort, not the one down by Stock Island. You might want to check it out."

Dave Ackerman was happy to hear that I had Snooks' Mako at my dock, ready to resume the Stebbins watch. "How about we start this thing tomorrow?"

"Sounds good. I'll bring my scope and camera. Anything else?"

There was just a moment's hesitation. "You took weapons training when you first worked as a consultant with Fish and Wildlife, right?"

"Right. And they issued me a sidearm."

"Then you might want to bring it along, just in case."

I didn't much like guns, and I'd rarely even carried mine, let alone used it. "Well, okay. What time will you be here?"

"Let's make it about six. We don't want Stebbins getting out ahead of us."

"See you then."

I had an uneasy feeling about this whole Stebbins thing. But I'd volunteered, and I didn't like the idea of Dave going out there all by himself. I tried to put the whole thing out of my mind, and turned instead to the files on Katie's desk. I made myself a cup of coffee and got down to business.

The stack of paper was bigger than anything I'd dealt with since the last time I'd read student exams in my vertebrate zoology class. They'd had their own special problems and frustrations, but at least I knew what I was looking for. What, exactly, could records from the Islamorada Building Department tell us about what befell Sebastian Brophy? I really had no idea.

I started by organizing things, first by date and then by topic. The years began with 1995 and ended a decade later in 2005, nicely bracketing 1998, the year Brophy disappeared. This suggested whoever had copied the files for us knew what year was important.

Paperwork from the Islamorada Building Department fell into three broad categories. First were applications for building permits themselves. Peter Robinson's name appeared on all the documents, which figured since he was head of the department. But for the permits his usually was the only name, along with the applicants, most of which were building companies or development corporations. The second category of files included the results of site inspections. These seemed to be divided about equally between Wallace Burke and Sebastian Brophy. Reading through these I got the distinct impression that Brophy's were much more likely than Burke's to contain comments about things that needed attention.

The third category of files was by far the most interesting. These were the "stop work" orders, where a whole project had been shut down for one reason or another. Most of these included an addendum indicating that the conditions had eventually been met, and when construction had resumed. But not all of them. I couldn't tell whether that meant a project had been permanently halted, which seemed unlikely, or whether the paperwork about project resumption was simply missing for some reason. What I could see was that a clear majority of "stop work" orders had gone out under Sebastian Brophy's name and not Burke's.

Finally, I scanned through the files to see if I knew any of the applicants. In short, I did not. Nearly all were the names of various companies, and not individuals.

There was a ton of information in the files, and a lot of work left to be done. But they confirmed what we already suspected about how Brophy and Burke did their jobs. Did Burke or one of the developers/builders have motive to kill Brophy? Yes, especially if Burke was on the take and there were deals made under the table. But I couldn't see how it got us any closer to finding proof.

My examination of the files got interrupted twice. The first was by a visit from Penny McMasters, head of the Monroe County crime scene unit. She came to dust our place for prints in case any were left by whoever had kidnapped Prince. I was impressed that the head of the whole unit would come all the way from Key West to deal with a dog case. I asked Penny if anybody from the department had had a chance to examine the note and envelope that came home with Prince. She said they had, but there had been no readable prints.

The second interruption took longer. I was about halfway through the files when I heard the familiar rumble of a motorcycle coming down the street. I ran to the door in hopes it was Nate Sturm making one of his rounds. I looked down and it was him. I waived and Nate pulled into the yard. He hopped of his bike and came up the stairs, along with his poodle.

"Got time for a beer? I need to talk to you about something."

"Nope. I like to stay sober while I'm working for the HOA. But a diet coke would be nice."

"You actually work for them?"

Nate chuckled. "Well, I guess it's more like a volunteer thing. But you never know when something might happen that requires my A-game."

We settled on the deck with soft drinks, the afternoon sun warm on our faces. We watched a pair of pelicans squabbling over some fish entrails in the canal two houses down. Prince, who had a thing about pelicans, started barking furiously. Nate's poodle, on the other hand, paid no attention. I told Prince to shut up, using a no-nonsense tone I knew he recognized. Prince huffed one last little bark, and then went over and lay down under a bench without making eye contact. Corgies are friendly dogs, sometimes almost too friendly, but they do know how to pout.

"How's it going with your investigation?" Nate asked, beating me to the punch.

I told him about the arrest warrant that was out for Santiago Islava, and that we were pretty sure Will Stebbins was in the conch poaching business but we hadn't yet been able to catch him with the goods.

"But what about Bash Brophy?" he said. "That's why I hired you guys. To find his killer." He stopped to drink some coke. "Or killers."

"Yeah I know, and I'm sorry. But we're making progress. Actually, that's what I wanted to talk to you about. What do you know about his work for the village building department?"

"I know he worked there. It was his day job. But like I told you, his passion was with the everglades and Florida Bay. Why?"

"Did he ever mention a man named Wallace Burke?"

Nate brought a hand up and twisted one end of his handlebar mustache. "Sounds sort of familiar. Who is he?"

"Today he runs the building department in Islamorada. He worked alongside Brophy back in the '90s, reviewing building permits and conducting on-site inspections. We've turned up some pretty strong evidence that they didn't get along."

"Meaning they sometimes disagreed on stuff?"

"More than that. Apparently it got personal."

"Are you saying this Burke guy might have killed Bash?"

"Maybe. We're looking into it. I just thought maybe Brophy had told you something about their relationship."

"Not that I recall. Sorry."

~ ~ ~

That evening, after Katie got home from work, she said she wanted to go for another boat ride. But thick, ominous clouds had built over the bay, and lightning lit up the gray sky down toward Key West. Prince went into the closet in our bedroom. He didn't like rain, which had begun to fall, and he liked thunder even less. So instead we stayed home, ate Marie Callender's chicken pot pies for dinner, and talked about the case. Store-bought pot pies were a secret indulgence of mine, going back to my bachelor days. Prince came out of the closet just long enough to scarf down his kibble. Then he went right back. The thunder had become even closer and louder.

While we ate I told Katie what I'd found in the files from the building department. It took her no time at all to focus on the one thing that might prove useful as well as intriguing. "We need to find the names of people who had their permits revoked," she said. "Wouldn't it be interesting if one of them knows all about the everglades backcountry, even if Wallace Burke doesn't?"

I showed her my list.

"You need to get that to Stella right away," she said.

The storm had blown itself out into the Atlantic by nightfall. When it got quiet, Prince came out into the living room and looked at his empty food bowl, no doubt hoping we'd forgotten he'd already eaten. When that didn't work, he settled for a walk down the street and back. Two cats were having a hissing contest under the bed of a pickup next door. The hairs on his back stood up while he tugged at his leash and pretended it was the only thing standing between him and a big cat fight. As if.

Chapter 31

Will Stebbins came out from his canal into Florida Bay a little past seven the next morning. Dave Ackerman and I already were out there, pretending to fish from Snooks' Mako. Actually, Dave was the one pretending. I was doing the real thing. No point in passing up the opportunity to snag a couple of mangrove snappers for dinner.

Stebbins went past without showing any signs that he'd recognized us. I stowed my gear and got ready to follow, but Dave put his hand over the ignition switch. "No hurry," he said. "We don't want to get too close and blow it."

"But we'll also blow it if he gets away," I said.

Dave grinned. "Which he's not gonna do. We got a judge's okay to put a tracking device on his boat. One of my people sneaked out to his dock last night and stuck it under the center console."

Dave opened up his big tackle box and pulled out something that looked like a glorified cell phone. He punched a couple of keys and an image of Florida Bay lit up, with the beginnings of a route marked by blue dots moving across the screen.

"We'll give him some time, and then follow. When he stops we'll close to within a hundred yards or so, and you'll get pictures. Hopefully, they'll show his mate throwing conchs on board. You brought that big camera, didn't you?"

"I did."

Stebbins drove north and west, skirting the flats along the southern edge of the Arsenicker Keys. He snaked between the red and green buoys marking the edge of the Arsenic Bank, and then headed farther out into the bay. Based on boundary markers, he was right on the edge of Everglades National Park.

"What if he works inside the Park?" I asked Dave.

"If he stays put long enough, I'll give the rangers a call. But Mike Nunez and I have worked this out. He's given me the green light to go wherever the man takes us." He stopped for a grin. "After all, there no law against anybody using a camera out here, is there? Maybe we're just watching birds."

Stebbins' boat was maybe five miles out beyond Sprigger Bank when the image on Dave's screen stopped moving. "Looks like he's laid up," Dave said. "Keep going until I say stop, but don't go in a straight line. And put out a couple of rods, so it looks like we're trolling."

Dave had me throw out an anchor when were about 100 yards from Stebbins' gray Yellowfin. With my ten power binoculars, I could make him out easily. He was standing in the stern, looking down into the water. After about five minutes somebody in a wet suit surfaced behind the boat and tossed something up over the transom.

I pulled out my camera and started clicking away.

"Was that a conch?" Dave asked.

"Think so. Looks like we got him."

Over the next half hour or so, the diver came up with at least a dozen more conchs. Or at least that's what I assumed they were. I couldn't be sure until I got home and downloaded the images to my computer, where I could blow them up. Finally, the diver came up empty-handed and hauled himself on board.

"Looks like they've finished here," I said. "Now do we move in for the arrest?"

But Dave shook his head. "No. Now we wait and follow again. I want to know where he's taking his catch. Based on previous experience, I'm pretty sure he's not going back to his own dock. I expect there's a middleman involved in all this, and we want to catch him too."

When Stebbins pulled up anchor, he headed in a direction I hadn't expected: not toward Islamorada, but pretty much due south. We tagged along, holding at a distance where I could barely make out his boat. Dave borrowed my binoculars and scanned the horizon. When we got close enough to make things out, Dave said: "Looks like he's headed right for Conch Key. Wouldn't that be ironic?"

But that wasn't Stebbin's target. Instead, he turned hard to starboard when he was about two hundred yards from shore. I asked to look at Dave's device with Stebbins' track on it. "Well I'll be damned," I said.

"What?"

"Unless I'm mixed up, he's on a course for Channel Key."

"Never been there. What's on Channel Key?"

"Nothing that I know of. But I'm told there might be an old houseboat tied up behind it. And if I'm right, there's better than an outside chance our conch middleman will turn out to be Santiago Islava, of all people."

"Holy crap," Dave said. "How do you know this?"

"I don't for sure. But a friend told me the Islavas keep—or at least kept—a houseboat there."

Somebody once said that it's better to be lucky than smart, if you have a choice in the matter. Whether or not that's always true, Dave Ackerman and I certainly had our share of luck that day, both good and bad. When we got close enough to check it out, both Stebbins' Yellowfin and a sorry-looking white lobster boat were tied up next to an old turquoise houseboat on the back side of Channel Key.

"What happens now?" I asked Dave.

"First I make a couple of calls, one to headquarters and the other to the Coast Guard. Then we wait."

"What if they make a break for it?"

"Then I suppose we'll have to move on our own. But if we stay back far enough, that shouldn't happen."

"Which is good. My guess is it would be even riskier than you think."

"Why?"

"Because this could be about a lot more than just fishing violations. I learned yesterday from Stella Reynard that there's a warrant out for Islava's arrest—on a murder charge. And likely he knows it."

"Holy shit."

Perhaps only fifteen minutes went by, but it seemed like an eternity. Dave had just finished saying "I guess we'd better get going," when two Coast Guard cutters and a Florida Fish and Wildlife boat came out from behind Channel Key. Somebody with a megaphone yelled something. We were too far away to make out what was being said, but the responses from Islava and Stebbins were immediate and predictable. They both jumped off the houseboat into their own boats and attempted to get the hell out of Dodge.

Stebbins' Yellowfin was a lot faster than Islava's lobster boat, and he made a run for it before anybody could stop him. We watched as he sped out north into the bay, with the State team in close pursuit.

"Hate to see him get away," I said.

"Not to worry," Dave said. "My guys have a fast boat, plus they can track him just like we did. Stebbins is toast. Let's see what happens with Islava. That could get a lot more interesting."

And it did, if "interesting" is the right word for what happened next.

The lobsterman's old plodding diesel was no match for the Coast Guard cutters. Islava must have realized it because pretty soon his boat just stopped. We watched him climb down from the bridge and duck into the cabin below it. When he came back up he was holding some sort of a gun. Even from a distance, it had the unmistakable profile of an AR-15 assault rifle. We watched as Islava walked back to the stern of his boat. Then he gave something that looked like a salute and pointed the gun, not at the Coast Guard, but directly at us.

"Holy shit," Dave said again.

Dave reached down into his tackle box and pulled out a pistol, while I took mine out from where I'd tucked it into my pants. We both looked at each other, and I think he had the same idea I did. Our sidearms would be no match for Islava's semi-automatic long gun. We both crouched down low behind the center console and kept moving forward.

Soon we were close enough to hear and see every detail of what ensued. An officer on one of the Coast Guard boats had a megaphone. "Throw down your weapon, Islava, and put your hands in the air!" she shouted. The response was a spray of gunfire, and the next thing I knew the plastic windscreen on Snook's Mako shattered. Dave and I ducked down into the well of his boat, as a second shot ricocheted off the outboard, and then another. Why was he shooting at us instead of the Coast Guard? Despite the continuing gunfire, I couldn't resist the temptation to stick my head back up over the gunwale. "Get down you idiot!" Dave said, tugging on my sleeve. "That guy's nuts! You wanna get yourself killed? Not on my watch!"

I got down a bit lower, but couldn't resist peeking up just enough to see what was going on. It was an all-out gunfight like I'd never seen before. Guardsmen on both cutters had some serious weapons, including long-range sniper rifles. Islava kept spraying fire around wildly, unlike the guardsmen, who clearly were taking their time. And it was only a matter of time before the inevitable happened. Two sniper bullets hit Islava almost simultaneously, one in the chest and one in the head. He went down and did not come back up. The image of Islava's face turning to bloody pulp still haunts me, especially on nights when I'm having trouble sleeping.

It was clear from the outset that Santiago Islava had no intention of going quietly. Was it suicide? We'd never know. He must have realized we had the goods on him, if not for killing Sebastian Brophy then certainly for killing his fellow lobsterman, Rudy Valdez. Tyler Brophy's testimony would have made sure of that. But it never came to a trial, let alone an interrogation. Instead, Santiago Islava met his end in a hail of Coast Guard gunfire, within sight of a turquoise houseboat where he'd once hosted weekend parties with his high school buddies—assuming Flo Delaney had it right.

Chapter 32

Dave and I motored in toward the old houseboat after the Coast Guard gave us an "all clear" wave. Despite the damage, Snooks' Mako chugged along, maybe with a bit of a hitch, but still mobile. We never actually got out of Snooks' boat because they told us the houseboat and Islava's lobster trawler now were officially crime scenes and we weren't welcome on either vessel. But I did have a question. "Are there any conchs on board?"

One of the crewmen ducked into the cabin on the houseboat and came back out holding one in his right hand. "You mean like this?"

"Yeah, that's a conch."

"Well, there's a big tank in there with more than a dozen of 'em inside. What should I do?"

"Do you have a phone?" Dave asked.

"Uh huh."

"Could you take some photos for evidence, and send them to me?"

"Sure. Give me your number."

Dave gave the man his cell number. "Thanks. And when that's done, please throw the conchs back into the bay. They're endangered and it's illegal to possess a live one."

The officer in charge of the Coast Guard crew was standing in the stern of Islava's lobster boat. She waved her hands around at the scene. "Is that what this was all about? Poaching conchs?"

"At least partly," Dave replied.

The officer shook her head. "Seems like a helluva reason for a gunfight. Or more like a suicide if you think about what he was up against."

"There's likely more to it," I said. "The shooter is a suspect in at least one and possibly two murders. Or should I say 'was' a suspect."

"That's a definite 'was,' gentlemen," she said, pointing to something we couldn't see lying at her feet. "This guy's poaching days are over."

We were on our way home when Dave got a call. All I heard was a serious of grunts and "uh huhs," followed by a "thanks, keep me posted."

"What was that about?" I asked, after the call had ended.

"That was my buddy with the department. They followed Will Stebbins all the way back to his dock, where they arrested him and his crewman on suspicion of poaching."

"Did they find any conchs on board?"

"A couple. He must have unloaded the rest of them onto Islava's houseboat before we caught up with him. When they hauled him off his boat in handcuffs, he claimed not to know anything about conchs or about Santiago Islava.

"We both know that's bullshit."

"That we do, my friend. This guy's had it."

We were bringing Snooks' wounded Mako back down our canal, when I saw Katie jump up off the deck and bolt for the house. It was obvious she'd been working on her all-over tan. Prince doubtless had barked like he usually did when he saw me coming, and that had alerted her. By the time we reached the dock, she was back outside, wearing a terrycloth robe.

"How did it . . . oh my gosh, what happened to the boat?"

"We sort of got caught in a crossfire," I said. "But the news isn't all bad. I'll talk to you in a bit."

"Are you hurt?" she asked.

"Nope. We're fine."

Dave and I climbed the back stairs, sat down, and accepted Katie's offer of iced coffee.

"Damn sorry about what happened to your friend's boat," Dave said. "Be sure to tell him Florida Fish and Wildlife will cover all repairs."

I had an idea. "Why don't you tell him yourself? Snooks and his partner Flo run the Safari Lounge. We could go over there for dinner. Unless you've got other plans, that is."

"Nope. No plans. And I haven't been to the Safari in years."

Katie came back outside, having changed into shorts and a t-shirt. "So tell me what happened today."

"We caught up with Santiago Islava and Will Stebbins."

"Both at the same time?"

184

"More or less. Rather than tell this story three different times—first to you, then to Snooks and Flo, and then to Nate Sturm—instead why don't we ask Nate to come along to the Safari and I can tell everybody at once?"

"Who's Nate Sturm?" Dave asked.

"He's a paying client, and the one who put us onto Islava and Stebbins in the first place. But please keep that confidential."

"I'll go give him a call," Katie said, "while you two finish your coffees."

My "tell everybody at once" plan didn't work out. When we got to the Safari, the place was jumping. Katie and Dave grabbed one of the few tables left—outside on the patio—while I dragged Prince inside and dealt with Flo and Snooks. Flo barely had time to say hi when I brought Prince into the kitchen and sent him downstairs to be with the cats. She was in the final stages of loading up a big platter of shrimp and onion rings, along with a couple of burgers. "Fresh fish today is mahi," she said, as she headed out with the platter hooked under one arm. When I went back out into the restaurant, Snooks was busy making complicated multicolored drinks for a bar full of thirsty patrons. I caught his attention, pointed outside, and mouthed "three margaritas, rocks and salt, and one sweet tea." Snooks signaled a thumbs up, but he didn't say anything. The tea was for Dave Ackerman. He was driving his State pickup, and wouldn't dare drink, even though he was out of uniform and undoubtedly could have used a drink as much as I did.

While I was walking back out the door onto the patio, I heard the familiar rumble of Nate Sturm's Indian motorcycle pulling into the parking lot. He joined us at the table, and I introduced him to Dave. We sat and watched a flock of laughing gulls circling over the beach below us. Two boys were throwing pieces of bread up into the air, which the gulls were deftly catching before they even hit the sand. There was no sign of Snooks. I knew it could be a while before he got to our margaritas, so I decided this was the time to fill in Katie and Nate about what had happened today.

When I had finished, Nate—not surprisingly—had a question. "Did one of those guys murder Bash?"

Dave looked at Nate. "Who's Bash?"

"Oh, uh, sorry. Sebastian Brophy. His friends called him Bash. Anyway, Sam—or Katie—what do you think?"

"I wish we knew," I said. "Of the two, Islava looks better for it than Stebbins, given his history of violence."

Bock

"Probably our best chance of getting him to admit it would have been part of a plea deal," Katie added. "But obviously now that's not gonna happen."

"So where do we go from here?" Nate asked.

"We'll keep on digging," Katie said. "That is, if you want us to."

"Damn straight I do."

At this point Snooks came out carrying a tray with our drinks, and menus tucked under his arm. He set down the tray and passed the menus around to the four of us. "Sorry this took so long. It's crazy in there."

"No problem," I said. "Crazy can't be all bad, can it?"

Snooks laughed. "No, I suppose not. It's just that sometimes I wish our customers would spread themselves out a bit more." He looked at Dave. "You're the Fish and Wildlife guy, right? How did it go out there today?"

We both knew this was coming, and, as I expected, Dave took the lead. "We have some good news and some not-so-good news." He went on to describe in detail how we'd tracked down both Santiago Islava and Will Stebbins out behind Channel Key, that Islava had died in a gunfight and Stebbins had been arrested.

"So the bad news is that Islava got killed?" Snooks asked.

"Well yes, I suppose that's part of it. But the other part is . . . uh . . . your boat kind of got shot up in the process."

Snooks frowned and fiddled with the rubber band holding up his ponytail. "How shot up?"

Dave went on to describe the damage: a broken windscreen, a dinged up engine cowling, and maybe some internal motor damage we hadn't yet had a chance to check out.

"But she runs?" Snooks asked.

"Oh, yeah. We made it back to Sam's dock with no problem. And here's what I'd like to do. If it's alright with you, I'll take the boat to our headquarters in Marathon and see to it that all necessary repairs are made. On the Fish and Wildlife Commission, of course. And that would include replacing the outboard if necessary."

"That's more than fair," Snooks said. "Thank you." He pulled a small pad of paper and a ballpoint out of his shirt pocket and clicked open the pen. "And now, what would you folks like to eat?"

The ends of Nate Sturm's mustache twitched. "You got any poached conch?"

I bit my tongue and waited to see if Snooks took the bait.

He did.

"No, we don't serve conch here, and I never heard of it poached anyhow. Now if you'll just look at the menu—"

Everybody laughed, including Snooks. Eventually.

Katie and Nate ordered the shrimp basket, while Dave and I opted for one of Flo's juicy quarter pound cheeseburgers with fries. We started in on the drinks, while Snooks went back inside with our orders. The boys down on the beach had used up all their bread, and the gulls had moved on. I watched a lone white heron stalking the edge of the receding shoreline, probably looking for crabs before they disappeared down their little holes.

About fifteen minutes later, Flo came out with a big tray full of food. She knew everybody at our table, of course. I think she knew everybody in the whole Village of Islamorada.

"I don't know if Snooks had a chance to tell you," I said. "But your tip about the Islava's houseboat on Channel Key paid off big time today."

Flo pushed back a stray lock of hair that had fallen in front of one eye. "He did tell me."

"And we thank you for that," Dave added.

"I'm sorry Santiago had to die, but from what Snooks told me he didn't leave the Coast Guard much of a choice. The guy always was trouble. I hope his wife is okay."

I saw Katie's eyes shift away from Flo and onto something farther down the patio. "Interesting," she said, almost to herself.

"What is?" I asked.

"See those men there at the end table?"

We all turned and looked where she was pointing. "The one on the left is Wallace Burke. He's head of the village building department. But I don't recognize the other man. Flo, do you know who that is?"

"Oh yeah. That's Skippy Knowland."

"Skippy?" Katie said.

Flo grinned. "That's what he calls himself. I think his actual name is Theodore."

"What do you know about him?"

"Quite a bit, actually. He lives in Key Largo, and he's big into buying up old restaurants and resorts, and remodeling them."

"Does he come here often?" I asked.

"Not recently. But he did a while back because he wanted to buy the Safari. Persistent as hell, but we kept saying 'no,' and finally he went away."

"I'd like you to do me a favor," Katie said. "Two, actually. First, would you happen to have his card? He must have given you one."

"I think it's around somewhere. I'll look. What else?"

"When he and Burke leave, find out who pays."

"I can do that. Is there something going on here I should know about?"

"It's probably nothing. Just curious is all."

Flo shot Katie a look, but she didn't say anything.

Once Flo had left, we set about attacking our food. Before we'd finished, the evening sky had faded to purple and then to gray over the Atlantic, while the deep waters below had lost all color. There was no wind, the only sound being the gentle lap of waves breaking on the beach below us.

After we were done eating, I went back to the kitchen to retrieve Prince. Flo handed me a business card. "This is from that guy Knowland. Oh, and he's the one who paid for their dinners."

I leashed up Prince, walked outside, and caught up with the others in the parking lot. Nate was getting ready to fire up his motorcycle, but I put a hand up and walked over in his direction. "You sure you want us to keep on with this?"

He took the time to mount his bike, then he kick-started the motor and revved it a couple of times. "You think it's worth your effort and my money?"

"That, my friend, is a good question. Things aren't looking too promising right now. But tell you what. I don't like to let go of something once I've sunk my teeth into it, and I know Katie feels the same way. So here's what I'd like to do. Katie and I will keep working, but we'll do it off the clock."

Nate put up a hand. "No, that wouldn't be—"

"But if and when we get somewhere with this thing, then we'll send you a bill. Okay?"

Nate gunned his Indian. "Deal. And if you can discover for sure who killed my friend, make it a great big bill."

I watched Nate rumble off toward the highway and then joined Katie and Dave, who were standing next to his truck. "I'd like to ask you a favor," she said to Dave.

"Of course."

"Can you find out if either Wallace Burke or Mr. Knowland owns a boat, and—if so—what kind?"

"Sure. I can do that. But do you mind me asking why?"

"Oh, just a hunch. There's something about that man I don't like."

"Which one?" Dave asked.

"Burke. But it's probably nothing."

I had the impression that Dave wasn't buying it, but he didn't say anything. Instead, he just got in his pickup and drove off.

Prince tugged on his leash, like he wasn't ready to get in the Jeep.

"He probably needs to pee," Katie said. "Let's take him over to the beach."

We walked while Prince sniffed. Eventually he did his business up against a big palm tree. "What are you thinking about Wallace Burke?" I asked. "Oh, and Flo said to tell you this Skippy fella paid for their dinner."

"I'm thinking that if Burke was on the take, and Sebastian Brophy found out about it, Burke would have had a pretty strong motive to get rid of him."

"And you're thinking if it were Burke, he must be a fisherman or at least a serious boater, in order to have killed him way over there in the everglades."

"Yeah, or know somebody who does have a boat."

"Maybe. But wouldn't there be simpler ways of getting rid of Brophy?"

"Simpler maybe, but not necessarily safer. After all, it was only a fluke that you found his canoe, and then the hurricane unearthed his flats boat. Otherwise, it could still be just a missing persons case."

We loaded up Prince and started for home. "Did Flo give you that guy's business card?"

"Oh yeah, I forgot." I pulled the card out of my shirt pocket. "Here it is."

Chapter 33

Because I had no official connection to law enforcement, I'd gotten used to the fact that when a case I was working on got to the prosecution stage, I almost always found myself on the outside looking in. At best I would end up in the observation booth attached to some interrogation room, or maybe not learn anything until they told me about it afterwards. Therefore I was surprised when Dave Ackerman called a couple of days later and asked me to join him and Assistant State's Attorney Walt Stone for a meeting with Will Stebbins.

"He's had a court appearance?" I said.

"Yep. Charged with poaching conchs. And because it appears to be a longstanding deal, we've hit him with a class four violation, which is a third degree felony. He pled not guilty and demanded a jury trial. That surprised both us and the judge, given the nature of our evidence in this case."

"Has the trial been set?"

"No. The judge wasn't willing to do that until we tried mediating the case, which is where you come in. We're set for a meeting tomorrow morning in Walt Stone's office in Marathon. Hope you can make it. And be sure to bring your photos of Stebbins in action, okay?"

"I'll be there, with a folder full of evidence. Is Stebbins in jail?"

"No, the judge released him on a $20,000 bond."

"Isn't that a bit risky?"

"We thought so, and we requested no bail. But the judge wasn't buying it. They rarely do with fish and wildlife cases like this. I got the very strong impression the judge wants this thing to go away without using up any more of his precious time."

"Does Stebbins have an attorney?"

"I think so. Stebbins claimed poverty, so it's going to be a public defender."

"What about his crewman?" I asked.

"Turns out he was from Guatemala and not here legally. Name's Alex Ortega. We made a deal with him. In return for his videotaped testimony, we agreed not to prosecute but instead to turn him over to immigration. He's being deported."

"What did he have to say?"

"Pretty much what we expected: that Stebbins was in the conch poaching business and has been for years."

"What about Islava?"

"He didn't know Islava personally, but he did acknowledge that the old houseboat is where they dropped off the conchs."

"Did you ask him about Sebastian Brophy?"

"I did, but it turns out he's only been in Florida since 2012, so that was a dead end. Our meeting starts at nine, but I expect Walt Stone would like some time with just the three of us before then. Can you make it by eight?"

"No problem."

Stone's office was in the county building in Marathon. It was a big room with a desk in one corner and a table in the other. Scattered palms outside a big window partially blocked a view of the highway. Dave and I got there about the same time. Walt offered coffee. We accepted and took seats around the table. He opened a file folder, cleared his throat, and clicked on a small recorder.

"For the record, Mr. Ackerman, would you give us a brief summary of the case we are here to consider?"

I suspect Walt Stone was fully aware of the details by now. In my experience he was a sharp guy who always did his homework.

"We have long suspected Mr. Stebbins of poaching conchs illegally, using a Yellowfin boat supposedly available for deep sea fishing charters. The problem has always been that we couldn't catch him out there doing it. And on those occasions when we inspected his boat after he came back to his dock, there were no conchs on board. We now believe this is because he was off-loading the conchs onto a houseboat owned by Santiago Islava that he kept anchored behind Channel Key."

"So Islava was in on this operation?"

"That is our belief, yes."

"And what evidence do you have that the relationship between Stebbins and Islava involved a conch poaching operation?"

Dave proceeded to describe our activities from three days previously, including our photographic evidence of Stebbins and his crewman harvesting conchs, and then the fatal encounter at Channel Key when they were in the process of offloading the catch into a tank on Islava's houseboat.

Stone shuffled some papers. "Is this Islava the same man we suspect might have killed a fellow lobsterman, and also possibly Sebastian Brophy?"

"It is."

I decided to add my two cents worth. "The same client who put us onto Islava as a suspect in Brophy's murder also mentioned Stebbins as another possibility."

"The motive in both cases being that Brophy had learned about their poaching operations?"

"That's correct."

"I assume the sheriff's department has no evidence linking Stebbins to Brophy's death, or I would have heard about it."

"That's also correct."

Stone glanced briefly out the window, and then back at me. "Would you like me to bring up the Brophy case today?"

"Couldn't hurt I suppose. You also might ask about our dog."

Stone frowned. "What about your dog?"

"One day last week a client and I accidentally ran into Stebbins out in the bay. We saw him take at least one conch. It got ugly. Then that same night, while my wife and I were out to dinner, somebody kidnapped our Corgi. The dog eventually came back home, but with a threatening note attached to his collar. It seemed like too much of a coincidence."

Stone raised an eyebrow. "But you have no actual proof Stebbins did this?"

"We do not. The sheriff's department dusted the note and our house for prints, but they turned up nothing useful."

"Well, gentlemen, it sounds like we're in no position to accuse Stebbins of anything today except poaching. But if either of you would like to ask him about Brophy or the dog, I suppose there's no harm."

Dave and I looked at each other. "You do it," he said to me.

The clock on the wall said 8:55. We expected Stebbins and his attorney to arrive any minute, but it didn't happen. We had seconds on coffee and waited. When nobody had showed up by 9:30, Stone got on his phone to call the public defender's office. Nobody answered, so he left a message.

"You think he skipped?" I asked Walt Stone.

"It wouldn't surprise me, but you'd think his attorney would at least let us know."

We were on the verge of giving up, when Stone finally got a call. He said "uh huh" a couple of times, and then rang off. "They're on their way in. That was his attorney, Janet Grebe. She said Stebbins didn't show at her office like he was supposed to at eight, and when he did finally get there he wanted to talk."

"Did she say what about?"

"Nope. Hopefully, it's about a plea."

Will Stebbins and his public defender, Janet Grebe, arrived an hour late, but at least they showed up. Stebbins and Grebe sat on one side of Stone's table, while he and Dave and I sat on the other. It was just like the standard arrangement I'd seen before in interrogation rooms, except the table was nicer, the lighting was a whole lot better, and I was right there with them instead of tucked away in an observation booth.

I'd never seen Grebe before. She was wearing an all-black pants suit, low heels, and no jewelry or makeup that I could detect. She had bags under her eyes, suggesting overwork. Her frizzy brown hair needed attention, and the pants suit was shiny, presumably from too much wear.

If Will Stebbins had in mind some sort of a plea bargain, he certainly showed no signs of it when the interview began. "These charges are crap," he said before Walt Stone even had a chance to state what they were. Then he pointed in my direction. "And what's *he* doing here?"

Janet looked as surprised by this as I was, which made me wonder what she and her client had discussed ahead of time.

Stone proceeded as if Stebbins hadn't said anything important. "You are accused of running a conch poaching operation, which is a serious violation of both Florida and Federal law. You're saying you didn't do this?"

"Damn straight."

Janet Grebe again looked stricken. She put her arm on Stebbins shoulder to get his attention, but he shook her off. "You wanna know why I was out by that old houseboat? It's not what you think."

"We know why you were there, Mr. Stebbins," Dave Ackerman said. "You were in the process of unloading your day's catch, which Santiago

Islava would then take on the black market, just like he'd been doing for years. But we interrupted your operation before you could finish, which is why we found a bunch of conchs in a tank inside the houseboat, and only a couple still on your boat when you got home."

"Bullshit. You wanna know why I was there? I was curious about that old houseboat. I thought it might be for sale. And those two conchs your guys found on my Yellowfin? I didn't even know they were there. It must have been Alex, my crewman. He must have sneaked 'em on board while I wasn't looking."

"That's not what he told us in a videotaped statement. According to him, you've been in the conch business for years."

Stebbins curled a lip. "And you're gonna take some greaser's word over mine?"

Stone was having none of it. "Actually we don't have to take anybody's word for anything, Mr. Stebbins, not that Mr. Ortega wasn't pretty convincing. Dr. Sawyer, would you please show the accused and his attorney your photographs?"

I opened the file sitting on the tabletop in front of me, and spread out eight of the two dozen shots I had, all of which clearly showed Alex Ortega tossing conchs up to Stebbins, who was standing in the stern of his boat. "These are all photographs of different events, with—as you can see—the date and the time in the lower left corner." I opened a second folder, this one containing images of Stebbins and Ortega tossing conchs to Santiago Islava. "And here you are unloading your catch onto the houseboat."

This time Janet Grebe took hold of Stebbin's shirt sleeve and didn't let go. "Is there someplace I can talk to my client in private?" she asked Stone.

"Absolutely. But before you do that, Dr. Sawyer has a couple of questions he would like to ask. If that's alright with you, that is?"

"Who, me or her?" Stebbins said.

"You," Stone replied. "This shouldn't take long. Dr. Sawyer?"

"I'm curious what you might be able to tell us about a man named Sebastian Brophy."

"What about him?" Stebbins snapped. "He used to live in our neighborhood. That's about all I know." There was a short pause. "Oh, and he had the reputation of being some kind of ecofreaky tree hugger. I remember that. None of us much liked him."

"He disappeared in 1998, and we have newly discovered evidence suggesting he was murdered. Would you happen to know anything about that?"

This brought Janet Grebe quickly and forcefully into the conversation. "Now just a minute here, Walt. Are you accusing my client of murder? Nobody said anything about that when we agreed to this meeting."

"No, we're not accusing Mr. Stebbins of anything except conch poaching. At least not at this point."

"Well okay, then. Now, can Mr. Stebbins and I *please* go somewhere and talk?"

"I believe Dr. Sawyer has one more thing he'd like to ask Mr. Stebbins. Right, Sam?"

"Yes. Not all that long ago, a client and I encountered you out by Cameron Key. We saw you take a conch on board. You claimed your crewman had made a mistake, and you threw the conch back in the water. I'm sure you remember that."

"Damn right I do. And for good reason. You threatened to turn me in for something I didn't do."

"Maybe and maybe not. But that's not what I wanted to ask you about. That same night, while my wife and the client and I were out to dinner, somebody kidnapped our dog. I'm wondering if you know anything about that?"

Was there just a moment's hesitation, or was it my imagination? In any event, right after that Stebbins really blew up. His face got red, and he pounded the table.

"What is this bullshit you people are throwing at me? First you accuse me of being a poacher, which I most certainly am not, and now I'm a dog thief?"

Stebbins paused and wiped away beads of sweat that had broken out on his forehead. Then he pointed directly at me. "Now listen, you self-righteous bastard. If I ever decide to come after you, it's gonna be straight on, you can count on that. It won't be with some chickenshit note!"

The room went dead quiet. First I, and then the rest of them including Stebbins, realized what had just happened. I hadn't yet said anything about any note. Stebbins spluttered around afterwards, saying he must have heard about the note from another neighbor. But he couldn't remember which neighbor, and I don't think anybody bought it, least of all me.

After the interview ended, Janet Grebe dragged Will Stebbins out of the room. They were gone about twenty minutes. When they came back she had a very different client on her hands. They quickly agreed to Stone's offer: Stebbins would plead guilty to felony poaching, permanently giving up his captain's and fishing licenses, pay a $5,000 fine, and serve six months in county jail. The sentence for a level four fish and wildlife violation could have included a five-year jail term, which probably explained why Stebbins went for the deal. That and the fact that I agreed to let the dog issue drop. I was pretty sure Katie wasn't going to like it, but Stone had pushed back, pointing out that we had no real evidence except for Stebbins' slip.

Dave and I met in the parking lot after the meeting. "Sorry about the dog deal," he said. "But at least we got Stebbins for poaching. He's out of business for sure. Still, I wonder if he was the one who killed Brophy."

"Me too. Maybe something will turn up. Katie's not gonna be happy about Stone's decision not to go after him about Prince."

"I get that. Oh, and speaking of Katie, tell her I did a search for boats licensed to either Wallace Burke or Theodore Knowland. As far as department records go back, Burke never has had one. Or at least not one he bothered to register. But Knowland is another matter. It turns out he's all about boats."

Just then my phone pinged, almost at the same time as Dave's. We both looked at our screens.

"Did you just get invited by the sheriff to a meeting about Islava?"

"I did. It's for tomorrow afternoon in Al Beaudry's office. I think Katie's invited too."

"Seems like it's our week for meetings, huh?"

"Yeah. One of the reasons I bailed on an academic life was the endless string of boring meetings. Now it seems like my life may be devolving back to that."

Dave grinned. "Maybe this one won't be all that boring."

"Hope not. See you tomorrow."

"At least the sheriff was willing to come up here, rather than make us drive all the way down to headquarters in Key West."

I laughed. "Yeah. What is it they say about small favors?"

Chapter 34

"**H**e did *what?*"

I'd just come back home and had given Katie the news. While it appeared Will Stebbins had, in fact, kidnapped Prince, Walt Stone had declined to press charges.

"I tried to talk him into it, but I guess he decided nailing Stebbins for conch poaching was enough."

"Well then you didn't try hard enough, dammit!"

There didn't seem anything left to do except change the subject. "You got the message we're invited to meet with Chief Spivey tomorrow?"

"Uh huh. Do you have any idea what it's about?"

"Not for certain, but I expect it has to do with what happened to Santiago Islava, and where the Brophy case goes from here."

Katie had been at her desk, shuffling papers, when I'd walked in the door. "Speaking of that, I think I found something interesting in these records from the building department. You remember that guy who was having dinner with Wallace Burke at the Safari the other day?"

"Skippy somebody? What about him?"

"And Flo gave you his business card, and then you gave it to me?"

"Yeah."

Katie picked up the card and looked at it. "His real name is Theodore Knowland, and he's president of something called Gold Star Renovations and Properties. There's a Key Largo address and contact information. But that's not the interesting part. It turns out he had lots of dealings with the Islamorada Building Department. They go way back, and guess what?"

"Something to do with Sebastian Brophy?"

"Damn straight. Prior to 1999 Brophy had filed a whole bunch of inspection violations on this guy's company, including three stop work

197

orders. But after that, when Wallace Burke took over, it stopped happening. They issued Gold Star multiple building permits, but I could find no records of any violations. Of course the files we got only go up to 2005."

"But he's still in business from what Flo said."

"And still buying Wallace Burke's dinner. Pretty brazen, don't you think?"

"Do you think we should bring this up with the sheriff when we meet with him tomorrow?"

"Along with what happened to Prince. Maybe he'll be more sympathetic than Walt Stone."

"Don't bet on it."

~ ~ ~

We met in a cramped windowless room two doors down from Al Beaudry's office in the Marathon substation. The six of us barely fit around the table: Monroe County Sheriff Michael Spivey, Detectives Al Beaudry and Stella Reynard, Dave Ackerman, along with Katie and me. There were two pots of what turned out to be stale coffee on a counter at one end of the room, along with a stack of Styrofoam cups.

We took seats, and the sheriff called the meeting to order. Michael Spivey was in his mid to late sixties, wiry and trim. He wore an immaculate brown suit, an off-white shirt with cufflinks, and a gold tie. I'd seen him on several previous occasions, and he always dressed this way. He had a small handgun in a holster clipped to his belt.

"Thanks for coming," Sheriff Spivey said. "We're here today to discuss the unfortunate shooting death of Santiago Islava. Not that it could be helped, mind you, but it left open the question of future directions for our investigation into the death of Sebastian Brophy back in 1998. I've already discussed this with Detective Beaudry, who has the lead in this case, and we have come to an agreement on how to proceed."

I couldn't help noticing his use of the past tense: "left open;" not "leaves open."

Spivey swallowed some coffee and made a face. Then he proceeded to confirm my suspicions. "And let me be clear about this. We have made a determination that Islava almost certainly was responsible for killing Brophy. He had the means, motive, and opportunity. Especially motive, given that Brophy apparently had the goods on him not only for poaching lobsters but for killing a fellow commercial fisherman."

Spivey stopped talking and looked around the room. Nobody said anything right away, but both Stella Reynard and Dave Ackerman made throat-clearing noises like they were about to. The sheriff let the silence hang, but only for about three seconds before he continued. "I have instructed Detective Beaudry to indicate this tentative conclusion in the file, and to discontinue work on the case until or unless any new information arises." Then he turned deliberately in my direction and Katie's. "As private citizens, I cannot of course order you off the case. But I would encourage you to turn your attentions elsewhere."

This was too much for Katie. "With all due respect, sheriff, I must disagree with your conclusions."

"What, specifically, is your problem?"

"There actually are two," she said. "First, if I understand the information you have gathered so far, Mr. Islava almost certainly is a murderer. I'll grant you that. But I believe you have no direct evidence that he killed Mr. Brophy, isn't that right?"

Spivey shook his head in dismissal. "Thanks to the hard work by Detective Beaudry, we have some new evidence you may not know about. Al, would you please explain?"

"Yes, Sheriff. We recently interviewed Santiago Islava's widow, and we ended up arresting her for aiding and abetting. We found phone records indicating she called her husband as soon as she learned we had an arrest warrant out on him, in order to warn him about it. He was working his lobster traplines at the time."

This answered one question I'd been asking myself. Why had Islava fled in his lobster boat instead of driving away in his car if he wanted to avoid arrest? It was because he was on the boat when his wife called, and he couldn't think of anything to do except go hide on the houseboat.

"What happened after you arrested Mrs. Santiago?" the sheriff asked.

"After an extensive interview, we agreed to drop the charges against her in return for information she had about Sebastian Brophy's murder."

"Like she knew he did it?" I asked.

Beaudry smirked. "Better than that. When we gave her a chance, she produced some documentation to that effect. It turns out Islava kept a diary, which is now in our possession."

Katie raised an eyebrow. "You mean he confessed to killing Brophy in his diary?

Beaudry glanced briefly at the sheriff. "Well . . . . no, not exactly. But there are numerous entries where he describes his hatred for the man, including one that says 'something needs to happen' to him, and that it would be easy to make him disappear."

"Forgive me, detective," Katie said, suddenly all polite. "But that hardly constitutes conclusive evidence."

"Now look here!" the sheriff interrupted. "It adds to the overall picture, I'm sure you'll agree." He stopped talking and ran a hand back over his hair. "We're not saying this case is absolutely solved, Mrs. Sawyer. But until some sort of evidence—*any* sort of evidence—comes to light suggesting who else might have killed Brophy and why, we—"

"Which brings me to my second point, Sheriff," Katie said. "Specifically, have you looked into any circumstances related to Mr. Brophy's employment? You do know that he worked as a building inspector for the Village of Islamorada, don't you?"

From his bodily reaction—almost a physical recoil—it was clear this was something the sheriff didn't want to talk about. But now he had no choice. "Of course we looked into that," he replied. "But it turned up nothing."

"Then perhaps I can enlighten you," Katie said. "As part of our investigation, we have uncovered evidence that Mr. Brophy had a well-earned reputation for being a stickler about the rules, which got him jammed up not only with customers, but also with his co-workers. Specifically a man named Wallace Burke, who currently runs the department."

"And how did you come up with this so-called information, about something that happened more than twenty years ago?"

"I'm afraid we are not in a position to disclose our source, Sheriff. But I'm sure you can find this information yourself, or your deputies can, if they take the trouble to look."

The sheriff's normally pale face turned bright red, and a sheen of perspiration glistened on his forehead. He fixed Katie with a hard stare. "I resent your questioning the thoroughness of our investigation, Mrs. Sawyer. But in the interest of quelling this apparent dissention among ourselves—all of whom I am sure are equally anxious to see justice done in this case—I am now asking Detective Beaudry to take another look at Mr. Brophy's history with the Islamorada Building Department." He stuffed papers back into a manila envelope he'd brought with him, and stood up to leave. "Not that I expect it to turn up anything useful. And now if you'll excuse me, I'm late for another meeting."

Chapter 35

Katie and I got back in my Jeep for the drive home from Marathon. "I thought you were going to tell the sheriff about what happened to Prince."

"I thought about it, but then thought maybe I'd poked the bear enough for one day."

"You certainly did that."

Katie frowned. "You think I went too far?"

"Hell no. But I can't help thinking you hit a nerve, and I wonder why. I also wonder why you didn't tell the sheriff how we got our information about the past history of the building department."

"Because I'm pretty sure it was that old janitor who sneaked us the files, and I didn't want to risk getting him in trouble."

"Which could happen if the sheriff and Wallace Burke are tight."

Once back home, and having given Prince his midday lunch, I decided to call Nate Sturm. Katie had gone off to teach an afternoon forensics lab. I didn't have any clients booked, and Nate deserved an update. Also, I wanted to ask him a couple of questions. Nate seemed to know everything about everybody in our part of the Florida Keys, which made him a potential goldmine of information. We'd already learned that.

Nate answered, but only after the fourth or fifth ring. "What? I'm at the barbershop."

"Sorry to interrupt, Nate, it's Sam. Any chance we could talk when you've finished having your mustache trimmed, or whatever?"

"They're under orders not to touch my mustache. But sure, I'll drop by on the way home. Should be about forty-five minutes."

This gave me some time to kill, so I decided to continue looking at the building department records somebody had copied for us. We'd already discovered that Theodore Knowland and his company, Gold Star

Renovations and Properties, had received harsh treatment from Sebastian Brophy prior to 1998, and an apparent green light from Wallace Burke after that. But were there other outfits with similar permit and inspection patterns? Could I go online and learn the names of individuals involved?

I worked my way through the pile of documents, restricting my search to companies and corporations who had done business with the Village of Islamorada both before and after 1998. It took me about a half hour to come up with a list of a dozen or so likely possibilities, though none of them had received such stark before and after treatment as Gold Star. Equally disappointing were the results of my computer searches, though given my limited abilities along those lines, perhaps it was not surprising. Many of the companies on my list appeared to no longer exist, and among those that did, the names of their executives meant nothing to me. I put the list aside, but did not throw it away. Maybe somebody else who'd been around longer than me might know something. Like Nate Sturm.

Then I had another thought. Were there companies that had dealt mainly with Sebastian Brophy up to 1998, but for which there were no records after that? This list proved shorter than the first. There were only three names, but one of them was vaguely familiar: Middle Keys Beachside Development. How could that have been, since I hadn't moved to Islamorada until many years after the company apparently went out of business? I got back online and typed in the name. There was no website, which was not surprising for a company that apparently no longer existed. It wasn't until I had scrolled down a rather long list of "hits" before I came to something that almost fit: "Middle Keys Beachside Enterprises." I clicked on the link, and it took me to a pdf copy of a bankruptcy notice, dated August 1998. And there it was, right on the first page. The owners of Middle Keys Beachside Enterprises were listed as Charles Alva Simpson and Patrick Henry Simpson.

Before I could read further, Prince—who had been asleep at my feet—jumped up and began barking. He went to the door, just as Nate Sturm walked in. "Hey, what's up?" he said.

A whole lot was up, but I wasn't ready to fill him in on what I'd just discovered. More work needed to be done. But I was anxious to tell him about our meeting with the sheriff, and to ask him a couple of questions.

We settled in the living room with iced tea. I said something polite about his haircut, even though I couldn't see much change. "Katie and I met this morning with Sheriff Spivey and his detectives, Stella Reynard and Al Beaudry. They seem convinced, or at least Beaudry and the sheriff were, that Santiago Islava killed your friend."

Nate took in a deep breath and let it back out. "So that's that?"

"Not necessarily. There's no doubt Islava was a bad dude with a violent streak, and that he had plenty of motive to murder Brophy. But they don't really have any hard evidence."

"Then the case is still open?"

"More or less."

"What the hell does that mean?"

"The sheriff made it clear that he wants the case put on the back burner, pending some big new information."

Nate frowned. "And he doesn't want his people spending a lot of time looking for it, right?"

"I'm afraid so."

He took a drink of his iced tea and set the glass back down on the coffee table in front of us. "What about you and Katie?"

"I said the other day that we're staying on this, and nothing's changed. There'll be no charge unless and until this thing gets resolved. But I do have a couple of questions. First, would you happen to know if Wallace Burke and Sheriff Spivey know each other?"

Nate got a knowing look in his eye. I hadn't been certain before, but now I was sure. Our client was one smart man. He didn't even bother to ask why I'd asked the question. "I expect they do," he said. "The three of us belong to the Marathon Moose."

"You're a Moose?"

"Yeah, mostly I belong for the bingo nights. It's every Tuesday from six to ten."

"Does the sheriff play bingo?"

"Not that I know of. But he and Burke are regulars at our weekly lunches."

Nate finished his iced tea and started to get up. "Time for my rounds."

"Before you go, I've got another question. You know we have a neighbor called Hank Simpson."

"Uh huh. What about him? I don't much like that guy."

"Do you know if he's related to a Charles Simpson?"

"Used to be. Charlie was his brother. But he died of a heart attach back maybe fifteen years ago. Why?"

"Just curious."

"Does this have anything to do with Bash?"

"Maybe. Probably not."

Nate twirled his mustache. "You're doing a dance on me here, Sam. Care to explain yourself?"

It was tempting. "Not right now, Nate. But trust me on this. If it turns out to be important, you'll be the first to know."

He shot me a look, but didn't say anything except to thank me for "all the help," before he went downstairs and hopped on his motorcycle.

I sat back down, thought about things for a while, and then made up my mind about something. I found his contact information on a list of fishing clients I had stored in my phone, and made the call.

"Hello, Hank? This is Sam Sawyer. You got a minute?"

Patrick Simpson had more than a minute. He seemed positively thrilled that I'd called, probably because he thought it was about selling our house. I did nothing to dispel that notion, which caused him to drop whatever it was he'd been doing and rush right over. He came in carrying a manila folder.

"Brought a contract with me, just in case," Simpson said.

"Sorry. It's not about that. Katie and I talked it over, and we decided not to sell at this time."

Simpson scowled. "You could be making a big mistake here. Something you might regret."

"I'm sorry."

I watched his face fall. "Then what am I here for? We could have set up a fishing date over the phone."

"It's not about that either."

"Oh."

I invited him to sit in the living room. "Something to drink?"

"Uh, no thanks. I can't stay that long."

"Then I'll make this quick. You may not know it, but my wife and I have become private investigators. Not in a big way, but as something to do in addition to our regular jobs, which—as you know in my case—is work as a fishing guide."

The look on Simpson's face was hard to read. Puzzlement, maybe?

"No, I didn't know that," he said.

"Anyway, we have a client who has asked us to look into the disappearance many years ago of a man named Sebastian Brophy. He used to live in our development. Perhaps you remember him."

"The name sounds familiar. Maybe I met him at an HOA meeting or something. You say he disappeared?"

"That's right. Back in 1998. Nobody knew what happened, but then just recently his body was discovered, and the evidence shows that he was murdered."

"Wow. That's terrible. But what does it have to do with me?"

"Probably nothing. But Katie and I are in the midst of interviewing anybody who might have known Brophy, in hopes somebody might have seen or heard something back when he went missing. Maybe give us a clue as to what happened."

Simpson frowned, like maybe he was trying to remember something. But then he shook his head. "Nope. I wouldn't know anything about it. Like I said, the best I can remember we only met a couple of times at homeowners' meetings."

I thanked Simpson for his time, and showed him to the door. I hadn't learned anything specific about Patrick Henry Simpson, except one thing. The man was a liar.

Chapter 36

When Katie got home that evening I told her what I'd learned about Hank Simpson.

"We need to talk," she said. "And I'd like to do it out in the Gulf. Privately, all by ourselves." Then, as an afterthought, "Except for Prince, that is."

"Fine. Any particular reason? Hoping finally to see the green flash?"

"Ha ha. I don't want any interruptions messing things up. Don't bring your phone. And no alcohol. This isn't a booze cruise."

She sounded serious. I loaded up the skiff with soft drinks and snacks and the dog, and we set off down the canal. After going about a quarter mile out into Florida Bay I cut the motor and let the boat drift. There was little wind. The sun had about an hour to go before it dipped below the horizon.

Katie got down to business. "I've never done a cold case before, and I had no idea how hard they could be. Time erases so much evidence, and peoples' memories fade, or they get set in patterns that don't fit what actually happened. We need to figure out what to do next, and we must make sure that you and I, honey, are on the same page. Bottom line: Who do you think killed Sebastian Brophy?"

I ducked. "You go first."

She shot me a look, but then she went ahead. "Obviously, Santiago Islava is a real possibility. No doubt the sheriff was rushing to judgment yesterday. But Islava had plenty of motive, plus—and this is a big one—he has a history of violence, including murder. From what Nate told us, Brophy had the goods on both him and Will Stebbins, so we can't rule out either of them." Katie stopped to sip her diet cola and eat a handful of Cheetos. "And then there's Wallace Burke. I'm betting he's been on the take all along. Brophy had plenty of opportunity to figure that out and confront him, perhaps with fatal consequences." She drank again. "Okay, now it's your turn."

"I can't disagree with anything you've said, Katie. But here's one additional thought. Whoever went to the trouble of following Brophy over into the everglades, then killing him and then hiding the body and his boat—he almost certainly couldn't have done that alone. He had to have somebody along to drive either his boat or Brophy's."

"Which means we're looking for two people instead of just one."

"Has to be. And I can think of several possibilities. One is that Islava and Stebbins did it together."

"Or it could have been Islava and his wife. From what the sheriff told us, she certainly was aware of what her husband was up to. But I'd like to come back to Burke for a minute. Didn't Dave Ackerman tell you that he didn't even have a boat?"

"Right. But what about one of those builders or developers Burke was winking at? One of them could have had one. Most likely did, in fact."

"Like that Skippy Knowland character who bought lunch for Wallace Burke at the Safari the other day."

"Sure, or some other person that Brophy went after."

"Like maybe Hank Simpson?"

Katie had been watching a line of cormorants flying low across the water, heading south. Now she turned to look directly at me. "What about Hank Simpson?"

"I was looking at those building department records again today, and it turns out Simpson once had a company along with his brother that went bankrupt back in 1998. And guess who probably was responsible for shutting them down."

"Sebastian Brophy?"

"You got it."

"So here's the bottom line, Sam. And you tell me if you think I'm wrong. We have multiple suspects—maybe as you say, pairs of suspects—all with motives to get Brophy out of the picture."

"And no solid proof any of them actually did it."

"In other words," Katie said, "we're stuck."

"We need a break. We need some luck."

"Who was it said that it's better to be lucky than good?"

"Some baseball player, I think. So I have an idea, Katie. Why don't we try the green flash?"

"What?"

"Seeing it is supposed to be lucky."

By now the sun was approaching the horizon, glowing a fiery red-orange against the darkening sky. We didn't have long to wait.

"Frankly, I think you're full of it, Dr. Sam Sawyer. But if I'm gonna do this, you can't watch."

"Why not?"

"Because even if it doesn't happen, you'll try to talk me into believing I just missed it. Again. So look somewhere else, okay?"

I did as she asked, turning my back to the east, thinking about what had brought us to this point, and waiting. One minute dragged out to maybe five.

And then:

"Well I'll be damned."

I whirled around, but by then the sun was gone. "You saw it?"

"I did."

"Told ya."

Chapter 37

The green flash good luck effect, assuming there was such a thing, didn't kick in for a couple of days. Julie Liptan had called, inviting us to a barbecue at their place. But it wasn't to be until the following Monday. She explained this was the regular day Flo and Snooks closed the Safari, and so they would be able to come. Also invited were Stella Reynard, Nate Sturm, Dave Ackerman, and (of course) Prince, who definitely was into parties.

When we arrived at 5:45 Rashaan was busy fussing around with the grill out on their patio. Julie was in the kitchen organizing trays of food, including burgers, brats, potato salad, deviled eggs, and condiments. Serena and Candace were carrying things outside, either to the grill or to a big table where we all would be eating. The girls had the boy named Hardy in tow, apparently as usual. I had met him before. He was the kid who had come upon the body of Rusty Montrose three weeks earlier.

Next to the big stainless steel grill were two big Yeti coolers filled with ice and beer and soft drinks. There also were bottles of red and white wine, along with pitchers of lemonade and iced tea. Plastic glasses were stacked on a tray next to the coolers. Nate Sturm was bent over one of the coolers, rummaging for a beer, when Katie and I walked outside. He stood back up and turned, with a cold bottle of Corona in his hand. He offered it to Katie.

"No thanks," she said. "I think I'll pour myself a glass of iced tea."

I took the beer, and turned to watch Rashaan spread a half dozen each of brats and burgers out on the grill.

"How's it going?" I asked.

"Good," he said. "You know Julie was really upset about that body we found in the water right next door. She even suggested maybe we should move. But I reminded her what life was like back up in Miami: the high

210

crime rate and problems with our personal security. I told her I thought things were much better in Islamorada, and she agreed."

"So you're not gonna move, are you?"

"Hell no."

Rashaan went back to grilling things. Nate came over and tapped me on the shoulder. "How's it going?"

"Okay, I guess. Nothing really new to report."

He grunted, took a sip of his beer, and wiped foam off his mustache. "You thinking of throwing in the towel on the Brophy case?"

"Oh hell no, Nate. At least not yet."

"Good. Maybe one of these days I'll get a good night's sleep."

"Yeah, maybe we all will."

I was about to tell Nate about my meeting with Hank Simpson, when Stella Reynard came out of the house with Dave Ackerman at her side. I'd heard maybe they had become an item—or at least they were thinking about it. Stella and Dave went over to say hi to Rashaan, and then joined us by the coolers. I introduced Nate to both of them. Stella was wearing a long black skirt, spike heels, and a colored blouse cut low across the front. She looked spectacular, and I could tell from the way Dave was staring at her that he felt the same way.

Nate, who apparently had designated himself bartender, set Stella and Dave up with their drinks of choice: a diet cola for Dave and white wine for Stella. We made small talk about the weather (warm but dry lately), and the fishing (Dave had heard the cero mackerel were lit up on the Atlantic side of the Channel Five bridge). I was about to ask Stella about the Montrose case, when a great yowling set up somewhere back inside the house.

"Uh oh," Katie said. "Sounds like Prince and Taylor may have gotten into it again."

"Who's Taylor?" Stella asked.

"The Liptan's cat," Katie said. "I'd better go check it out."

As Katie headed back into the house, she passed Flo and Snooks on the way out, followed closely by the two girls and Hardy. "Is it our dog?" Katie asked.

Candace and Serena both laughed. "No, actually it's our cat," Serena said. "Prince is just trying to be friendly, but Taylor has other ideas. I wouldn't worry about it. They'll work it out."

"Maybe," Katie said. "But I think I'd better check it out anyway."

The young people had started walking out toward the canal, when Julie stuck her head out the door. "Where are you all headed?"

"Hardy wants to go for a swim in the canal, Mom," Candace said. "Is that okay?"

Rashaan and Julie both said "no" at the same time.

"But why not?" Serena said.

Julie held up two fingers. "One, your father saw a crocodile out there just last week. And two, I still need your help in the kitchen. Now please get back in here. At least you girls." All three teenagers disappeared back into the house. The cat racket had stopped. I assumed Katie had things under control, and didn't need my help mediating the feline versus canine event.

By this time Snooks and Flo both had beers. Dave took a handful of Cheetos from a bowl and started munching on them.

I took Stella aside. "Any news about Montrose?"

"No. But I did hear from Rhonda Wilcox yesterday. They were able to get IDs on the DNA and dental records from that body back in the glades. No doubt it was Sebastian Brophy."

"No surprise there, I suppose. We were all pretty sure it was him."

"And there's more. She asked me to tell you. The slugs from under the red canoe and the one from inside Brophy's skull? They're a match. Both .38 caliber."

"Now all we have to do is find the gun that fired them," I said. "And I need to tell Nate Sturm we have a final, positive ID on Brophy's body. I don't know if I've told you, but he's the one that hired us to look into the disappearance of his friend."

Stella nodded. "You want me to tell him?"

I thought about that. "No. It's a touchy subject for him. Let's not spoil this party. Katie and I will tell him another time. And frankly, it won't be that big of a surprise."

When we rejoined the group, Snooks was in the middle of telling everybody about some character at the Safari who claimed he'd seen a likeness of Donald Trump in an onion ring. Apparently the man wouldn't stop talking about it.

"What did you do about that?" Nate asked.

"Not much we could do," Flo said.

"Not much we *had* to do," Snooks added. "Because right after that he fell off his bar stool and hit his head. We had to call an ambulance to take him to emergency."

"And now he's gonna sue, right?" Stella said. "For having a floor that was too hard."

Snooks shook his head and laughed. "At least not yet."

"Did it?" I asked.

Snooks looked puzzled. "What?"

"Did it look like Donald Trump?"

"I don't know. He ate it just before he fell off the bar stool."

By this time Rashaan had finished loading up a big platter of burgers and brats. "Julie?" he yelled back into the house." Tell the kids their food is ready."

Evidently the plan was for Candace and Serena and their tag-along Hardy to eat first, which made sense because the table wasn't big enough for the adults plus them. Remembering back to when I was their age, they probably preferred it that way.

Once they finished eating and—under Rashaan's watchful eye—carried their dirty dishes and silverware back into the house, he set about taking food orders from the rest of us. Then he loaded the grill with the requested numbers of burgers and brats, and fired up the barbecue. In less than twenty minutes we all were seated around the table with our food. The chatter was what you might expect from a group of interesting and animated people.

Dave wanted to hear Rashaan talk about his basketball career, especially when he was in college. "What do you think about all the transferring of schools going on today, and the pay involved?" he asked.

Rashaan shook his head. "I don't like it much at all. I think it's fair that the kids get compensated for what they do, given the positive impact it has on the institutions they play for. But it ought to be standardized in some way, so the so-called student athletes don't shop around like they're buying a new car or something."

"Do you think that's gonna happen?" Dave asked.

Rashaan shrugged and chewed on his brat. "Probably not."

Snooks was in the process of telling a story I'd heard before, about how he got one of their cats from a mounted policeman in Key West, when the three teenagers came out of the house and asked again if they could go swimming in the canal.

"No you may not," Julie said.

"But we're bored," Candace replied. "There's nothing to do."

"Maybe we could play video games," Hardy said. "Would that be okay, Mrs. Liptan?"

"Yes. Okay."

The kids went back in the house, and the chewing and chatting and drinking resumed around the table. Everybody seemed to be having a good time, but I could sense an underlying tension. Somebody had drowned under suspicious circumstances in the canal right next door, and not all that long ago. And for those who knew him, the murder of Sebastian Brophy still loomed large. Nate Sturm usually was as talkative as any of us, maybe more than most under normal circumstances. But the situation wasn't normal, especially for him. He talked little for the remainder of the meal, and his eyes kept wandering out toward the canal.

We were close to finishing our meal, when Serena Liptan came out of the house and quietly approached her father. She tugged at his sleeve and made a motion with her head that indicated she wanted to talk to him alone. Rashaan wiped some mustard off his chin, excused himself, and followed her back into the house. We all acted like nothing had happened, except everybody stopped talking and concentrated on their food.

Rashaan was back in about fifteen minutes, and he did not look happy. "Stella and Katie and Sam, may I see you for a second?"

We joined him on the other side of the patio. "What is it?" I asked.

"The kids, they—I can't believe this—they found a gun in our attic."

"What sort of a gun?" Stella asked.

"A pistol. I'm not sure what kind."

"Is it yours?"

"Hell no. I don't even have a gun. I used to keep one in my car when I played for the Miami *Heat* because sometimes I had to drive around town late at night. But it's long gone. What would a gun be doing in our attic?"

"What were the kids doing up there when they found it?" I asked.

"Exploring. That's what they said. Just exploring. I didn't even know this house had an attic. Apparently they found a panel in the ceiling of one of the upstairs bedrooms, and Hardy got the big idea they should go up there."

"Is the gun still there?" Stella asked. "I hope the kids haven't moved it."

"Serena said they hadn't even touched it, and neither did I."

"That's good. Here's what we're gonna do. I have a flashlight, some evidence bags, and my phone out in the car. I'll go get them, and then you or one of the kids can show me the weapon."

I looked back toward the table, and noticed that people were getting fidgety. "I'll go tell the others what's going on while you do this."

"Good idea," Stella said.

I went back and jointed the others, told them what had happened, and watched their faces for any sort of odd reaction, especially Julie's. But she looked as puzzled and surprised as the rest of us.

Sometime during the next ten minutes, while we waited for Stella and the others to come back, I remembered something. Something important. At the recent homeowners meeting, Hank Simpson told Rashaan that not only had he built the Liptan's house, but he was the first person to live in it. I must have jumped or flinched or something when this hit me because Katie shot me a look. I mouthed the word "later," and she gave me a subtle nod.

Was I adding two and two and getting five? Or maybe even ten? But if the gun in the Liptan's attic turned out to be Simpson's, and if it matched the slugs we found in Brophy's canoe and his boat . . . ?

Chapter 38

Things moved very quickly after that night at the Liptan's house. They moved without help from Katie or me, but that was okay. We'd made our contributions, and we knew Nate Sturm would finally get some closure. Stella, by dint of determination and momentum, simply took the Brophy case away from Al Beaudry, and from the sheriff as well.

The first thing she did was trace the gun found in the Liptan's attic. It had been registered to Patrick Henry Simpson. Next she got hold of the slug that Anthony Hernandez had taken from Sebastian Brophy's skull, and compared it with Simpson's gun. It was a match. Based on this evidence she persuaded the State's Attorney to bring a charge of first degree murder against Simpson. His motive? Almost certainly it was revenge for Brophy's role in halting some of Simpson's developments and causing his subsequent bankruptcy. This, coupled with the hope that somebody else in the building department would treat him more kindly in the future, would have been more than enough.

Stella agreed with me that Hank Simpson could not have hidden Brophy's boat back in the glades without some help, but we weren't sure who it had been. She was unable to find any evidence that Wallace Burke had been in on the murder, even though he probably benefited from it. We both decided that Simpson's brother and business partner, Charles, could well have been involved, since he had the same motives. We hoped it might get resolved at Patrick's trial.

Patrick Henry "Hank" Simpson pled not guilty at his arraignment and requested bail. The State's Attorney objected, but the judge granted it anyway. Bond was set at a half million dollars, which Simpson raised.

Katie and I met with Nate Sturm the day after Simpson's arraignment. He came to our house when we called, and we settled on the deck with iced tea. It was a warm afternoon, the air was still, and the canal had a rich organic smell, probably coming from a bunch of dead seagrass that had blown in off the bay overnight.

Nate was as disappointed as we were that the guy was out on bail, but we reassured him that justice would be done.

"The match between his gun and the slug is powerful evidence, Nate," Katie explained. "That by itself would probably be enough. But his motives also are crystal clear. Your friend hit Simpson right in his pocketbook, and put him out of business at least for a time."

Nate watched a group of a half dozen brown pelicans fly overhead, then looked back at us. "So neither of my tips was any good, I guess."

"You mean for Islava and Stebbins?"

"Yeah."

"They're both bad guys, and they both got in serious trouble because of it. But for Brophy's murder? No. Brophy got in trouble not for his environmental passions, but for doing his day job like he was supposed to."

I was about to say something about Wallace Burke, when my cell phone came to life. It was Stella Reynard.

"Hi Stella, what's up?"

"Something important, thought you'd want to know about."

"Don't tell me Simpson skipped bail?"

"No, nothing like that. We're keeping close tabs on him. It's about Sheriff Spivey. He just handed in his resignation."

"No kidding. Any ideas why?"

"His resignation letter was nothing but platitudes. He'd had a long career. He wanted to spend more quality time with his family. The time was right for new blood. Blah, blah."

"You should run for sheriff, Stella."

"Are you kidding? I bring you all this interesting news, and that's all you've got to say?"

"Well, you should."

The connection went dead.

Nate drank some tea, and sighed. "Anyway, it sounds like Simpson's the one who did it. But there's something about this whole event that keeps bugging me, whoever did it."

"What's that?" Katie asked.

"If Simpson was so anxious to get rid of Bash, why do it like that, way back in the glades?"

"I guess so nobody would find him."

"Yeah, I suppose so. But even if there was some reason to shoot him while he was paddling around in his canoe, why not just haul him and his boat out into the ocean and sink it?"

Katie already had come to the same conclusion. "We've wondered the same thing. In some ways it doesn't make sense. Maybe it'll come out in his trial."

"One thing's for sure, Nate," I said. "Wherever your friend died, he and his boat ended up deep inside Everglades National Park."

Nate nodded and sighed again, and drained the last of his iced tea. "Well, I'd better go do my rounds. And thanks. Thanks a lot. You guys are the greatest." He headed for the door, and then turned back. "Now you be sure to send me that bill, okay?"

"What was that call about?" Katie asked, once Nate had left. "Why would Stella run for sheriff?"

"Spivey just resigned, so the job's open."

"Is she interested?"

"Apparently not."

"She'd be great, but I wouldn't blame her if she ruled herself out. Being a sheriff is largely about politics."

"And while we're on that subject, I can't help wondering if it was Simpson who pushed Spivey to concentrate on Islava for the Brophy murder. Somebody sure was."

Katie raised an eyebrow. "You think the sheriff was in on it?"

"You mean in on the killing? No, I don't think he's that foolish."

"You're probably right."

~ ~ ~

That night Katie and I decided to go to the Safari for dinner. Partly it was for a celebration of sorts, and partly it was to tell Snooks and Flo about the Brophy case. I knew Snooks in particular would be pleased it was over. Any lingering suspicion about his possible involvement all those years ago should now be erased.

It would be the three of us, Katie and me and the dog. We loaded Prince into the Jeep and drove the short distance down to the Safari. There were only a half-dozen other cars in the parking lot. This was good because it increased the odds we could get Snooks and Flo alone together and bring them up to date on things. Snooks was at the bar washing glasses when we walked in. There were four patrons at the bar, and another group of five eating at a table, but from what I could see everybody was well supplied with food and drink.

"Can we see you for a sec?" I asked Snooks, pointing toward the kitchen.

"Uh, sure. Be right there."

We proceeded into the kitchen with Prince, said hello to Flo, and watched as she shooed him downstairs to the cat house. She came back up wiping her hands on a towel, as Snooks came in the door. "What's up?" he said.

We proceeded to tell them about Simpson's arrest. The look of relief on Snooks' face was unmistakable. "You're sure he's guilty?" Flo asked.

"We certainly believe so," Katie said. "Simpson pled not guilty, which means there probably will be a trial. But the forensic evidence is very powerful, and it turns out he had plenty of motive. Stella Reynard is pretty sure he's going down."

"Did he make bail?" Flo asked.

I nodded. "Yeah, for a half million."

"So that's it?" Snooks asked. "What about that man who drowned next door to the Liptans? You think Simpson might have done that too?"

"That's not at all clear," I said. "He might have drowned accidentally, and even if it was foul play, there's no solid evidence that Simpson was involved. Really, no evidence at all. But I have my suspicions."

"Why's that?" Flo asked.

I told them about how Rusty Montrose had pried information out of me about the Brophy disappearance, and my concern that he may have shared it with the wrong person, namely Hank Simpson.

Snooks looked skeptical, and I couldn't blame him.

"Maybe something will come out at the trial, assuming there is one," I said.

"What do you mean by that?" Snooks asked.

"I'm just speculating here. But if the case goes to a plea bargain, it's possible Simpson would admit to drowning Montrose—maybe by accident—in return for some sort of leniency for the Brophy murder."

I could see Katie wasn't buying it. "Leniency for a first degree murder? What would that be?"

"Life without parole instead of execution?" I asked.

Flo apparently had had enough arm waving. "Why don't you all go back outside, and let me get back to work? And Snooks, we've got thirsty customers out there."

We all dutifully headed for the door, but Flo stopped us with a snap of her fingers. "You know I have an idea. Now that this is over, why don't you two guys go fishing tomorrow, have a little fun? You've earned it."

"But what about the bar?" Snooks said.

"I can handle that," Katie volunteered. "At least for one day. I'm not busy tomorrow. What could go wrong?"

"What do you think, Snooks? Wanna go?" I asked.

"Sure."

"Any preferences as to where?"

He thought for a bit. "You know, there's a spot out in the bay, about 15 miles past Sprigger Bank, used to be full of fish. There's some sort of structure down there. Not sure what it is, but we called the place 'The Rocks.' I haven't been there in a couple of years. You know it?"

"I think so. At least I've fished something like it, about where you're talking about. Lots of different species: jacks, mackerel, bluefish, even the occasional cobia."

"Let's do it. What time?"

"Be at my dock by seven-thirty?"

"You're on."

Chapter 39

Snooks showed up at my house at a quarter past seven with a cooler full of food and drinks from the Safari, along with his favorite spin and fly-fishing equipment. I had bait and chum and my own gear.

I kissed Katie goodbye, and we got in the boat. The day was clear and calm and full of promise. Fishing with Snooks was a special treat that I didn't get a chance to indulge all that often since he started helping Flo at the Safari. He, along with my uncle, had taught me almost everything I knew about fishing the Keys.

"I love this time of day," Snooks said, as we pushed off down the canal. "Looks like we're ready for anything." It was the sort of thing optimistic fishermen (is there another kind?) always say at the start of a day on the water. I couldn't have imagined at the time just how inadequate our readiness would turn out to be.

Before we reached the end of the canal, Snooks—who was sitting on the cooler in front of the center console—turned around to face me. "Say, I have an idea. Before we head out to those rocks, what about stopping off at the Arsenic Bank? It's on the way."

"Sure, I suppose we could do that. Any particular reason?"

"Yeah. I heard from a customer the other day that there were some bonefish hanging around the shallows out there. We could try for one. It's been a long time since I've even seen a bonefish in the Keys, let alone caught one."

I knew bonefish were spooky as hell. "Okay. We'll go in quiet, and when we get about 75 yards off I'll cut the motor and pole us in. You be ready in the bow. You gonna try a fly?"

"Thought I might. I tied up some shrimp flies the other night. Could do the trick."

The tide was such that the Arsenic Bank was entirely submerged, but it showed clearly as a lighter colored band of water as we approached. I knew Snooks was right-handed, so it would be easier for him to cast toward the bank if I moved along it from south to north, with the shallows to our left. It also meant the sun would be slightly behind us, which would give Snooks better visibility.

I got up on the poling platform and pushed us to within 50 feet of the bank, then turned right. Snooks stood in the bow, with the rod in his right hand, holding the fly in his left. He was ready to cast the minute we spotted anything. But the first thing we saw wasn't a bonefish. It was another boat up ahead of us, perhaps a half-mile off.

"Hope that guy doesn't get any closer," Snooks said.

"Me too."

I'd worked our way along the bank for perhaps 300 yards without anything happening, when suddenly Snooks started to strip line off his reel, obviously preparing to cast.

"You see something?"

"Yeah, several somethings."

"Bonefish?"

"You tell me. You're the one up on the platform. You could see 'em better than me."

He was right about my higher vantage point. The fact that he'd spotted the fish before me was testimony to his years of experience. It was true that he spent more time behind the bar these days than he did out fishing, but obviously he still had an eye for the "gray ghost of the flats." That's what they call bonefish around here.

And Snooks was right. There were four, maybe five bonefish, not all that big, but not all that small either. They were working a sandy point that jutted out from the main bank.

"Is this close enough?" I asked Snooks.

He looked up at me for just an instant, before turning back to the fish. "It would have been twenty-five years ago. Maybe a little closer?"

I poled in to within thirty feet, and somehow did it carefully enough that the fish didn't scatter. Snooks made a perfect cast, out beyond the fish by four or five yards, and then began a slow retrieve that would bring the shrimp fly toward them, moving along the bottom. One of the fish flashed in the sun, and Snooks set the hook. He held his rod high as the fish screamed off out into the bay. "Look at that sonofabitch go!" he shouted.

Bonefish are famous for their long, deliberate, lengthy runs, and this one lived up to its reputation. But Snooks held on, letting the fish run when it needed to, then keeping the line tight when he could bring it closer. The sequence repeated itself three times before the fish tired enough that he could get it all the way to the boat. He held it steady, while I reached down over the gunwale and gently unhooked his fly. I cupped the fish in my hand. "You want a photo?"

"No, it's okay. Better to let it go."

Which I did.

The other bonefish had scattered when the first one hit, so that was it, at least from this particular spot. "That was great," Snooks said. "Now let's head for those rocks."

The rest of the drive across Florida Bay was uneventful, until we were about a half mile from our destination. Then Snooks tapped me on the shoulder. "Looks like there's a boat following us. I think it's the same one we saw at the Arsenic Bank."

"How far back is he?"

"Maybe three hundred yards. I'll bet he's headed for the same place we are. Damn."

"That shouldn't be a problem. Even if he is, we'll get there way before him. By the time he catches up, we'll already be anchored up and fishing."

I had "The Rocks" marked on my GPS from previous visits, which meant we had no trouble finding it. Snooks tossed out the anchor, while I tied the chum bag to the stern and dropped it in the water. A strong tidal current pulled the bag straight out behind the boat, which was a good sign. It would leave a good chum trail to attract the fish.

"Is this the place you remember?" I asked Snooks.

He looked around for landmarks. There weren't many, only a handful of keys far off to the north and northeast. "Feels right. And we're right on the edge of the Park, aren't we?"

"We're just inside it. That's why there's no more lobster floats."

"Let's go fishing. We need to get busy before that other guy shows up. He's still headed right for us."

I turned to look. "Let him come. We got here first."

Snooks picked up his spinning rod, threaded a shrimp onto the quarter-ounce jig, and made a cast. The bait had barely hit the water when his line came tight. It was a nice sized jack cravalle. He fought it to the side of the boat, while I made ready to cast.

Neither of us was aware of the other skiff until it was almost right on us.

"How's fishin'?" said the man in the other boat.

We turned to look. He was alone, driving a clean white Action Craft flats boat. He was wearing a sun gaiter pulled up over his nose and ears, and a green cap with a big visor. There was something familiar about his voice, but there was no way to recognize him all covered up like that.

"Just got started," I said.

"Mind if I join you?" he said.

Snooks and I looked at each other. It was pushy, and I was tempted to tell him to go to hell. It wasn't something a guide or even an experienced fisherman would ever think of doing. I decided maybe he just didn't know any better. "I suppose not," I said. "But maybe you could stay off a hundred feet or so? That way we'll all have room to cast and play our fish."

"Nope. We both know you've got the good spot. We're gonna share. In fact, we're gonna tie up together."

In all my years' fishing and guiding in the Keys, I'd never seen anything like this. He gunned his craft, and came up within four or five feet of us.

"Now listen, mister—"

"No, *you* listen. And look." The man reached up and pulled down the gaiter with one hand. Then he came up with a pistol in the other one and pointed it right at Snooks.

I remembered where I'd heard that voice. It was Hank Simpson. If either Snooks or I had been thinking this was some sort of a robbery, that notion had just evaporated.

"Now you're gonna do exactly what I say—and I mean *exactly*—or your friend here is gonna die. You got that?"

I thought about what I could do besides what the man asked, and I couldn't come up with anything except to position myself between Snooks and the gun. "Sure, sure. Take it easy. What do you want me to do?"

He tossed me a rope. "First, tie that up to one of your cleats and bring us right in so we're touching. Then take out your ignition key and throw it into the back of my boat."

"Good," he said, once that was done. "Now we're gonna have a little talk."

Talking seemed like a much better idea than getting shot. "What about?"

"I need to know what you know." Simpson paused long enough to wave his gun back and forth between Snooks and me. "Before I shoot both of you, that is."

"Why Snooks?" I said. "He doesn't have anything to do with this."

"Don't be stupid, Sawyer."

"I'm not trying to be stupid, Hank. I'm trying to understand what this is all about. Maybe we can work something out." It sounded desperate because it was.

Simpson laughed, and then his face turned deadly serious. "Tell me what you know about Rusty Montrose."

"I know he drowned in the canal behind his house, and they found a shoe near his body that could have been yours. That's it."

"Good. That's a good start. It tells me they really don't have anything on me for that one."

"Should they have something?" I knew it was risky, pushing the man like that. But all I could think of was to keep him talking, and maybe look for some sort of an opening. But to do what?

"That thing with Rusty was an accident. We tussled and both fell into the canal together. He hit his head on the concrete wall on the way down. He wasn't breathing. I panicked and drove off."

"What were you fighting about?"

"Not that it matters, and not that you deserve to know, but I was trying to get him to sell his house. Just like I tried to get you to sell yours." Then he pointed at Snooks. "I wanted to buy the Safari Lounge too. You and your wives or girlfriends or whatever—you were all being stupid."

"And killing Bash Brophy? Was that an accident too?" Snooks asked.

Simpson glared, but didn't answer. Instead he asked a question of his own, looking back at me. "How did you know that canoe was Brophy's?"

I told him about the dog collar.

"Shit! You mean that dog was yours? If Charlie or I had known that, we'd have taken it along with Brophy's body."

Simpson had just answered one of my questions, probably without even realizing it. His accomplice had indeed been his brother, just like Katie and I suspected.

"If only we'd gotten to him that day before he went off in his canoe, none of this ever would have happened." The man sounded almost wistful, and I seized on it.

"What *was* your plan?"

"You know what? That's none of your fucking business. Damned Park Rangers."

Where had that come from? "You don't like Park Rangers? I think they're the best." I hoped that would bring a response, and it did.

"Shit, we were all ready to haul Brophy, along with his boat, out into the bay and sink it where nobody would ever find him or it. But your precious rangers were doing some kind of goddam safety check of all the boats, including ours, and we had to make another plan."

Simpson stopped talking and shook his head back and forth, three times. "But I'm not here to answer your questions. You're here to answer mine."

I almost said "fire away," but caught myself. "Okay."

"Yeah, okay. Look, I know they found my gun, and they're saying it matches the murder weapon, but here's my question. Is that all they've got?"

"They know you had motive."

"Sure, sure. But I mean do they have any actual evidence? Because the gun is just circumstantial."

My mind had been racing, trying to figure out where this was going. If Hank Simpson had come all the way out here just to kill me—out of revenge I suppose—why all the questions? But then it dawned on me. He was probing for information and plotting a strategy, albeit a pretty deranged one. He was worried about what the sheriff and the D.A.'s office had on him, and whether a good attorney could get him off homicide charges. If the law had other hard evidence, his only option probably was to flee. But if all they had was the gun—which he could claim was stolen— he'd go back and take his chances. Maybe that was it? I could only guess.

Snooks and I looked at each other, and I sensed he'd figured out the same thing. Simpson might well go back and face charges, but only after he'd killed both of us.

226

I don't know who heard it first, but the sound of a helicopter is unmistakable. The three of us turned and looked, as a big chopper with distinctive Coast Guard colors came in low and fast from the southeast. It stunned Hank Simpson just long enough. I grabbed the only thing I could reach, a compact Yeti cooler that Snooks had brought with snacks and food, and threw it at Simpson.

My aim was good. The cooler hit him right in the face. He recoiled and fell backward against the outboard. Unfortunately, he came right back up, still holding the gun. Fortunately he never got to fire it. Somebody on the chopper was faster, and deadly accurate. There was a loud crack, and then another. The last time I ever saw a live Hank Simpson, he was staring down at two red stains spreading across his chest, a look of bewilderment on his face. Then a third shot hit him square in the forehead and he toppled over into the water.

Epilogue

Two days later we found ourselves once again at the Safari Lounge. Much had changed, but much remained the same. The Atlantic was still an infinite blue, bending below the horizon, its waves rolling in from someplace even farther away. Snooks was behind the bar as usual, Flo was rattling pans out in the kitchen, and Prince was downstairs with the cats. Stella Reynard had come with us, and Snooks and I squabbled over who should pay for her meal. She'd literally saved our lives, along with a Coast Guard sharpshooter named Jason.

Snooks and I had gone to his barracks in Islamorada to thank him. He deflected our thanks, explaining that his regular job with the Coast Guard was to disable outboards on drug boats, shooting either from the air or from a cutter. Jason must have been a superb shot, but Hank Simpson had been his first kill, and he was reluctant to talk about it.

Stella had explained—first to Katie and me and then to Snooks—how she happened to come to our rescue. She said it had been a lucky accident, but I didn't buy it and neither did Snooks. She was the one who planted tracking devices on Hank Simpson's cars and in his boat. When the boat had left the dock that morning, and showed no signs of coming back, she was the one who alerted the Coast Guard. She'd given them the tracking receiver, described Simpson and his boat, and explained that a probable murderer was on the run. She hadn't known that Simpson was after us and not just running away, so I guess that was the lucky part.

The Monroe County Commissioners needed to find a new sheriff to replace the retiring Mike Spivey. Not surprisingly, in my opinion, they tapped Stella Reynard for the position. She accepted the job as Acting Sheriff, but made it clear to them that it was only temporary. They would need to find somebody else when election time came around. But that was almost a year away, which gave me time to persuade her otherwise. There couldn't possibly be anybody else in the Florida Keys who could do it better than Stella.

As for Katie and me, things would get back to normal, if only for a while. Flo probably was the first one besides me to figure it out. When Katie ordered her second club soda with lime, instead of her usual margarita, Flo gave her a knowing look. But she didn't say anything.

After dinner was over, Katie and I retrieved Prince from the cat house and took a walk along the beach. A yellow-crowned night heron was hunting at the water's edge, its big red eyes better than mine at spotting little crabs as they scuttled across the sand in the fading light.

Katie hooked her arm into mine as we walked. "I wonder if Sam Jr. will turn out to be as good a fisherman as you are."

I stopped, turned Katie toward me, and looked into her dark eyes. "Or maybe Samantha will turn out to be a first-rate detective. Even with only half your DNA, she'd still be world class."

THE END

ACKNOWLEDGMENTS

Our thanks to Captain Steve Friedman for sharing his passion and deep understanding of Florida Bay and the Everglades backcountry. Thanks to our family for all their support, and especially to our daughter Laura Hernandez, a loyal reader and booster. Fellow members of the Red Herrings writers' group, Milt Mays, Jean McBride, and Beth Eikenbary, provided critical feedback in the early stages of writing this book. Thanks to our Florida neighbors for their interest and support: Gary Nichols and family, Dominic and Susan Orofino, and Steve and Eileen Johnston. Thanks to Beth Steele and Brandon Fies, who have made our stays in the Keys more comfortable than we have a right to expect. Finally, we are grateful to John T. Colby Jr. and his colleagues at Absolutely Amazing eBooks for their encouragement and editorial assistance.

ABOUT THE AUTHORS

Carl and Jane Bock are retired Professors of Biology from the University of Colorado at Boulder. Carl received his Ph.D. in Zoology from the University of California at Berkeley, while Jane holds three degrees in Botany, a B.A. from Duke, an M.A. from the University of Indiana, and a PhD from Berkeley. Carl is an ornithologist and conservation biologist. Jane is a plant ecologist and an internationally recognized expert in the use of plant evidence in criminal investigations. She is co-author with David Norris of *Forensic Plant Science* (Elsevier-Academic Press, 2016). The Bocks have co- authored numerous articles and two books based on their fieldwork in the Southwest: *The View from Bald Hill* (University of California Press, 2000), and *Sonoita Plain: Views from a Southwestern Grassland* (with photographs by Stephen Strom; University of Arizona Press, 2005).

Now largely retired from academic life, the Bocks have turned their creative efforts toward fiction writing, and are co-authors of two ongoing mystery series, the Arizona Borderlands Mysteries and the Florida Keys Mysteries, both published by Absolutely Amazing eBooks of Key West, Florida, and J. T. Colby & Company, Inc., New York.

Today the Bocks divide their time between Colorado, Arizona, and Florida, mostly fly-fishing, writing, and reading.

Thank you for reading.
Please review this book. Reviews help others find
Absolutely Amazing eBooks and inspire us to keep
providing these marvelous tales.
If you would like to be put on our email list to receive
updates on new releases, contests, and promotions, please
go to AbsolutelyAmazingEbooks.com and sign up.

AbsolutelyAmazingEbooks.com

or AA-eBooks.com

For sales, editorial information, subsidiary rights information
or a catalog, please write or phone or e-mail
AbsolutelyAmazingEbooks
Manhanset House
Shelter Island Hts., New York 11965-0342, US
Tel: 212-427-7139
www.AbsolutelyAmazingEbooks.com
bricktower@aol.com
www.IngramContent.com

For sales in the UK and Europe please contact our distributor,
Gazelle Book Services
White Cross Mills
Lancaster, LA1 4XS, UK
Tel: (01524) 68765 Fax: (01524) 63232
email: jacky@gazellebooks.co.uk

www.ingramcontent.com/pod-product-compliance
Lightning Source LLC
Chambersburg PA
CBHW061520020726
47502CB00006B/2162